Caintuck Lies Within My Soul

The Jemima Boone Story

Caintuck Lies Within My Soul

◆

The Jemima Boone Story

C.M. Huddleston

Interpreting Time's Past Press
2020

Caintuck Lies Within My Soul:
The Jemima Boone Story

Published by:
Interpreting Time's Past Press
Crab Orchard, Kentucky

Cover design by Samantha Fury
ISBN-13: 978-1-7328333-2-6
Library of Congress Control Number:2019916510

Publisher's Cataloging-in-Publication Data
Names: Huddleston, C. M., author.
Title: Caintuck lies within my soul : the Jemima Boone story / C. M. Huddleston.
Description: Crab Orchard, KY: Interpreting Time's Past Press, 2020.
Identifiers: LCCN 2019916510 | ISBN 978-1-7328333-2-6 (pbk.) | 978-1-7328-333-3-3 (ebook)
Subjects: LCSH Callaway, Jemima (Boone) 1762-1829--Fiction. | Boone, Daniel, 1734-1820--Family--Fiction. | United States--History--Revolution, 1775-1783--Fiction. | Pioneers--Kentucky--Fiction. | Frontier and pioneer life--Kentucky--Fiction. | Kentucky--Discovery and exploration--Fiction. | BISAC FICTION / Historical / Colonial America & Revolution | FICTION / Action & Adventure
Classification: LCC PS3608 .U32 C35 2020 | DDC 813.6--dc23

For all the brave girls and women who
dared to follow the men in their lives
west, beyond the Appalachians.
In particular,
Susannah "Sukey" Thomas Miller
my fourth great grandmother,
a Kentucky pioneer.

Table of Contents

Part I: A Childhood Remembered
Chapter 1. September 30th, 1767 1
Chapter 2. October 1st, 1767 9
Chapter 3. October 3rd, 1767 17
Chapter 4. Late April 1768 25
Chapter 5. John Finley 33
Chapter 6. Another Year Passes 41
Chapter 7. Planning 51

Part II: Jemima's Story
Chapter 1. September 25th, 1773 61
Chapter 2. Tragedy 69
Chapter 3. Lord Dunmore's War 77
Chapter 4. Moore's Fort 85
Chapter 5. Boone's Trace 93
Chapter 6. A Home in Caintuck 105
Chapter 7. July 14th, 1776 113
Chapter 8. Rescue 123
Chapter 9. Our Lives in Danger 137
Chapter 10. Indian Troubles 149
Chapter 11. The Salt Boilers 155
Chapter 12. One Man Returns 165
Chapter 13. The Siege 177
Chapter 14. Squire's Cannon 185
Chapter 15. The Trial .195
Chapter 16. Home in Kentucky 205
Chapter 17. My Soul Lies at Rest 215

Author's Notes 219
About the Author 222

Part I:
A Childhood Remembered

Chapter 1
September 30th, 1767

"No, Lil' Duck, you can't go with me," James hollered. "I'm goin' sangin' and you're too little. You can't keep up. You don't even have on shoes. Now, go back to the cabin." With that stern command, he turned, placed the short-handled shovel over his shoulder, and scampered up the steep slope across the now almost-dry Beaver Creek, leaving the scrawny girl to splash in the few puddles lying scattered among its rock bed. Her bare feet caused what little water remained to splash only as high as her bony knees, showing white as she held up the bottom of her shift, hoping against hope of keeping it dry.

She continued to stomp, wildly, with great glee, and considerable anger until no puddles remained and her shift hung soaked mid-calf around thin, scratched, and bite-covered legs.

"I can too, go sangin'. I know how sang looks, I seen it before. Just 'cause James be older, don't mean he knows everything. I'll go if'in I want to. I'm big enough to help," she muttered to herself, growing more confident with each breath, each thought, and each word.

Abruptly, she marched across the damp, rounded creek stones and began to climb the steep, tree-covered hillside, deliberately going away from where James' towhead had disappeared. Thick, shrubby undergrowth of mountain laurel, rhododendron, blackberries, and thousands of vining plants fought each other for space and sunlight beneath the heavy autumn canopy formed by multi-colored leafy trees. She recognized oaks, chestnuts, sugar maples, sycamores, and even a few magnolias. As a child of the woods, Jemima tried to remember landmarks such as large stones, particular trees, and other such things, just as Daddy'd taught her. Then she remembered she had set out to hunt ginseng, *sang* they called it. Sang brought good money, Daddy and Mama said. Briefly, she wondered what *bad* money was. She knew from listening to them talk, long after she'd gone to her pallet one night, 'bout how they needed cash money. Round and round her thoughts flew, coming to rest on the exact thought that started her up the hillside—James was not the only one who could sang. She'd show them.

Jemima continued to hunt ginseng among the Yadkin Valley's hills until almost dark. Finding the first olive green-leafed plant, standing high amidst the surrounding undergrowth, with its red berries shining, had been easy. Not having brought a shovel, she used her fingers to dig the plant from the root-filled soil. As she grasped the plant's roots and pulled with all her might, she fell into the surrounding briers. Despite small bloody pinpricks along her legs and arms, she pulled the root free. She stood, dusted off her behind, and turned to continue her search. Only a few steps later, she stopped, walked back, and picking up the discarded berries, buried them in the shallow hole created by her pulling up the root. "Mama always tells James to remember to bury the berries so more plants will grow," she murmured, using her dirty bare feet to stomp the soil flat around where the green leaves once stood.

Later, her now grubby hands each held tight to a bumpy-looking root. "Sang, glorious sang, I found sang," she crooned happily and off key, changing the made-up tune for another whenever she grew tired of singing the current one. She watched for her landmarks, confident in her sense of direction. She drank from streams and picked the last autumn berries, constantly moving toward home, that small cabin near the spring where Mama, and maybe even Daddy, waited with supper. Only the rising dark among the trees and shrubs, making the shadows of each trunk and branch create spooky specters across the landscape, awakened her to the understanding of being somewhat lost. She stopped and turned in a slow circle, observing every direction for familiar landmarks or smoke from a cabin fire, for theirs was not the only cabin along the Yadkin. She listened, but heard only the tree frogs begin their songs, a few crows, and then a whippoorwill. Not close. She knew the will's loud call carried for miles. "Oh, my," she whispered, "some soul done gone to heaven. Sure hope it wasn't mine."

She tried smelling home, supper cooking, even the cows and pigs. Anything. Nothing but the heavy scent of vegetation filled her nose, which dripped, mixing with the tears now sliding down her cheeks, until she grabbed her grubby shift's bottom, wiped her eyes, blew her nose, and declared aloud to no one in particular. "No, it wasn't my soul that darn ol' whippoorwill sent on to heaven. I'm right peckish, and dead people are not hungry. Leastwise I don't believe so."

Jemima walked until she could no longer see, always downhill till she found a gurgling stream running with clear water. Sure it wasn't Beaver Creek, which lay near the cabin, she remembered Daddy saying, *always go downstream if you're a might confused in the woods. When you find a bigger stream, follow it downstream until you find a river, then go downstream some more. If there's a river, there's most likely people livin' along it somewhere.* So, she walked, at times stumbling. Stopping often to drink. Trying not to think about the grumbling in her stomach. . . or home. At last, true dark slid in amongst the trees, obscuring her sight, and she could walk no longer. She heard wolves howling in the distance and other smaller woodland creatures creeping nearby. Looking about, she located a large, old, multi-branched oak tree, one with low-hanging branches she could climb, and she worked her way up, about six feet off the ground, still holding tight to her sang. As she sat back against the trunk, one scrawny, dirt-covered leg hanging down each side of the branch, Jemima relaxed. She whispered her prayers, praying for her Mama, James, Israel, Suzy, and the baby, Levina, all back at their cabin, for cousins Jesse and Jonathan off helping family with the fall harvest, and Daddy and Uncle Squire, off hunting west in the mountains. She prayed she wouldn't fall, she prayed no bears would climb the tree, and last and most fervently, she prayed Daddy would not get killed by Indians, would not get lost in the mountains, and would come home in time to find her.

— ● —

"Suzy, grab up Levina and quiet her down. I need to hear James," demanded Rebecca. "Now, son, where did you say you last seen Jemima?"

"Down to Beaver Creek, Mama, just where she prefers to go wadin' and catchin' frogs. I told her to *go on home* when I went past earlier today," ten-year-old James replied over Levina's wails of hunger, Israel's dumping of split hickory logs on the hearth, and Suzy trying her best to sing the baby quiet. With Daddy gone hunting, James believed he was the man of the house. Eight-year-old Israel, being the only other male family member until Daddy, Jesse, or Jonathan returned, often resented James giving him chores and such. But tonight, he stood listening, sure glad he wasn't responsible for Jemima not being home at dark. Suzy, not yet seven, remained too busy with Levina to do much more than turn the hoe cakes cooking over the hearth fire, and try to keep the baby from spilling the milk cup she'd placed on the rough-hewn table.

"She's not home," Rebecca said. "Best we go look for her. James, grab the rifle and a jacket. Suzy, you and Israel go ahead with supper, feed the baby, and then put her to bed. I'll help look for Jemima. She's probably still down to the creek." Rebecca grabbed her shawl and shoes as she left the cabin. Once outside, she collapsed wearily on the bench sitting beside the door, pulled on her shoes, and wrapped and tied her knitted shawl against the evening cool. "James, best we take two torches along for light. We'll need to split up."

At first, Rebecca and James stayed together as they walked down to the place on Beaver Creek Jemima haunted during any free time she had from her chores. Rebecca thought back to the day, earlier in the summer, when Daniel found her wet from head to toe, splashing after the small creek minnows. That child loved to play in the water more than anything else. Their fourth child, only a few days from her fifth birthday, Mima possessed a willful nature, often trying to do more than she was physically able. Rebecca knew the child's mind was sharp, since she understood and remembered most anything she heard. James, the only one of her children to ever have any schooling, tried to teach Mima her numbers and letters. She learned to recite each by heart, but rarely remained still enough to recognize them when James scribbled them out on his broken tablet.

Not finding Jemima at the stream, Rebecca and James repeatedly shouted out her name, facing north, east, south, and west in turn. Except for the usual forest night noises, nothing returned their plaintive calls. "James, exactly what was Mima doin' when you passed by?"

"Wadin', splashin'. She wanted to go sangin' with me, but I told her no. I told her she was too little. Besides, she didn't even have her shoes!" James exclaimed.

"You don't think she went off sangin' alone, do you? Oh, Lord in Heaven, where is Daniel when I need him?"

"Most likely she's done climbed a tree by now. I'll keep lookin', Mama. Guess you better send Israel off to fetch Uncle George or Uncle Ned."

"I'll send him at dawn, I don't want two lost children. You and I will search till then. How 'bout you go south along the creek, and I'll head north. Don't go so far we can't hear each other," Rebecca decided, knowing that two lost children would be more than she could deal with.

Long before dawn, both James and Rebecca returned exhausted to the little cabin. After a bowl of stew apiece, Rebecca sent James up for a couple hours sleep, stirred the fire, fixed herself a cup of milk, and ate another bowl of the leftover stew, which hung just barely warm over the smoldering fire. Sitting, she watched over her sleeping daughters, bedded down on a bearskin pallet beside her and Daniel's bed. It was nothing more than a platform built in against the cabin's back wall. She could hear Israel's quiet snores from the loft, and James sliding in beside his brother. She would let them both sleep until dawn and then send one each for Daniel's brothers. Brother Neddie and his wife Martha, her own sister, lived closer. Brother George and Ann lived a mite farther away. Both brothers would come to help search. Until then, all she could do was sit, pray, and worry.

Too tired to stay awake and too worried to sleep, Rebecca's thoughts turned to all the times Daniel had been away from home. "Tis a wonder we have five children," she thought. Why, he'd been a wandering man even before she met him. One of eleven children from a Quaker family, Daniel learned to hunt and tend the family's cattle long before he was full grown. Then, in 1755 at age twenty, he'd joined the North Carolina militia as a wagon driver and blacksmith. Under Major Edward Dobbs, the North Carolina militia formed part of Braddock's Expedition to Fort Duquesne during the French and Indian War. Daniel rarely spoke of going north toward Pittsburgh, driving a wagon loaded with military supplies, and later fleeing for his life. She'd learned more about what had happened from others who told of the horrors. British General Braddock had led a 2,100-man army out from Fort Cumberland toward Fort Duquesne. Young Colonel George Washington served as his guide and aide. By early July, the Braddock force had split into two columns and worked strenuously each day to build a road through the forest and to advance toward their objective, the French-held Fort Duquesne. That same evening, Indians, fighting alongside the French, sent a delegation to the British, requesting a conference. General Braddock sent Washington and Lieutenant John Fraser to listen, speak for him, and report back. The Indians wanted the British to halt their advance so an attempt could be made to talk the French into a peaceful withdrawal from Fort Duquesne. After hearing this request, knowing the French were stalling for time, Braddock refused.

The very next day, after crossing the Monongahela River about ten miles south of Fort Duquesne, Braddock's advance guard of three hundred grenadiers and colonials with two cannons under Lieutenant Colonel Thomas Gage encountered the French and Indian forces. This became the first skirmish in what everyone now called *Braddock's Defeat.* Under heavy fire from the French and their Indian allies, Gage's men retreated along the narrow road, only to collide with the main body of Braddock's forces. Daniel had once told his brother George about how Braddock's entire force fell into disorder as they recognized their predicament, surrounded on three sides by the enemy—Canadian militiamen, Indians, and the French regulars. General Braddock fell to enemy fire. Although Colonel Washington tried to rally the forces and restore order, Braddock's army continued to retreat, running for their lives. Soon, they encountered their own supply wagons positioned to the army's rear. Wagoners, such as Daniel, many unarmed, recognized the coming disaster if they stayed with their wagons. Daniel unhitched his team and fled on horseback. Many wagoners—those who had followed orders and stayed behind—died or were captured, tortured, and burned at the stake. Daniel's was a timely escape.

Since their marriage, Daniel had been away more than he was home. Sometimes only overnight or at the most for a couple of weeks. She remembered his impromptu trip to Florida just two years earlier. Along with friends from Virginia, Daniel, his brother Squire, and his brother-in-law John Stewart had left home in late summer. Traveling south to South Carolina and then on to Savannah and St. Augustine, Daniel had returned on Christmas Day to announce their upcoming move to Pensacola, all the way down in Florida. It was the first time she had refused to move. She'd been expecting a new baby in the spring and wanted so much to have her own family close by when her time came. Daniel gave in fairly easily. He reckoned the hunting had not been good in Florida.

"Oh, why could he not stay home?" she wondered aloud as, very late into the night, her tears began to flow.

Just weeks ago, Daniel, Squire, and neighbor William Hill had traipsed off west into the Blue Ridge and Smoky Mountains for an extended hunt. Still, she knew the meat they would dry and bring home would help carry them through the winter, and the hides could be sold to pay their debts and taxes. With one last thought before sleep overtook her, she thought back on how Daniel'd once tried to stay home and farm his land, yet the pull of places he'd never seen and the land he'd never walked constantly drew him away from her and their children.

Just before dawn, as her tears subsided and exhaustion overtook her, Rebecca fell asleep still sitting at the table, her head on her arms.

Chapter 2
October 1st, 1767

Rebecca awoke to Levina's soft giggles, as her baby pulled tufts from the bear hide and tickled Suzy's face and nose. Glancing toward the cabin's one window, she saw dawn had passed an hour or so ago. Glad her older children had not seen her crying, she grabbed her shawl and the smelly chamber pot before hurrying out toward the privy ditch. On her way back inside, she gathered a few split logs and some kindling, glancing anxiously toward the woods. A soft prayer left her lips as she pushed aside the door and spoke to her children.

"Suzy, go fetch some water. I'll take Levina. James, Israel. . . boys! I need you," she called toward the loft. When no sound issued from either boy, she turned, "Suzy, climb up and wake the boys."

"They're not here, Mama. Neither one," said Suzy, hanging from the top of the ladder. With the loft only about six feet off the floor, Rebecca seldom worried about her children falling as she watched time and time again when they climbed and then hung from the top rung by their hands, swinging to and fro, much as the pendulum of her mother's clock had done. Memories of Jemima hanging by only one tiny hand brought a smile to her face, easing only slightly the ache in her heart.

"Oh, I must have been tired. I wonder when the boys left?" Rebecca said to herself, as Suzy grabbed her own shoes and the bucket.

"Go, go, go," cried Levina, toddling after Suzy.

"No, Suzy can't carry you and the bucket," Rebecca whispered, picking up the child and turning back toward the hearth. Minutes later, while she sat feeding Levina warm honey-sweetened cornmeal mush, Rebecca heeded George's call, "Becca, you to the cabin?"

"Oh, Brother George, thank ye for comin'. Did James tell ye Jemima be lost?" she yelled, dashing out to meet him.

"That's why I'm here, Sister. Israel came for me ridin' that old nag. He said James is goin' for Ned. Now where did you see Mima last.?" George inquired quietly, taking her hands and squeezing each in brotherly affection. "Ned and I'll find her. Don't you worry. Israel stayed to eat with my Ann and the girls. You know that boy, he's always hungry. He'll be along later. I asked him to carry in some wood and water before he comes home. I'll go down to the creek and head north, tell Ned to go south." George had taken the easier path as he'd walked with a serious limp since childhood and most often carried a cane when on rough terrain.

James, Brother Ned, and Israel arrived within a half hour of each other. Ned headed south, while James and Israel divided up the chores.

"Mama, don't you cry no more about Mima. We'll find her. I promise," James whispered, pulling up against Rebecca and hugging her tight before he went off to help Israel. Rebecca could still feel the heat of his head against her shoulder when he walked away and recognized how her oldest was truly becoming a man instead of a boy.

⬤

As the day progressed, Rebecca tried spinning the last raw wool on the large walking wheel her father had passed to her, before she gave up and joined the search party. In her mind, it just seemed wrong that she was not out looking for her child, her darling Mima. Rebecca stayed directly beside the creek, first going upstream and later downstream. At least with the water being so low, her heartache lessened at the knowledge it was unlikely the child had drowned.

James walked to the ridge top behind the cabin and fired off his Daddy's spare rifle, hoping Jemima would hear it. Yet, no one could find even a trace of the child. Midday came and passed. Rebecca's concern grew, and she paced the cabin and the yard, turning at every little sound, hoping to see her daughter appear.

As the sun crept across the autumn sky, the weather turned cooler. Soon a strong breeze whipped dry leaves from the hardwoods surrounding the cabin and bent treetops first in one direction before quickly whipping them around in the other. Suzy kept watch over Levina, who tried to collect leaves in an old slat basket, fussing and jabbering as the wind often whipped them back out, swirling them around the baby's head. Thereafter, Rebecca paced from one chore to another. She'd turned to gather up the baby, meaning to change her wet nappy, when she heard the first rifle shot and the second before a minute passed. It was their signal that one of Daniel's brothers had found Jemima, and from the echoing sound, several miles away. It would not be James firing, as he could not yet reload quite that fast.

"Mama, does that mean Jemima's comin' home?" asked Suzy, guiding Levina by the shoulders, away from their sleeping cat.

"Yes, Uncle George or Uncle Neddie will fetch her home soon. Let's get supper going. She'll be hungry," Rebecca replied, hoping and praying her child was alive and well.

"Did so find more sang than you, James! It's in Uncle Neddie's huntin' shirt pocket. Show him Uncle Neddie, show them all I can too sang. I told you I could sang. And I was not lost! I knowed 'xactly where I was all the time. I just didn't knowed where the cabin lay. I did right as Daddy said to do. I followed the creek downstream till I found that big creek, and I went downstream some more along its banks. I drank water and ate berries. I hollered out for you. I even tried smellin' smoke from the cabin. I would have found home, but it got dark, and I climbed a big old oak tree so wolves and bears wouldn't get me. I did fall out once durin' the night, but I climbed back up right sharply. And this mornin', I kept walkin'. I found more sang, and I kept walkin', stayin' right beside that big ol' creek. And, and, well, Uncle Neddie didn't find me. I found him. Ask him. Go ahead, just ask him." And she breathed, still standing with her hands on her hips, elbows out, chin forward, daring anyone to disagree.

"Can't be dissimilar to her," Ned replied smiling. "There I was sittin' eatin' an apple, takin' a rest, and I looked up after hearin' a really strange bird call. It kept repeatin' *I can sang, I found sang.* Kind of off key, but I reckon some larger birds have a kind of an off-key call," he finished, while rummaging in his large hunting shirt pocket and pulling out four large and two smaller ginseng roots. "I reckon the child can sang. Been days when I've walked up one ridge and down another all day without findin' even one root as nice as these."

"Neddie, exactly where was she, how far away?" asked his brother George.

"Oh, 'bout a mile from the Upper Yadkin, say three or so miles from the cabin. I'd circled around some after findin' a torn bit of her shift where she had dug up some sang. Figured her bein' Daniel's child what was lost, she'd try followin' a creek."

"Brother Ned, Brother George, will you stay to supper?" asked Rebecca glancing back over her shoulder, while taking Jemima's small grubby hand in hers and heading toward the wash basin.

"No, thank you kindly, Becca, I don't believe I will," said Ned. "Better get along home and tell Martha we found her. She'll be frantic with worry. Want to walk a ways with me, George?"

"Becca, we'll all be back come the fourth for Jemima's birthday. I expect you'll have her cleaned up by then. I must say, the child smells right much as a bear might after a long winter's sleep. I'll take that sang to the market for ye next time I go. Send one of the boys if I be needed again," George replied. "Ann will be as anxious as Martha, so I'd better git along. Oh, and I'll see if I can round up Jonathan and send him this way. Jesse'll be busy earning enough to marry that gal next spring, but Jonathan should be here helpin' out while Daniel's away."

"Wait, wait," Jemima called, pulling loose from Rebecca's strong grip and running up to Ned. "Uncle Neddie, you promised, remember you promised."

Kneeling to look her in the eye, Edward Boone, Neddie to his family, hugged his niece's small body and kissed her forehead before whispering, "I won't forget. Now, go do as your mama says before we both gets ourselves in trouble."

<hr>

Bathed, scrubbed, scratches and cuts doctored with lineament, and wrapped up in a soft flannel gown, Jemima lay on Mama's bed, waiting for supper. "Mama, I didn't mean to worry ye. I was sangin'. You know Daddy taught us how not to get lost."

"Jemima, I don't care what you think your Daddy taught you. You cannot go past Beaver Creek without James or Israel. Now, help your sister with the spoons, and we'll eat. Suzy, call in your brothers and make sure they wash up."

Rebecca watched as her five children settled in for supper. Bear bacon, the last autumn greens, cornbread, and fresh butter, along with cold milk from their dairy cow, sat on the table. She crushed Levina's cornbread into her milk and added butter and honey. Only a year and a half old, Levina had come along almost four years after Jemima. During those years, the family had moved farther west, but this time their extended family had moved with them and lived nearby. For once, Rebecca did not feel so much alone when Daniel hunted. Daniel had chosen a place near, but not across, the Governor's Proclamation Line of 1763, called by some the Donelson Line. The colonial governors had proclaimed, after a period of conflict with the Indians, that settlers were not to move west of this line into Indian territory. The border line followed closely on the Blue Ridge Mountains.

Able, but not really willing, to be only a farmer, Daniel provided for his family by selling hides—mostly deer and bear—but also some smaller game. Their adopted sons, Jesse and Jonathan most often planted the family's corn crop and garden. Sons of Daniel's older brother, Israel and his wife Martha, who had both passed in 1756, the two boys had joined the family even before their own son James, born nine months after their wedding. Jesse had been eight and Jonathan only six. The boys' two sisters had gone to their mother's relations to live, before each succumbed to consumption, as their parents had before them. Jesse, now nineteen, planned to marry soon and often labored for others in the family to earn cash. Seldom separated from his brother, Jonathan had followed him on their latest trip to help Daniel's family.

Her children remained silent during the meal, each occupied with their own thoughts and filling their constantly empty stomachs. As the evening darkness grew even closer, encroaching on the little cabin, Rebecca counted her blessings one by one, first James, who had taken it upon himself to seek help from their uncles, sending Israel for Brother Neddie. Israel, her second boy, and fourth to raise, who listened quietly, learned quickly, and so resembled his father in looks. Susannah, already a mother in the making, doted on Levina, the baby, now walking and beginning to talk. Her thoughts turned last to Jemima, headstrong, willful, rambunctious, so much her father's daughter. In three days, on October fourth, the child would be five years old.

After the meal, when each was settled, she'd return to her work making the child a new shift and overdress for her birthday. Her own father, Joseph Bryan, a weaver, had sent a length of linen back in the summer. With cold weather approaching, she had already knitted each child a new pair of stockings. Poor Israel's feet remained crammed into James' old boots, and Suzy had only thin slippers. Jemima wore Suzy's hand-me-downs—when the child wore shoes. Watching Jemima scraping her wood bowl for the last of her cornbread, Rebecca settled her thoughts and rose to light the grease lamp. All her children sat safe, healthy, and fed in their cabin. Jemima's ginseng would bring enough money to pay the taxes and to purchase a few necessities, such as shoes. Yes, she could do without Daniel some bit longer, but she missed him mightily on days like the last few. He would have found his daughter long before morning, carrying her home on his back, both singing at the top of their lungs.

Most often birthdays and holidays came and went on the mountain, noticed with no more than a mention or perhaps a small treat. Yet, Rebecca always tried to make the day special for her children, usually with a favorite meal. As no churches stood nearby, once a month the Sabbath meant Daniel's brothers, George, Ned, and Squire, his sister Hannah, and their families, would gather on the day before at one family's cabin or another. Each brought food to be shared. Early on Sunday, the families would hold a quiet service, men sitting in one area and women in another, much as their Quaker families had always done, though many had left the brotherhood years before and several now worshiped more in the Baptist style. The families would spend the day together, departing barely long enough before dark to reach their own homes.

Gatherings such as this gave the womenfolk a chance to talk and catch up on family news. The men would talk as well, planning crops and long hunts, while debating the latest news from the coast, especially the latest in taxes and tariffs. The children would play, wrestle, fight, and generally have a day free from most chores. With Jemima's birthday falling on the day before the Sabbath, the coming weekend would bring family members to Rebecca and Daniel's small home. Often, if weather allowed, the families would sleep outdoors. In rough weather, the womenfolk and smaller children bedded down inside the cabin. With today's changing weather, Rebecca knew the cabin would be more crowded than normal. At least the men folks and older boys could bed down in the lean-to built to stable their horses.

Rebecca started counting families and children. She and Daniel, him being the oldest in the immediate area, had five of their own and his late brother Israel's two boys, Jesse and Jonathan. Brother George and Ann had the two girls, Elizabeth and Ellender, the baby. Brother Ned and dear Martha—oh, it would be good to see her sister—would bring their three girls and two boys. Their little George, only about six months old, would be the youngest at the gathering. With Brother Squire off on the long hunt with Daniel, she doubted Jane would travel with one-year-old Jonathan. Still, there would be the five adults and their twelve children. Mentally, she prepared food and beds for the company, her hands busy with tiny stitches along a seam in Jemima's new shift.

Late in the evening, when the light grew too dim to continue her work, Rebecca fell to her knees beside her bed, folded her hands in prayer, and thanked the good Lord for returning her child. Tears leaked out once again as Rebecca remembered her fears of losing Jemima to some calamity of the wilderness. She prayed for her children, her family, and especially for Daniel and Squire. Then she washed her face and hands, climbed into bed, and slept.

Chapter 3:
October 3rd, 1767

"Mama, Mama, let me go out and wait. Uncle Neddie promised, he did, he promised," begged Jemima.

"Exactly what did Uncle Ned promise?" demanded Rebecca and Israel together.

"Won't tell you. It be a secret. Just 'tween me and Uncle Neddie."

"Jemima, it be cold and rainin' outside. Content yourself with sweepin' up these ashes and puttin' them in the hopper. Then help Suzy with Viney. If the rain lets up, you can go outside later. After all, they won't get here until mid-afternoon."

With only one window to provide any light at all inside the cabin, and it covered with a thin skin rather than glass, Rebecca carried out her morning chores. Usually she tied back the door to let in more light, but today's wind blew in the rain and cold. Having arisen at dawn, she'd already washed Levina's nappies, hanging them to dry on pegs about the cabin, where they emitted a slight smell of ammonia and lye soap, and fed the children. As she sat peeling a large pile of late apples for Jemima's favorite fried apple pies, she hoped the aroma of frying the pies would overcome the wet-nappy smell.

Rebecca listened for sounds of James' return, as she always worried just a bit about him wandering the hills on his own. He had left at dawn to check all his snares and with hopes of bringing down a doe. She doubted they'd have venison, as not once had their old musket's sound rung across the surrounding hills. Taught by his father, James carried on the family tradition, as he was a right good hunter. Without venison, rabbits and squirrels would serve for the stew pot.

Suzy continued to churn while additional pans of milk sat on a bench beside the door, covered by a linen towel. Levina played on the girls' pallet, content for a moment as she happily chewed on an apple slice.

"Mama, someone passed by the window. Did you see?" asked Israel, reaching for the cabin's remaining musket and passing it to his mother.

"Hello cabin," a deep voice shouted.

With the long gun looped in her elbow, Rebecca motioned her children toward the ladder. Israel grabbed Levina and watched as Jemima and Suzy climbed up before him.

Wrapped in her wool shawl, Rebecca stepped from the door into the small clearing before their cabin. The wind and rain blew the cold into her face. Standing a respectful ten feet away stood three Cherokees. "Good day, may I help you?" Rebecca responded with a nod in their direction.

"Be lookin' for Wide Mouth," the oldest of the three announced.

As most Cherokees currently lived peacefully with the western settlers, Rebecca debated before answering, "Daniel's gone huntin', south along the Yadkin. May I help you?"

"Tell Wide Mouth stay home. Not to go west." Pausing, he gestured toward the eastern hills and continued, "Son of Wide Mouth bring venison." Then the three turned and headed up the slope west of their cabin and soon disappeared over the ridge line. All the while, Rebecca watched and wondered. Within minutes, James came across the opposite ridgetop, following the creek, and carrying a venison haunch.

"Mama, is there trouble? Why you carryin' the rifle?"

"James, did you see three Cherokee men?"

"No ma'am, didn't see anyone at all. I shot a doe about a mile across to the south. I could only carry this much back. I'll go back with the horse for the rest. Just let me get this hung for you, Mama."

"No, son. Not until one of your uncles can go with you. Three Cherokee men just came by askin' for your Daddy. I want you to stay close," demanded Rebecca.

James understood better than to argue.

* * *

Mid-afternoon brought the sounds of welcome company. Brothers George and Ned arrived together with their wives, numerous offspring, and baskets and pokes full to overflowing with foodstuffs. Rebecca already had venison steaks ready for frying and stew cooking over the hearth fire. James and Israel grabbed Uncle George and traipsed off to the hillside to retrieve James' deer, while Rebecca ushered Martha and Ann into the cabin. Nine-year-old Charity handed the baby to her mother, Martha, and grabbed up Levina instead. As the oldest girl, she took charge, ushering them all into the loft to play. Rebecca's Suzy joined Martha's Jane and Mary to giggle and talk, relaying to each other all the family goings on. Martha put George to her breast and settled at the table while Ann helped Rebecca about the cabin.

"Rebecca, you must've been frantic with Jemima lost all night long," exclaimed Martha. "Ned said he found her wanderin' along the creek, filthy, and singin' so loud as to be heard across many a forest mile."

"Yea, the child 'tis her father's daughter. No fear, stubborn, and speakin' of Jemima, where did she go now?" questioned Rebecca.

"Oh, she passed me as I was comin' in. Headed straight toward Neddie. I'm sure they're examinin' her birthday gift."

"Gift? What in heaven's name did Neddie bring her?" demanded Rebecca turning toward the cabin door.

"Becca," whispered Martha, "just you wait here. Let that child and Neddie have their time together."

Before Rebecca could respond the door flew open and a wet Jemima ran in holding a struggling, speckled pup. "Look Mama, Uncle Neddie brought me a puppy. See 'tis just beautiful. Don't you think? I'm goin' a name him Ezekiel and let him sleep with me and take him everywhere I go. I'll even teach him to swim in the creek. Uncle Neddie promised me a pup, and he brung me one."

Turning to face Ned, who had entered the cabin directly behind Jemima, Rebecca smiled, as her brother-in-law resembled Daniel both in looks and temperament. "Neddie, seems I have another mouth to feed, thanks to you."

"Ah, shucks Becca," Ned answered, hanging his head, his hands turning his hat to and fro. Daniel often commented on how Neddie could worry a belonging to death when anxious. "Besides, Jemima needs a dog. He just might keep her from trouble and show her the way home next time she goes sangin', don't you think?" he finished, finally looking Rebecca in the eye and smiling.

"Oh, Neddie, don't fuss yourself. I'm happy about the pup. Ever since our old dog died, we've had no warnin' when visitors are a comin'. Why, just this morning, three Cherokee turned up right on the doorstep askin' for Daniel with no warning at'll. At least a dog might bark and let on someone's about."

"Did you recognize any of the Cherokees, Sister?"

"Nay, but they called Daniel *Wide Mouth* and told me to tell him to stay home, not to go west. Didn't ask for anything, not even food. Just wandered off over the ridge."

"Sounds as if more company's comin'. Bet I know who 'tis," replied Ned, before whispering in Rebecca's ear, "we'll talk this over with George when they return."

Before anyone could move toward the door, it opened to reveal Daniel's sister, Hannah, and her two small girls, accompanied by Jonathan. "Good day, Auntie Becca. I brought you some more company. I'll be back in for one of those pies soon as I bed down the horse. Sure is wet out there." And he fled from the cabin before anyone could respond.

"Well, he didn't even mention my birthday or my new puppy. Didn't even ask what I plan to call him. Well, Jon'll see. I named my pup Ezekiel, 'cause he'll be such as that ol' prophet, he'll give us warnin'. Might even warn us Jon is back. Serves him right if my dog barks at him," Jemima stated as the door closed.

Sunday morning brought noise and laughter to the cabin. Rebecca, Martha, Ann, and Hannah worked first to feed all the children. Rebecca had hung Jemima's new shift and overdress on her wall hook, over the everyday clothes the child generally wore. Jemima had scarcely noticed the new clothes as she grabbed the pup and ran for the cabin's door. Several minutes later, she ran by Rebecca, gave her a huge hug and a word of thanks, declaring this to be her best birthday ever. Rebecca recognized her child's words for what they were. She was proud and thankful for the new clothes, but much happier for the pup.

After dispersing the children to perform a few chores, the womenfolk fed the menfolk and continued their daily routine. Ned, Jonathan, and George, helped by Israel and James, gathered what chairs, benches, and tree stumps they could for seats and readied the little cabin's front clearing for the Boone clan's service to God. Disturbed only by forest sounds, and the occasional cry from one or more little ones, George and Martha shared the scripture that morning and the little group sang the familiar hymns between prayers and thoughts of others absent from their worship service. Amongst the prayers, they thanked God for Jemima reaching her fifth birthday and for Squire Boone, who would be twenty-three the following day. Off on a winter's long hunt with Daniel, Squire was the seventh and last Boone brother. Only Hannah was younger than him.

———————— • ————————

"Becca, I be headed into Salisbury in about a week. Make a list of what you need, and I'll fetch it back. I'll take Jemima's ginseng and see that you have some coins if possible," stated Ned over the remains of the midday meal. The children had scattered after eating quickly. The older girls had the little ones, and each adult sat quietly relaxed, enjoying a day filled with spotty sunshine and a few peaceful moments from their children and their duties.

"I appreciate your offer Brother Ned. Can you pay our taxes, too, if'in there's enough? I can't stand the thought of the tax collector comin' around when Daniel is not to home. That man frightens me," replied Rebecca.

"He scares us all, especially since the Regulators have taken to harassin' all the tax collectors and merchants. I understand they mean well, yet at times, it seems they do more harm than good, although none care to pay more than what's deemed fair," George acknowledged.

Rebecca kept quiet on her views concerning the Regulators, as members of her own Bryan family had involved themselves in the movement. Daniel himself held that those living in the colony's western regions, near the proclamation line between the settlers and the Indians, were sorely underrepresented in the provincial assembly. Despite his beliefs, Daniel had no time to devote to politics beyond the occasional conversation with his brothers. Her own brothers, being more prosperous, fumed about the governor's taxes and high tariffs on essential goods. Several had joined the men determined to fight back against their lack of representation, and often rode with the Regulators.

Summoning her thoughts back to the ongoing conversation, Rebecca heard George ask about the Cherokees' visit the previous day. "No, George, I didn't recognize any, but since they called Daniel by his Cherokee name, I assumed they knew him. Seemed friendly enough and told me James was headed in with venison before walkin' off over the ridge. I can't say I was afraid, just concerned that they approached without us having any warnin'."

"Well, perhaps little Zek will grow to be a good guard dog. His sire's a good watch at our cabin. He keeps track of the girls, especially Mary," replied Ned. "Rightly so, that Jon should be back to the cabin. His presence will be a relief for you, make life easier."

"Where is Jon?" asked Hannah. "I haven't seen him since dinner."

"Oh, Jemima is showin' him how to find ginseng," laughed George. "He walked along, just as proper as a student listenin' to a teacher, that pup followin' somewhat along behind the two. Whispered as he passed by that at least he might be able to keep Mima from getting lost. Personally, I think we might have to go lookin' for them both. Jon's a hard worker, a good farmer, and an excellent shot, but he can lose his way between the house and the privy. I've noticed he always tries to follow worn paths when there's no one about for him to follow."

"Daniel's said many a time *the boy will never be a long hunter, as he'd never know how to get back home,*" stated Rebecca. "Yet, I depend on him and Jesse. I'm glad he's back."

Conversations continued, the men walked toward the stream and planned a short hunt for winter stores of deer and bear meat. Rebecca enjoyed the quiet autumn weather, the wind whispering quietly today amongst the leaves. Near time for her guests' departure, Martha asked, "Sister, how far gone are ye?"

Startled, Rebecca glanced down at her stomach and realized she had been rubbing it without even thinking about what she was doing. "Oh, the babe should arrive about the end of May."

Ann answered as well. "Looks as if mine will come not long before yours, I suspect the end of February. George hopes for a boy this time. Says two girls are aplenty. Yet, he adores them both and spoils them somethin' awful. Reckon he will with a boy, just the same as a girl."

Chapter 4
Late April 1768

With stealth, quiet footfalls, and silent breath seldom seen or heard in white hunters, the man, dressed all in dirty tan, patched buckskin, except for his felt hat, crept down the hillside toward the small cabin. He could make out children's voices and the occasional barking from a not-quite-grown dog. He watched as one child, a girl, fetched water from a springhouse sitting behind the cabin, while a half-grown boy skinned rabbits near the lean-to attached to the cabin's rear wall. Having passed by him earlier, he knew another boy, only about nine years of age, milked a large, black and white dairy cow in a pasture, one-quarter mile from the cabin. He had also seen an older boy, almost a man, preparing a field for planting in a nearby patch of cleared bottom land.

Yet none mattered, the man centered his thoughts on one and only one cabin occupant. He stood as still as a sentinel and watched as the children carried out their chores, most barefoot on this beautiful spring day. His thoughts turned to the last time he had seen his children. Today, James looked almost a man, although he was not yet eleven. Israel, now nine, seemed to have grown a foot. Seven-year-old Suzy, his darling daughter who looked like her mother, yet with his brownish-blond hair, stood tall for her age. He knew her to be clever and full of energy. He had not yet spotted Jemima or Levina. He wondered if his youngest, little Levina, was talking; surely at two she talked and walked? "Would she recognize me?" he wondered, knowing he had left when the child still crawled on the cabin's floor. Giving a good sniff, he could smell the sourness of his body and the stench of his buckskins. He thought about stripping down and engaging in a good wash in the roaring stream, despite knowing the water to be ice cold. Yes, he thought, it would be worthwhile to arrive home clean and clean-shaven. Instead, unable to pull his gaze away from the scene below, he simply stood and watched, finding joy in seeing his children and right glad to be home.

"You there, smelly, scruffy ol' man. You wander on off to where you came from. You're not wanted here," demanded a small feminine voice over a puppy's growling bark. "I'm armed and will shoot you dead, you hear? Now move along."

Daniel didn't know whether to laugh or to be afraid. Did Jemima really have a rifle? Surely Rebecca would not let the child near a gun at only five years of age? While still considering his options, he experienced a hard poke in his back, right above his belt. He knew she couldn't reach much higher, unless she had grown a mighty lot during his absence. Perhaps the child did have a rifle.

"I said move on along," she demanded.

"Don't believe I will, daughter. Reckon you'll have to shoot me."

"Daddy, Daddy, is that you? I don't have a rifle. James won't let me. I only got this big ol' stick and Zek here. He's our prophet and tells us when someone comes sneakin' around, Uncle Neddie gave him to me. That's how I knowed someone was here, prowlin' around," Jemima cried, throwing herself against Daniel's legs and hugging him so tightly he lost his balance, felling them both to the forest floor, where they rolled over and over, both laughing and rejoicing in the other's presence.

Once she had regained her breath, her questions started. "Where's Uncle Squire? Did you lose him? Don't you got any hides and furs and meat? Did you make it to Caintuck? Did you Daddy? Did you?"

"Mima, how 'bout one question at a time," Daniel suggested, pulling his daughter into a tight squeezing hug. "I expect Brother Squire and Will to be along shortly. I came ahead to let your Mama know we was home. Yes, I've got hides and furs and meat. It was a good hunt. Now let's go on down toward the cabin."

Discarding the stick and calling to Zek, Jemima led the way down the hill calling loudly to James and Israel, who now returned with a bucket of milk, "Look who I found. I found Daddy!"

The boys ran to greet their father as he approached the cabin's swept yard. Daniel noticed the good firewood and kindling supply, the yard's cleanliness, and their old cat sunning on the bench beside the door. With both the boys and Jemima making a racket, he almost didn't hear Rebecca's soft call.

"Daniel, oh, Daniel, blest be the Lord, you're home."

At the sound of her voice, he hurried toward her, planning to take her in his arms and swing her around and around, the same way he had returned to his girl time after time. That was until he looked closely. Seems he'd arrived home barely in time for another addition to their family.

Days and weeks melted into late spring as Daniel adjusted to farming and hunting near home. James' birthday fell on a Saturday. On May 7th, all the various families planned to be together. Unlike Israel's birthday on January 25th and Levina's on March 23rd, the day sprang forth warm, clear, and bright with a light breeze. The family gathered at George and Ann's, as they'd recently welcomed a son, little William Linville Boone on February 22nd. George spoiled this one as he did his two girls and was anxious to show him off to the entire family. Rebecca rode their old mare the short distance to their residence, where all the family stayed the night. Of course, George preached the following day. This time Brother Squire and Jane joined the gathering, bringing not quite two-year-old Jonathan and baby Jane. The men spoke about Daniel and Squire's long hunt. They planned trips into the village, while the womenfolk talked about babies and children and the menfolk.

Near May's end, the 26th to be exact, Daniel listened to their sixth child's birth. Rebecca labored alone for a while before sending for Martha. James felt lucky, as he found his grandma, Aylee Bryan, visiting at his aunt's cabin. The two women hurried the mile or so to be with Rebecca. Once there, they settled the children outside and prepared for "women's work." Daniel and the boys paced back and forth in the cabin's clearing until Daniel sent James and Israel off to hunt. Suzy watched over two-year-old Viney. The three returned to the cabin not long after the baby's first loud wail to welcome the baby girl. After one look at his new daughter and his wife's face, Daniel insisted she be named for Rebecca.

Soon James and Israel returned and joined the family, welcoming their new addition while Martha and Grandma Aylee served supper. Only as the family took to the table did they realize Jemima's seat on the bench remained empty.

"Daniel," Aylee whispered so as not to wake Rebecca and the babe, "we seem to be missin' a child."

"Has Mima not been in to see the baby?" asked Martha.

"I seen her earlier down to the creek fishin'," mumbled Jonathan, his mouth full, all the while helping himself to several more hoe cakes.

"I be the one to go," replied Daniel, glancing to his wife. "Don't tell Rebecca the child's gone missing once again."

Daniel grabbed his rifle and hat, and an unlit torch, should it be needed later, and walked from the cabin toward the woods and Beaver Creek.

He passed his child's favorite fishing and wading spot. Five good-sized fish, strung on a line, lay in the cold water. A cane fishing pole stood propped against a nearby cedar.

Daniel stood and listened, finally hearing his daughter's small voice coming from somewhere downstream.

"Mima?" he said quietly as he approached where she sat singing, leaning against a large dead oak trunk with Zek's head resting on her knee.

"Yea, Daddy."

"Don't you want to bring those fish and come on home for supper?"

"No, sir. I don't believe I will, if'in you don't mind."

"Well, what if I say I do mind?"

"Oh, if'in that's so, I reckon I'll come along. . . Daddy, has Mama birthed the baby?"

"Yes, it's a little girl. She has a head full of dark hair, as does your Mama, so I named her Rebecca. Don't you want to come see her?"

"Not particularly, no. But, well, I do wish to see Mama. Can I? Is she well?" whispered his daughter.

"Yes, child, your mother be well and asleep with the babe in her arms. Sister Martha and Grandma Aylee took good care of them both. Is that what you be frettin' about?"

"Well, Daddy, you know, some mamas die birthin' a babe. I overheard Mama talkin' with Aunt Martha and Aunt Ann and Aunt Hannah about how it happens. And well, Mama seemed to be right troubled this morn. She even cried and, well, Mama never cries or shouts, she never does. Didn't it worry you some?"

"Jemima, I worry each time your Mama births a baby, or one of my children lies hurt or sick or lost. Still, I can't go hide in the woods, although it's not a bad idea. No, I stay and try to help out, and I pray."

"Oh, Daddy, I prayed. I prayed a peck and a peck more—'xactly as Uncle George tells us to. I even said that whole Lord's Prayer he taught us," Jemima stated, grabbing Daniel's hand and heading back to her catch.

"Well, seems your prayers had some right powerful influence on the good Lord today, daughter. So, let's go have some supper before Jonathan eats all the hoe cakes. I believe Martha even brought a custard pie."

"Daddy, can I have a knife, a sharp knife?" Jemima asked, changing the subject.

"No. Why, in heaven's name do you need a sharp knife?"

"To clean these fish, of course."

"Lil' Duck, that's why you have brothers. I'll make Jonathan clean your fish. We can have them for breakfast. Now, quit pokin' along. I be right hungry."

⟶ ● ⟵

Over the summer, Daniel, James, and Israel often stayed away for days at a time on hunting trips. Israel worked hard to carry the family's second rifle and to learn from his father the wilderness ways. Daniel taught the boys to hunt, to track game, to spot Indian sign, and to clean and prepare anything they shot or trapped. Always with a book, mostly the Bible and *Gulliver's Travels*, Daniel read to the boys at night around the campfire. Having attended school and later instructed by his older brother Samuel's wife, Sarah Day, Daniel could read, write, and do necessary mathematics. The trio roamed wide and far among the Blue Ridge Mountains and into the Smoky Mountains, but seldom stayed gone longer than a week.

Back at the cabin, Rebecca rose on the day after she gave birth and resumed the tasks of daily frontier life. Grandma Aylee stayed for another week to help and to care for her daughter and the baby, before Neddie came to take her home to Grandpa Joseph. After a tearful parting, life in the little cabin returned to somewhat normal. Suzy now watched after baby Becky and Levina. After finishing with her chores, Jemima often disappeared into the woods and returned with enough fish for the evening meal. Occasionally, despite her size and abilities, she helped with the other tasks left undone by her father and brother's absences. Without comment, Jonathan pitched in to supervise her attempts at chopping wood and carrying water from the spring. To prevent injury, he moved the ax to a place Jemima couldn't reach. Otherwise, with occasional help from Daniel and the boys, Jonathan put in the family's corn crop and helped Rebecca with the vegetable and herb patch.

When at the cabin, and as they all rested outside after the evening meal, Daniel would thrill his children and Rebecca with tales from his and Squire's adventure of the previous winter. "Well, first you have to cross the Blue Ridge, took us right near a week as we hunted along the way. We followed the rivers when possible, but often camped in rock shelters, high on the hillsides. The Cherokee also travel along the rivers, and we felt it might be right smart to avoid their company on this hunt. We left some of our furs and hides hidden in various dark shelter recesses as we traveled farther northwest. Next came the Appalachian Mountains. Seems we found mountains no matter which way we turned. Squire, Will, and me, well, we hunted and kept to ourselves. Didn't see another white soul the entire trip. Us being west of the Proclamation Line, we didn't want to stir up no trouble. We saw a few Indians, mostly from a distance, so we took care not to be noticed, so to speak.

"We wanted to find that hunting ground John Finley told me about back in 1755. We followed the Holston River and the Clinch. At the Clinch's headwaters, we had to climb more mountains. High mountains. Plum tuckered us out, walking or riding rough, rocky mountainsides day after day. After a long uphill climb, we discovered the start of another stream, flowing almost due north, it became a river as we walked or rode mostly downhill day after day. Figured we were well into Indian land by that point. As the mountains became hills, Squire and I found a salt lick surrounded by buffalo, deer, elk, and other animals' tracks. We settled into a convenient camp nearby and began a serious hunt. Wasn't long before the snow fell. We found ourselves trapped as the snow became deeper and deeper. At least the hunting proved good.

"Squire, Will, and me stayed right there most all winter. Ate bear and buffalo meat. Tried to stay warm and hunted most every day. Bears, oh my, oh my. . ., the place was crawlin' with them. We might have killed a hundred or more but figured even with our three pack horses we could not return with that many hides."

"Daddy," James interrupted, "did you find the cane fields and the meadows and the huntin' ground Mr. Finley told you about?"

"No, son, I reckon we didn't go the right way. Seems there's a lot more country out west than I expected."

"Uncle Daniel," asked Jonathan, "do you reckon to go back?"

"Not directly, but I've found that curiosity is a natural part of man's soul and creates influencin' powers to those that embrace that curiosity. So, I reckon, the good Lord put the curiosity of Caintuck in my soul. Guess I'll have to go again, someday."

"My soul, too," piped Jemima's small, sleepy voice from where she lay on the hard-packed dirt.

"Well, not mine," answered Jonathan. "I expect I'll stay right here in North Carolina."

Chapter 5
John Finley

"Daddy, a peddler's at the cabin. Mama says for you to come," shouted Israel as he scurried up the hillside, stopping near where his father sat cleaning a few rabbits for the evening meal.

"Sure, son. Be down presently."

Placing the rabbits in his rawhide sack before picking up his knife and rifle, Daniel thought over the list of things his family needed. He hoped the peddler might have a few items for Rebecca, but he needed gunpowder and a new skinning knife, having passed his oldest one on to Israel just a few days previous.

As he started for the cabin, Daniel noticed the largest hardwood trees around the cabin showed autumn's first colors, some yellows and just a few oranges amongst the green cedars and still green hardwoods. In the cabin's clearing, Daniel saw his children bunched around the peddler as he demonstrated a little wooden toy. It was shaped like a man and its arms and legs flew about when the peddler pulled the attached string. The peddler handed it to Daniel's oldest daughter to try. Viney giggled wildly every time Suzy pulled the string, reaching for the toy while jabbering her nonsense words. He watched the boys, along with Jemima, examining the peddler's supply of folding knives. Rebecca rummaged through a selection of cloth yardage. She had already placed two pieces aside.

Focused on his family, Daniel didn't pay much attention to the short, scruffy-looking peddler until he walked past the single-axle wagon's end, watching as the man entertaining his daughters with yet another toy.

"Well, I'll be a suck egg mule, if it isn't John Finley," Daniel declared.

"Daniel, Daniel Boone? Is that you, truly? I haven't seen you since our escape from Braddock's Defeat. My, what a lovely family you've gotten for yourself," replied the trader.

"Becca, come meet my friend John Finley. John, this is my wife Rebecca and my children, James, Israel, Susannah, Jemima, Levina," pointing to each one in turn, "oh, and the baby's asleep in the cabin. Rebecca, children, please welcome my old friend John Finley."

"Will you stay to dinner, Mr. Finley?" asked Rebecca.

"Will you tell us more about Caintuck?" requested James.

"Ah, so your Pa's done told you about the promised land. Have you been yet, Daniel?"

"No, not yet. Now let's find a place to talk. Can you sit and stay awhile?"

"No place I need to be except with old friends, beggin' your pardon, Mistress Boone."

"No need, Mr. Finley. Daniel's spoken fondly of you and your tales of Caintuck. I feel I already know you," answered Rebecca.

Later in the day, after making their trades and purchasing what goods they needed, John joined the family for the evening meal.

"Mr. Finley, do you have family hereabouts?" asked Rebecca politely.

"No Mistress, my parents and I came over from Ireland many years past. Over the campfires of Braddock's Campaign, Daniel and I discovered we had grown up near each other in Pennsylvania. That's where I first learned to speak and trade with the Delaware and Shawnee. Later, I joined with several other men in a tradin' post of sorts at the Forks of the Ohio. In 1752, us five traveled by canoe, down the Ohio and Louisa rivers to trade at the Shawnee village called Blue Lick Town. The tradin' was good, and we stayed on a bit with some other traders until a party of Frenchmen and Canadian Indians attacked and killed three of my men and several other traders. Afterward, we returned to the Forks of the Ohio and our old camp. As you can see, I've never settled long in one place."

⟢ ● ⟣

"Seems to me as you children wanted to hear more about Caintuck," John stated, after lighting his pipe. He leaned back against the cabin wall and, settling his feet on a stump Israel had placed near the bench for just such a purpose, started in with his tale. "Well, now let me think. I first saw Caintuck back in 1752 when I floated down the Ohio River to trade with the Shawnee. Ah, it was the Good Book's land of cane and clover, must resemble Eden, as it reminded me of the Bible's tale of the land of milk and honey. Few Indians lived below the Ohio in Caintuck, but many tribes hunted those lands. Some tell how Mingoes, Delawares, even Iroquois and a few Mohawks, hunt amongst its riches. Of course, those Shawnee are the most likely ones to be encountered. And, I encountered quite a few as I traveled on down the Ohio to the great falls, where I made camp and traded until all my goods sold and I no longer felt welcome." He stopped to tap his pipe and check if it needed relighting. Then, looking about at all the intent faces yearning for him to continue, he nodded to Daniel, who lazed nearby, and said, "Since I last saw your Pa, I've explored more of that dark and bloody ground. Last year, I led a huntin' party down the Ohio and to the Louisa River. We hunted and trapped the whole season.

"Let me tell you, the land is full and fruitful. It's also a howlin' wilderness full of savages and beast of all kinds," John explained, waving his arms here and there. "I've seen buffalo herds at salt licks that could not be counted, for the good Lord didn't create numbers to count that high. There be bobcats and panthers, wolves, coyotes, streams filled with beavers, polecats, deer and majestic elk herds, and turkeys. A man might feast most every day on a turkey should he so choose. Course, why would a man choose to eat only turkey when there is so much variety to fill yer stomach? I found nuts and berries and persimmon trees; oh, and fox grapes as big as apples, hanging alongside creeks just after the first frost. I almost forgot the fish in the streams. Trout jumpin' high in mountain streams and lesser fish in the rivers. See, I prefer trout when I eat fish.

"There's bottom land with rich soil, yet covered in thick, waist-high grass. I discovered rivers and small streams. Springs and salt licks abound where animals of all sizes and sorts come to lick the ground. Why, a man could camp alongside those salt licks and never go any farther to keep himself fed. He'd gather enough pelts and hides to enrich his pockets to overflowin'."

"John, just last winter my youngest brother Squire, a friend, and myself camped at such a salt lick. We fed on bear and buffalo all winter," Daniel stated. "I was never sure if we'd reached Caintuck, as we never found those valleys and plains covered in grass. Yet, we lived and hunted well all winter."

"Bears, oh, yes, the bears," John declared. "Daniel, did you tell these children about the number and massive size of Caintuck's bears? Why, I figure some are so large and so mean it takes three good shots to bring them down."

"Not if I be doing the shootin'," demanded Jemima, interrupting and jumping to her feet and pretending to hold a rifle. "Daddy says to aim for the brain, not the heart, for the heart lies buried under all that bear fat."

"Well, Miss Jemima, can you fire a rifle?" inquired their guest.

"I rightly could if Daddy or James would let me. I know how to load. Course I needs to stand on a stump to reach the end of the barrel."

John and the others laughed at Jemima's determined expression. Just before Daniel started to ask another question about Caintuck, Rebecca called her children to finish their nighttime chores and ready themselves for bed.

As John and Daniel settled in to talk at length, he thought to call Jonathan back.

"Jon, has Mima actually loaded a rifle?"

"Not so's I know, Uncle Daniel. James and I have taken care to keep them from her reach ever since we found her tryin' to pull one down off the hooks. James says she's been beggin' him to teach her to shoot. James and me, well, we don't reckon she can even heft a rifle, much less a musket. She's a mite scrawny little thing."

Days passed. John often camped just outside their cabin. He had proceeded on to several family members' cabins and returned alongside Squire not long after the first light snow. Rebecca welcomed him in each evening and listened as Daniel spoke with him about Caintuck. Some evenings, John Stewart, Hannah's husband, and Squire joined them. Their discussions roamed around all the problems and solutions for a long hunt into Caintuck. Rebecca listened, knowing more certainly than ever before that Daniel would once again be leaving her. She often caught James and Jemima listening intently to the conversation. James wanted to join the trip, and occasionally seemed on the verge of suggesting he might go along. Mima, on the other hand, understood she would never be allowed to traipse off over the mountains with a hunting party, yet Rebecca and Jonathan had seen her pretending to hunt and trap on the hillside above the cabin and at Beaver Creek.

"Daniel, I've heard tell, you can reach the valleys and great meadow of Caintuck through a gap in the Cumberland Mountains. The trail's mostly used by the Cherokee who come from the south to hunt buffalo," John offered, late one evening in early winter. "I've never been that route, but with enough men, and if we follow Indian trails from the Clinch River, I suspect we might suss it out."

"I agree, most say you can follow the Great Warrior's Path to the Clinch River, then on to the Powell Valley. Some call the gap *the Cumberland Gap.* I've been told Dr. Thomas Walker named it after the Duke of Cumberland back in 1750," replied Squire.

"I've given it some thought myself. I reckon it could be found. I think I might be able to gather a few good men to join our party if you be willin' to join us," Daniel proposed.

"Well, now I just might. First, I must get my tradin' done and ride back into Salisbury to pay off some debts. When might you reckon we'd depart?"

"Not until next spring," Daniel suggested. "I need to make sure my family has provisions enough for me to be gone a right good spell."

Winter progressed much as any other winter. Snow came and left. The cold drove them all into the little cabin for days and nights together. John Finley traipsed off to finish his trading and then into Salisbury, where Daniel joined him to purchase what supplies they could afford. John and Daniel, sometimes accompanied by Squire, talked with other long hunters among their neighbors, hoping to increase their party's size and strength. Hannah's husband, John Stewart, recently returned from a trip all the way to New Orleans by river, promised to go along. News of the Treaty of Fort Stanwix, signed in the New York colony and relinquishing Iroquois rights to hunt in Caintuck, reached them in early winter. They listened to stories told around the village about how the British paid about forty thousand pounds of trade goods to the Iroquois for the agreement. This treaty followed shortly after the October treaty with the Cherokee at Hard Labor, South Carolina. Most local hunters thought as how these two treaties seem to open Caintuck's lands to hunters and settlers. Yet, word arrived as to how the Shawnee did not agree and had declared all-out war against any hunters encroaching on their traditional, treasured hunting grounds.

Jemima watched as the first day of May 1769, the date set for departure, approached. The hunting party gathered pack horses, and their own rifles, powder horns, and shot pouches. The horses would carry extra flint for starting fires and creating the new flints for rifles, along with powder, shot and extra lead to make shot. They took along traps in all sizes and types. Camp equipment included blankets, kettles, salt, and various provisions. She saw them include lineaments and potions for possible illnesses and injuries , and gave a little prayer these things would not be needed. Then three additional men rode in and joined their party— James Mooney, Joseph Holden, and William Cooley, all Yadkin Valley neighbors. Daddy said Mooney, Holden, and Cooley agreed to remain in camp to process and prepare hides for shipment back east, while he and the two Johns carried out the hunting and trapping.

Late one April evening, just before the planned departure date, after everyone had settled down to sleep, Jemima listened as her parents spoke quietly together from their bed. "Daniel, I understand you have to go, but you should know, we'll have another child late this year, I expect in December," whispered Rebecca. Before Daniel formed his reply, she continued, "Squire is stayin' home because little Moses is only a couple of months old. John is leavin' Hannah with the three daughters to care for, and another on the way. Your poor sister. No wonder she plans to stay with family durin' his absence. I can cope. I have James and Israel, and Jonathan. Yet, I worry, and I'll miss you terribly. I've become accustomed to having you home."

Jemima heard no more from either parent, except her father's soothing whispers and her mother's soft answers. Several mornings later, she stood firmly clutching her mother's hand and watched as her father and his companions rode off toward the west where the mountains, obscured by an early morning mist, swallowed them whole.

Rebecca shed no tears in her children's presence when Daniel left. Instead, she carried on in her usual way. Only James noticed how his mother sometimes walked to the top of the western ridge and stood looking toward Caintuck, as if hoping to see Daniel return.

Chapter 6
Another Year Passed

Once again, the trees surrounding the Boone's small cabin stood emboldened with color, signaling another winter's arrival. Not long after dawn, Zek whined and barked, running toward the door from his place before the fire, growling and scratching to be let out. While James gathered up his rifle, Rebecca pushed her children away from the breakfast table toward the loft ladder, handing Viney to Suzy before turning to grab the musket. Hoping the baby would still sleep, Jemima placed a cover over little Becky's crib, before climbing the ladder.

As Rebecca and James, each cradling a rifle in the crook of their arm, moved toward the cabin's door and single window, Jemima crept forward toward the loft's edge, calling softly to Zek. She knew better than to raise her voice above a whisper as James slid the hide covering away from the window frame and peeked out to view the swept yard for intruders.

"Can't see no one yet," James whispered.

Rebecca stood, rubbing her aching back, and hoping the pup had only heard a passing deer or turkey and not a stranger. He rarely barked at family, even the extended Boone family. Since either Squire and Ned checked weekly on how Rebecca and the children managed, Zek had become accustomed to their visits. She'd almost made up her mind to turn Zek out and let him run when an unfamiliar voice shouted, "Mistress Boone, hello the cabin. It be Alexander Neeley."

"James, go and greet Mr. Neeley and let Zek run. I'll get my shawl and shoes," Rebecca instructed, breathing a sigh of relief. Indian trouble was rare these days, but that didn't mean their own kind could be easily trusted either.

"Good mornin' Mr. Neeley. Is Uncle Squire with you?" questioned James, propping his rifle against the cabin's front wall.

"He'll be along sharply, young James, had to stop and get a rock from his horse's hoof. May I speak with your mother?"

"Good day, Alexander. I guess you and Squire be off today to Caintuck. Is Squire far behind?" Rebecca inquired as she stepped from the cabin.

"No, ma'am, he'll be along shortly. I came on to tell you we're headed to the hunt and to check if you be in need of supplies. My wife's headed into Salisbury later in the week. She'll be happy to pick up what you need, if'in you'll send young James or Israel over with a message."

As they talked, Squire rode down the creek's bank and tied his horse and pack horses to the rail Daniel had placed there for just such a purpose. As he jumped off and walked toward Rebecca, Daniel's youngest brother smiled and waved at the children now piling from their home.

"Why, Rebecca, you look as if you could deliver that babe most any day now. Don't you want me to send a boy for Martha or Jane? I'm sure either one will be happy to come over," suggested Squire quietly.

"No, Brother, I believe it will be weeks yet before the babe comes. How long do you expect before you see Daniel?"

"Right near four weeks or so, if'in we can find him in that wilderness and don't meet with bad weather," answered Squire, purposely not mentioning the danger of encountering any Shawnee. "I remember your messages for him and will make sure he knows how you and the children are farin'."

Anxious to be on their way west, Squire and Alexander chatted only briefly before they mounted and rode off, each trailed by four horses loaded down with supplies for Daniel's hunting party. Rebecca and Suzy watched until they rode from sight before returning to the cabin. Inside, Levina had finished off all the bowls of cornmeal mush and spilled her cup of milk. Tail wagging furiously, Zek stood licking away the drops as they hit the puncheon floor. Rebecca, stooping to clean up after Levina, said a silent prayer for Daniel and Squire's safe return, adding in the other hunters' names as she finished her thoughts to the Lord.

Susannah grabbed little Becky from her crib and changed her nappy, serving as a second mother to her many siblings. Their own breakfast eaten by Viney, the boys finished with some cornbread and honey before beginning their chores. Rebecca watched as Jemima gathered their pallet, stored it away, and proceeded to wash the bowls, cups, and spoons. *Six children, the oldest only twelve and another on the way,* she thought. *How many more winters can I go without Daniel?*

"Blessed be the Lord, I'm mighty tired," declared Jemima as she clambered wearily onto the bench and settled herself at the table.

"Mima, why might you be so mighty tired? What have you been up to all day?" questioned Rebecca, realizing she had hardly seen her daughter since breakfast.

Not seeing the quelling looks from James and Israel, Jemima proclaimed, "Why, I've been huntin'. Haven't I, James? James and Israel been learnin' me, haven't you James?"

Rebecca stared at her two sons and turned to Jemima before asking, "Well, Jemima, did you actually shoot anythin'?"

"No, ma'am, today was just loadin' practice. James put me on that ol' stump out back of the lean-to to practice loadin'. I got right good at it, but he won't let me shoot nothin'. He claims I'm too small still to hold the rifle steady.

I told him how Daddy sometimes props his rifle in the crook of a tree, but. . .”

“Enough talkin’, Mima. Eat your dinner and go finish your chores,” Rebecca interrupted, hushing all conversation simply by her voice’s soft quiet tone.

As the children finished eating and Mima had gathered all the bowls and spoons and headed for the hot water kettle, Rebecca pulled her two eldest aside, and they exited the cabin.

“Mama, we got plum tired of her. . .,” started James.

“No! You listen here. Mima is only six years old. I know she has been pesterin’ you to let her shoot, but it is not your responsibility to teach her to use a rifle. James, you and Israel, go bring in enough firewood and water to last the night. Then feed the cow and calf and tend to the horses. When you finish, off to bed, and not one word, not one word to me or Mima, do you hear?”

Standing before their little cabin, Rebecca surveyed their holding. Yet another winter had passed, and spring approached as evidenced by buds on the young trees. In the surrounding forest, she noticed ferns and other forest plants sending up their first new shoots. Soon she’d need to send for Jonathan or Jesse to help with the planting. She pondered, just sitting outside and letting the girls tend their siblings. She listened as an approaching rider calling her name rode down the hillside. She watched with fear as Alexander Neeley, alone, proceeded down the slope and into the yard, leading two fully loaded pack horses.

Both anxious and scared to know the answer, she challenged him with, “Mr. Neeley, are Daniel and Squire headed home?”

“No, Rebecca. I have some news, so I stopped in on my way home. Might should get on with tellin’ you. Daniel and John Stewart had some trouble with the Shawnee back some time ago, early on in winter. When Squire and I arrived, we found the other four men preparin’ to leave, believin’ Daniel and John to be captured or dead. Now don’t you worry, they both turned up two days later fit as a fiddle; however, the party had lost their pelts to those thievin' Shawnee. Squire and I stayed with Daniel and John and continued to hunt. Afterward, away on an overnight hunt, Daniel and John Stewart separated. Daniel returned to camp two days later. But, well, I be plum sorry to tell you, Rebecca, but . . ., well, John never returned. Daniel and us searched far and wide. He and Squire decided to stay and continue the hunt to replace the hides that was stolen and to look for John, but I returned. I'll go find Hannah tomorrow and give her the news. Daniel sends his best wishes for you all. He and Squire were well when I left them near on five weeks ago." After entertaining Rebecca's few questions, Alexander tipped his hat and rode off toward his cabin and his family.

Moving to the bench and sitting heavily, Rebecca worried over the news. Poor, poor Hannah, partially scalped by Indians when only four and still bearing the scar, she now raised three young daughters. A babe expected any day now and her husband likely dead. Oh, Lord, oh, Lord. Rebecca mused, praying a silent prayer that John had returned to camp by now. Thinking back over Alexander's message once again, she realized he didn't seem to think that was likely. She knew about the camp keepers returning last winter, as brothers Ned and George had passed along the news of their return. Not one of the three who'd returned came by the cabin with the news. John Finley'd turned north on their journey home. Seems he, like the others, never imagined she might want news of Daniel or were afraid to be the one to tell her the trouble with the Shawnee. With Caintuck's dangers fresh in her mind, Rebecca bowed her head in prayer, silently thanking the Lord for her children and asking his blessing for Squire and Daniel, remembering John Stewart and poor Hannah, now a newly made widow.

⬤

Rebecca watched as Suzy gathered up little Daniel Morgan and placed him on the bench outside the door, before changing his nappy. Levina and Jemima helped James and Israel, alongside Jonathan, plant the vegetable patch and herb bed. Jonathan had returned to oversee the spring planting. Little Daniel Morgan had arrived on December twenty-third, according to Alexander Neeley, at near the same time as Daniel and John had been first captured by the Shawnee. The boys and Daniel's family had provided them with fresh game during the winter. After Suzy handed Daniel Morgan back, Rebecca nursed her son and watched her children argue and play.

She thought on her two older sons. Only thirteen years ago, she had once held her oldest this way, marveling at her and Daniel's new babe. James now hunted as well as most men and better than many. Her second, Israel, only eleven, could shoot and trap. He worked hard around the cabin, keeping all their livestock fed and watered.

Next, her thoughts passed to her four daughters, each one so different from the others. Susannah, oh, how would she ever cope without her Suzy? Tall for her ten years, with long light brown hair, she resembled the many Boones, Suzy had grown into a polite, caring girl. Seemed to Rebecca that black-haired Jemima might never be as tall as her and Susannah. Still small for her age, Jemima unfailingly did her chores, never complaining, as long as she had time to fish, hunt ginseng, and wander the surrounding hills. She still begged her older brothers to teach her to shoot, but always out of Rebecca's hearing. Rebecca had promised her daughter that she could learn just as soon as she turned eight years old. That would be this coming October. Levina and Becky kept them all busy, keeping each safe and away from trouble, especially now that Becky walked. Each day, her youngest, Daniel Morgan provided them with laughs as he tried to sit alone, gurgled, and smiled. If only she had her Daniel.

As the summer grew hotter, Rebecca and the children visited family and tended their crops. June brought their most important visitor as Squire returned from Caintuck with four pack horses loaded down with beaver pelts and deer hides. Each horse carried more than two hundred and fifty pounds of the hunters' hard work, enough to pay their debts and Squire's. Squire stayed only long enough to gather more supplies and fresh horses before heading back to join Daniel. He'd take the news about Daniel's new son, named for his father and Daniel's mother Sarah Morgan. Brother George and Ann also had a new son, also named for his father. He'd be sure to share the news from Boston, about the massacre by British troops on March fifth. Ever since the Stamp Act of 1765, tempers had flared across the colonies. New taxes and demands from the King and royal governors continued to make many colonists yearn for more freedom to govern themselves. Also, Squire had visited their sister Hannah, now living with her mother, Sarah Morgan Boone. Squire would report to Daniel how Hannah's four daughters thrived while their mother still mourned her missing husband. This would go some ways toward easing Daniel's mind over John Stewart's disappearance. He rode past Rebecca's cabin one more time on his way back to Caintuck.

"Rebecca, I suspect the next time we meet Daniel will be ridin' beside me. Can't imagine he'll want to remain away much longer."

⬤

"Mama, tomorrow's my eighth birthday, and you promised, truly you did," demanded Jemima.

"Yes, daughter, I promised. Tomorrow, the boys will do all the chores and watch the babes. You and Susannah and me will go out back and learn to load a rifle and shoot."

"But, Mama. . ." wailed Suzy, "I don't want to learn."

"Susannah Boone, I've put this off far too long at your insistence, but you must learn to use a rifle properly. At some time in your life, you'll need to defend yourself and your family, probably from Indians in some far western home, if'in I know your father. So, you *will* learn."

While Mima rose early, dressed, and gobbled down her breakfast, Suzy lingered over each and every step of the cabin's morning routine. Before long, Rebecca had had enough and demanded she hurry along.

"Boys, chores first, but watch Levina and Becky constantly. Becky loves to run outside anytime the door is opened, as you well know. Israel, little Dan is your responsibility. We'll be down toward the cornfield if you need me. I'll leave that ol' pistol here for today and take both rifles."

Suzy started whining about not wanting to learn but was quickly hushed and handed both powder horns and the cabin's shooting kit. Jemima carried one rifle, taller than her by several inches while Rebecca carried the other. The day dawned clear and warm for early October. As they walked, Jemima thought back on learning to load a rifle earlier in the year from her brothers and hoped she could remember all the many steps.

Once they reached a safe way from the cabin, Rebecca sat the girls down and started instructing them on how to handle a firearm, much as her father had with her many years ago. Jemima listened intently from the beginning and so did Suzy after being warned once again to pay attention. In order to make this possible for Jemima, James had placed two stumps at the cornrows' edge for each to stand on. All morning the girls practiced loading and firing under Rebecca's constant instruction. Standing the rifle on its butt end, they would load the coarse powder into the barrel after measuring it in the powder horn's cap. Next came the small round fabric patches and the lead ball. Jemima soon learned to place the patch on the barrel end and then the ball, pushing the ball in place, barely within the barrel end by using the round knob on the short starter rod. The hardest part for her was placing the ramrod in the barrel's end and pushing the ball in place. Rebecca suggested she hold the rod by the middle until she had it partly inserted and then to push it the remaining way. Mima never once forgot to tap the rod and check to see that the ball was in place by lining up the small notch marked on the end of the rod with the barrel's end.

Suzy hated the next part, the actual firing of the rifle. After the ball was in place, each girl had to pull back the frizzen to prime the pan with additional black powder. This step took careful practice, as too much powder could clog the pin hole in the frizzen. Too little and the shot might wedge itself in the barrel. The girls used their respective tree stumps to support their rifles while pouring the correct measure of powder and making sure the pin hole was visible before closing the frizzen. They practiced placing the hammer at half cock to make it safe to carry and placing the hammer at full cock for firing.

Rebecca showed each how to aim. She demonstrated her prowess by shooting a squirrel from a tree at the cornfield's far end. For most of the morning, Suzy aimed high and missed every target, despite Rebecca's constant instructions. Jemima, on the other hand, soon hit the large oak where James had earlier tacked a bright red cloth scrap from Rebecca's mending basket. Just past noon, Jemima hit the cloth. Jemima's resulting celebration brought both brothers outside to see if someone had been shot. Suzy stood and stared at her sister before declaring herself to be done for the day.

Dinner that night was filled with Jemima's bragging constantly about hitting the target, loading faster than Suzy, her knowledge of gun safety, and getting her own rifle someday. Suzy instead complained about how her arms hurt and Mima's constant bragging. Rebecca smiled, remembering her and Martha's first lesson. She kept that memory to herself, yet relived every moment as she listened to her own daughters.

Squire's prediction proved false. Instead, he returned to the Yadkin Valley alone in the late winter, again loaded down with furs and pelts, leaving Daniel back in Caintuck. Squire rushed around gathering supplies and left once again to meet up with his brother. The two continued to hunt into the next year, 1771. Other long hunters now walked and hunted Caintuck. Daniel and Squire occasionally encountered other hunting parties or saw signs of their activity near salt licks and springs. In March of 1771, Daniel and Squire began the return home with their spoils. Rain-swollen creeks and other natural obstacles hindered their return. When they reached Powell's Valley, they camped, planning to hunt for meat to carry home. Instead, they discovered a gaunt, unwashed, barely clothed man, obviously suffering from hunger and exhaustion. That man proved to be their Yadkin Valley neighbor, Alexander Neeley, who had become separated from and lost on his way to Cumberland Gap with another party of long hunters. Squire and Daniel nursed him back to health, gave him powder, shot, and food, along with directions to find the gap since Neely seemed determined to rejoin his party.

Days later, as they continued their homeward journey, Daniel and Squire came across six or seven Indians, who robbed them of much they carried, including their rifles. The two men proceeded to a nearby settlement where, after an attempt to regain their stolen goods, the Boone brothers gathered enough supplies for their journey home.

Chapter 7
Planning

"Mama, mightn' I join in the dancin'?" asked Suzy, curiously glancing around at their neighbors at the frolic while smoothing the skirt of her new dress.

"Of course, you may. Only not with the boys, if any ask. You can dance along with your girl cousins and friends over toward the woods," replied Rebecca smiling at her oldest and her many nieces, who listened intently to her reply, knowing their own mothers would answer the same.

"But Mama, Charity gets to dance with boys!" wailed her own daughter.

"Yes, she does. Charity is nigh on thirteen, and you my dear daughter are only ten. Now run along and watch after Levina."

As the girls wandered over to the clearing's edge, Rebecca turned to see Jemima hurry away with yet another piece of apple pie. James stood nearby, awkwardly talking to a Bryan girl, a distant cousin. Israel appeared to be more interested in a neighbor boy's new folding knife. The younger children, the babies and toddlers, were nearby being looked after by several older women, everyone a grandmother many times over.

Listening to the fiddlers tune up for another song, dressed in her best gown, Rebecca thought back on her first dance with Daniel. He'd just returned from Pennsylvania and joined in with some young people going to pick cherries. Rebecca remembered spotting Daniel among the older boys as the party headed to a nearby orchard. As the afternoon progressed, when no one was watching, she often peeked in his direction. She'd recognized his name, knew his family, and his reputation as a hunter; all the girls did.

Later in the day, the cherry pickers returned to an informal gathering where a fiddler tuned up and called for dancers. Rebecca recollected Daniel's invitation to dance, him asking quietly, but not demonstrating the least shyness or embarrassment. They danced the evening together, barely noticing those around them. Her being taller than most girls and barely shorter than Daniel, her black hair against his brownish blond, they made a striking couple. The next day Daniel and Rebecca's names, linked together, became the talk of the village.

Tonight, as the dancers moved around the hard-packed dirt, Rebecca watched her sister Martha and Neddie step lively to the "Virginia Reel." The evening air was filled with the smell of a hickory fire, roasting pork, and fine liquor. Each neighbor seemed to have turned out in their best clothing. Some of the men wore suits of fine cloth rather than buckskin or homespun. One or two had patterned waistcoats and gold watch chains that glimmered in the firelight. A few women had even donned silk gowns of glorious colors and carried fringed shawls. Her own dress, several years old, had been a gift from her father several years past. The linen overskirt was bright red, while her underskirt and bodice were a lovely pale blue. A fine silk scarf covered her shoulders and the top of her bodice.

The tune ended, and she stood, still tapping her foot, listening as the head fiddler called for "The Flowers of Edinburgh." Suddenly, before her stood an unshaven, dirt-covered, slightly smelly hunter holding out his hand in anticipation for the next dance. Rebecca saw several family members, Bryans and Boones alike, staring at her, wondering if she might dance with this stranger in Daniel's absence.

As she opened her mouth to respond in the negative, the stranger softly demanded, "You need not refuse me, for you have danced many a time with me."

Rebecca recognized Daniel's voice and threw herself into his arms, startling the many onlookers. Only Squire's appearance in front of Jane, also begging for a dance, revealed the men's presence to their friends and neighbors. Soon, both Daniel and Squire found themselves surrounded by their respective children and various family members. The evening grew late as the two hunters' return added to the frolic's atmosphere. Daniel rarely left Rebecca's side during the dancing. He swung her around the dance floor with abandon, just as he always did his girl upon returning from a long absence.

Late, late into the night, many men gathered to hear Daniel and Squire tell about their previous two years' adventures. The conversation added unknowingly to the buzzel about Caintuck. Settled at Daniel's feet throughout the late evening's story time sat Jemima and his sons, James and Israel. Each marveled in their father's many adventures, finding yet again the draw of Caintuck in their souls.

During his absence, Daniel's debts had mounted. They continued to do so after his return with nothing to show for his last year hunting with Squire. Soon, the family lost their Yadkin Valley farm to their creditors, and once again, they moved. This time Daniel took them west and south to the Watauga River Valley, near Sycamore Springs, where the Watauga Association had illegally created a community of like-minded families who wanted more freedom, especially from taxes and government. Here the Boone family settled in an even smaller cabin, one that did not belong to them. Daniel hunted the lands west of the settlement after their arrival.

Jemima rejoiced when her father returned them all to the Upper Yadkin Valley in 1772, not long before he returned to Caintuck with other long hunters. Once again, he'd left her mother expecting a babe.

This time, friends from the Yadkin valley, Hugh McGary, Samuel Tate, and Benjamin Cutbirth, joined Daniel. The buzzel about Caintuck had spread far and wide, with many a wandering man desiring to see that land for themselves. Many an evening before their departure, Mima had once again sat listening to their tales of that promised land.

In late April 1773, James' voice rang across the small clearing around the cabin, "Mama, Daddy's comin' down the creek." As the children gathered, Rebecca made her way slowly from the cabin to welcome her husband. This time, she could see his pack horses, loaded with furs and pelts, following in single file. The boys and Jemima helped Daniel unload, while Rebecca sat on the bench outside the door, waiting for his greeting.

"Seems Daddy made it home in time for this babe, didn't he Mama," stated Suzy, carrying Daniel Morgan on her hip.

"Put him down and make him walk," Rebecca instructed. "He has to get used to walkin' before this next one comes."

"Yes, Mama. Shall I add more to the stew pot?"

"Your Daddy and the boys will be hungry, so go ahead and start another pot. I'll ask Jemima to bring butter from the spring house and some bacon."

Walking toward the cabin, Daniel smiled at his wife, sitting and waiting for his approach. "Glad to see I'm in time for this one's arrival, my girl," he whispered in her ear, while holding her against his chest.

Weeks later in late May, Jesse Bryan Boone, named for his cousin, whom Rebecca and Daniel had raised, and his mother's family, entered the world. Following the birth, the family contemplated seriously a move to Caintuck. Daniel and others had enlisted to the venture, and they decided to leave in the early autumn. Nephews Jesse and Jonathan chose to stay in North Carolina, but Squire, Jane, and their three sons decided to join Daniel's party into that promised land.

Not long after mother and babe were fit to travel, Daniel and Rebecca packed their belongings and headed to the Forks of the Yadkin River to visit with Boone and Bryan family members. Daniel hoped to persuade them to join in his venture.

"I've spent the last year dreamin' of returnin' to Caintuck with my family, this time to stay," Daniel insisted. "Squire and Jane have agreed to go. George, Neddie, I find it might make Rebecca and me easier about such a move if'in you and your family will join us. Such a move means we can escape our debts for a while, and instead, own hundreds, maybe even a thousand, of acres in Caintuck. With such riches, we could each pay off what we owe here in North Carolina. I've recently spoken with Captain Russell, and I believe he and his partners will furnish us with the supplies needed to make such a move. In return, we'll need to survey and establish tracts of land for each investor, and likewise, ourselves.

Rebecca and Jemima, sitting nearby shelling peas they'd recently picked from the family's communal garden, listened intently. Rebecca knew they'd have to move, as their previous farm and cabin had been seized for payment of the family's debts. Currently, they occupied a cabin belonging to family members, and owned not much more than what they wore and used daily. Rebecca sat and thought on moving westward once again. She and Daniel had spoken of the possibility of moving into Caintuck. She knew Daniel had spoken with others such as James Harrod, who already planned a large expedition to establish a fort there. While purchasing land in Caintuck remained illegal, others, such as the McAfee brothers and Captain Thomas Bullitt, had already surveyed and claimed large tracts for themselves. Even the famous Virginian George Washington had shown great interest in land prospects beyond the Appalachians.

It seemed probable that Daniel would organize the move for militia Captain William Russell of Castle Wood in Virginia. Russell owned extensive lands on the Clinch

River and had even served in the House of Burgesses. He and Daniel had first met in the spring of 1773. Daniel would serve as guide and make all the arrangements for the journey. Although he'd be one among thirty or so men to join the expedition, he was recognized as Russell's right hand man. In exchange, Russell promised to provide their family with the wherewithal to make yet another move and to survive the coming winter.

Rebecca listened as Daniel approached their respective Boone and Bryan family members, presenting them with the opportunities each could enjoy once they crossed the mountains.

As the conversation rolled on, with each brother expressing his views and decisions, Rebecca moved toward the cabin to add the peas to a pot simmering on the fire. Jemima stayed put and listened, dreaming and hoping for a new life without creditors' demands, as each older child had witnessed firsthand the tax collectors' and sheriffs' arrivals. Her head filled with the pictures of a new world—impressions created in her thoughts and dreams by the words spoken by John Finley, Squire, and her own father. Jemima often thought on the dangers of Indian attacks, but unlike Susannah, she had total faith in her Daddy to keep them safe. Why, he had been to Caintuck many times, faced Shawnee, and always lived to tell his children about bountiful hunts and encounters in that wild and wondrous place called Caintuck. Besides, she could now take down a doe at almost fifty yards, shoot and clean enough squirrels to fill the pot, and fish better than her brothers.

The men carried on various loud, and occasionally argumentative, discussions on Indians and their rights to the lands west of the Appalachians. Lord Dunmore believed the native men and women had a right to this land and had created treaties giving white settlers only scarce parts of the wilderness they desired to settle. Mostly, it seemed, Lord Dunmore wanted to keep the Cherokee, Shawnee, and other tribes happy so that they wouldn't raid into white settlements and cause trouble. Indian troubles meant King

George's troops and the militia had to be called up, which meant money wasted protecting the western settlements. Some men expressed the idea that Dunmore cared more for his own comforts than he did the colony's residents. Others repeated the rumor circulating throughout the western settlements that Lord Dunmore, himself, had sent a man named Bullitt, along with surveyors, west of the Donelson Line, ultimately planning to grant himself large land tracts.

After many evenings' discussion, Uncle George gave Daddy their decision. "Dan, Neddie and I'd go," replied George, "but we're settled for now and with all the Indian trouble, and it bein' illegal, we've decided to hold off on goin' to Caintuck, at least for a spell. Perhaps, someday we'll join you in your glorious wilderness."

As the men talked of Caintuck, the women talked about babies and receipts. Jemima sometimes heard her mother and Martha whisper about Hannah and the girls. While Charity led the older girls off to a quiet place where they whispered about boys and dances and dresses, Jemima stayed put beside her Daddy, often falling asleep against his knee, bound and determined to dream of that dark and bloody ground called Caintuck.

Part II:
Jemima's Story

FORT BOONESBOROUGH

Chapter 1
September 25th, 1773

Finally, finally! We were moving to Caintuck. I danced around all morning—when Mama wasn't looking—singing *goin' to Caintuck, goin' to Caintuck.* We've been at the Forks of the Yadkin for weeks and weeks, gathering, packing, planning, and saying our goodbyes to family that wouldn't be coming along. The hardest came when we left Grandma Boone's home, leaving behind Aunt Hannah and the girls, and, of course, Jonathan and Jesse. I knew I'd be missing those two the most. Mama's eyes shone with unshed tears all morning, watching Jon and Jesse help pack the horses, knowing it might be the last time she saw her *boys.* Then, Daddy made the day so sad I could hardly stand all the goodbye-in'.

"Mother, come hug me once more before I go. Or decide instead to join us on yet one more adventure. It'll be as in the days long past, when Father moved us from our home in Pennsylvania to North Carolina," Daddy called to his mother, Sarah Boone. As she walked across the yard, wiping tears on her white cambric apron, I thought Daddy probably remembered all the days when just him and his mother spent their time tending the family's livestock back in Pennsylvania. 'Twas she who, many years ago, taught him how to shoot, to live rough in the woods, to identify different animal tracks, and enjoy nature's peace. Many an evening by the fire as we sat and listened, Daddy reminisced on his youthful days in those woods, now far to the north. I remembered how Daddy's father, Squire Boone had moved his family, all his married and unmarried children, south, first into Virginia, and later to the Yadkin Valley, after the Quakers had disavowed him. The good Lord had called home the elder Squire some three years after my birth. I had no memory of the man, only the image formed in my mind by my father's many stories.

"Ah, son, I be much, much too old to make another move such as you're plannin'. I be settled here with Hannah and the girls. I've my own bed, my garden, and the rest of my family. Here, I plan to remain till the good Lord calls me home," she whispered, now breaking into sobs with the thought of her dear Daniel leaving her life forever.

Holding her closer, taking in her smell of fresh linen, lavender, and homemade bread, I watched as Daddy patted her back and wiped his own tears with his sleeve corner. Finally, Grandma Boone stepped back, smiled once more on her son, and walked steadfastly toward her cabin door. She had said her goodbyes and given her best wishes to all else as the early morning progressed. I jumped as the men fired a salute to her and Daddy, recognizing the significance of their feelings, at the instance when she turned to wave one more time. With sad, farewell smiles from all the party, Daddy mounted his horse, and we rode toward the Cumberland Gap.

At that moment, my joy renewed. My dreams of Caintuck would soon be fulfilled.

Of course, first we'd travel to Virginia or thereabouts to meet up with Captain William Russell's party. Despite Proclamation Line restrictions, Captain Russell had settled a large swath of land west of the Blue Ridge Mountains in the Clinch River Valley. Here he supported and protected several communities that surrounded his land. His militia men provided protection against Indian attacks. Russell and Captain Gass, his associate in the Virginia militia, had both agreed to supply and join the expedition west into Kentucky.

Hickory splint baskets or cloth sacks hung from the sides of our many pack horses, holding all our household goods, foodstuffs, or chickens and other fowl. Even the smallest baby pigs rode in baskets. On my horse's back, one basket held our mother cat and three newborn kittens. Zek, now full grown, ran along beside. Each person rode a horse, or at least shared a horse. I rode with Viney, who, at only seven, could not be trusted to ride alone. Suzy rode with five-year-old Becky, while Mama had baby Jesse in a sling across her chest and three-year-old Daniel Morgan rode in a basket strapped across the rump of Mama's horse. Uncle Squire and Aunt Jane had made similar arrangements. Both four-year-old Moses and one-year-old Isaiah mostly rode in baskets strapped across Auntie's horse, while Uncle Squire tended to seven-year-old Jon, who often sat perched atop a pack horse when his father was busy with other responsibilities.

"James, Israel, take care to keep the livestock moving. One or two men will join you throughout the day, Now, boys, call out if you have any problem you can't handle," directed Daddy as our caravan moved deeper into the North Carolina woods. He had previously fitted each cow, ox, sow, boar, and piglet with a bell. The racket they made moving along the trail proved tremendous. I didn't envy my brothers at all, until we'd proceeded miles down the river's bank. The boys passed the journey on foot, free to wander while moving along the livestock, while I had the responsibility of Viney.

Our caravan traveled in single file, often stretching over two miles in length. Sometimes, the older boys and men dismounted to guide our horses up or down steep slopes. At creek and river crossings, the womenfolk and children would be led across. Often, one of the stronger men took a child or baby into his arms at deeper river crossings. Being autumn, most creeks and rivers ran low and proved easy to cross. Throughout the day, at various times, we dismounted and walked to rest our horses. Daddy soon realized exactly how slowly such an undertaking would proceed across the many miles to our new Caintuck home.

Along our route, men who Daddy recognized to be good hunters, such as Michael Stoner and William Bush, ranged far and wide to provide us with fresh meat for the evening meal. At midday, we often ate cold corn pone and jerky while riding. We drank cold stream water from a gourd dipper. Several pack horses each carried two small water barrels for times when fresh water proved inconvenient. Of course, there would be short breaks here and there as mothers tended to children's needs, changing nappies and settling squabbles.

At dusk, tired from riding, the children played and ran while our mothers created a camp wherever Daddy chose. We camped rough. Baskets conveniently packed with bearskins and hide blankets provided pallets to spread on the ground, usually in family groups. Daddy always posted several guards, especially around our livestock. On those few nights when rain fell, a brush lean-to built of saplings covered with extra deer hides kept us mostly dry. While we had seen no Indian sign, or encountered trouble or threat of any kind, Daddy understood we had to be diligent.

Several days into our journey, we had all bedded down, and Daddy had come from checking the guard when I had a chance to question him.

"Daddy, Daddy," I whispered, "will Caintuck's stars look the same?"

"Mima, they'll shine brighter, but, yes, you'll see the same figures in the sky. Now, hush daughter and go to sleep, dawn will come before you're rested," he insisted.

"Just one more question, please?"

"What be on your mind, Mima?"

"When I'm eleven, can I ask Uncle Squire to make me a rifle?"

"Child, you can ask, but I suggest you put that question to your Mama. Now, sleep!" He'd answered with a smile in his voice, telling me I had his permission. Now I had only to convince Mama.

❦

Long time neighbors such as the Haworth boys, James and George, had agreed to join our adventure. I don't know why we called them boys, as both were grown men. I knew both, as they'd hunted many a time with James and Israel, though they were several years older than my brothers. George had recently married a second time to Susannah Dillon as his first wife had died. Both men could be relied on in a fight and had even served in the militia, though they had been raised as Quakers. Their older sister, Jemima Wright and her husband and family also joined our party.

The Mendinall cousins, John and Richard, decided to come along as well. John, only twenty-five, traveled alone, him being a bachelor. Richard had considered bringing his wife and eight children, but as did many other men, decided to leave her behind until we had settled and built a fortification against possible attack. All together our party contained two Boone families, several men from Mama's Bryan family, and five other families, most we identified as neighbors from North Carolina.

⁕

"Viney! You got to sit still," I demanded.

"I got to go potty," Viney whined.

"You do not, you went not two miles back. Now sit still before you fall off this dang horse and get trampled to death. Mama's likely to skin me alive if'in that happens."

"I want down," she whined again.

"Mima, pull off to the side and let her down," called Mama over her shoulder, "then walk with her a while. Now don't fall behind."

"Not to worry, Sister," called Uncle Squire, "I'll let Jon walk a while as well. We'll keep up."

Once we had taken to walking, after both Viney and Jon relieved themselves in the woods, I decided to talk with my uncle as Viney was not much on talking about serious things. "Uncle Squire, tell me again how many days until we get to Caintuck?"

"Mima, now, do you mean where Caintuck meets Virginia? Or where we plan to settle on the Louisa River?"

"Oh, I guess I mean where Caintuck meets Virginia at the Cumberland Gap. I want to gaze on that land filled with rollin' meadows, buffalo, deer, elk, and such. You know, that promised land."

"Mima, you forget the bears, the snakes, the wolves, and the Shawnee. You'll see them in Caintuck, as well, don't forget," answered Uncle Squire with a fierce scowl in his voice.

"Oh, I can't likely forget such things as that! How can I? Suzy talks about all that nonsense constantly. She's scared of Caintuck."

"And you're not?"

"Oh, I got sense enough to be scared, but I got you and Daddy with me. Besides, you give me a rifle, and I can deal with those horrible creatures."

"Don't doubt you can, Mima, but you still can't have a rifle," answered Squire as he grabbed up Levina and placed her back on our horse and positioned his son up behind his own saddle before turning to mount up.

"Need help, Mima?"

"No, sir, I can mount up a horse on my own, long as I got a saddle or a stump," I answered defiantly. To prove my point, I laboriously pulled myself up and slid in behind Viney. With us being small, we both fit inside the seat, though Viney enjoyed riding on the cantle when I'd let her. As we rode, I thought more and more about having my own rifle. Why, with Uncle Squire being a blacksmith and a gunsmith, he could make me one in no time. I'd have to work some, though, in convincing Mama.

⬛ ● ⬛

Two weeks of travel and Daddy said we'd covered about a hundred miles and had passed Horton's Summit and Powell's Mountain. A few days back, Daddy'd sent

James, along with John and Richard Mendinall for extra supplies for the journey. Our slow rate of progress meant we would need more provisions for the trip and to keep us supplied in Caintuck until Captain Russell's supply party joined us later. Now that Captain Russell seemed mighty rich to me, and he kindly sent the boys back loaded down with supplies, additional horses, and some cattle. To help them along, he sent a guide named Isaac Crabtree, a hired man named Drake, and two slaves, Adam and Charles. Captain Russell's son Henry, James' new, great friend, begged to go along and his father relented and allowed his son to travel with our supply party. Of course, I learned all this much later after it all happened.

On their return journey, not realizing they were only two or three miles or so from our camp, the boys decided to stop overnight along the trail near where Wallen's Creek meets up with Powell's River. It was the night of October ninth.

I remember that night so well. The day had been clear and warm. The sun dappled through the remaining leaves, and the cedars served as about the only green left in the forest. We had traveled a good bit that day, Daddy said we made good time. Come evening, we roasted squirrels and rabbits over the campfires, and Mama and Aunt Jane made hoecakes. We covered them in honey, piled on the hot meat, and folded them in half to eat. I finished off three, but Israel said he ate seven. I think he exaggerated a mite. We drank fresh milk since the dairy cows were milked twice each day and the bounty passed out among the children and mothers.

Around the campfire, Uncle Squire told us stories from the Bible. Him being Baptist, he knew those stories by heart. My favorite was the one about the Israelites wandering in the desert for forty years. Why, we hadn't been on the road for even a month yet, I couldn't imagine traveling around for forty years. I'd be old and gray in forty years. And those Israelites didn't even have horses!

As we sat and listened to Uncle Squire, darkness encircled us. Mama wrapped the little ones in blankets and shawls against the October evening's coolness. Viney and baby Daniel Morgan fell asleep first, then Becky. As the remainder of us sat, knees pulled up to our chests and listened, the sun dropped from sight.

Israel and I heard and saw it first—a screech owl sitting beside a hollow on a hickory branch some fourteen feet or so above the ground. Suddenly, she trilled out her soft warbling call a second time. From somewhere in the distance, an answer came, and she replied. Next, she spread her mighty wings and flew directly over our little gathering, calling once again. Shudders ran down my back and my arms broke out in goosebumps. Uncle Squire glanced up at the rustling noise that flew by, almost touching his head. Quietly, in conclusion to the evening, he offered up a prayer for all our souls, just as the evening's first whippoorwill sang out its melodic, repetitive song.

Sleep came slowly to me that evening. I could hear wolves howling far in the distance. Zek snuggled by my side, but at moon rise, he rose up and howled a long plaintive call, perhaps in answer to the wolves. Since that day, I have believed he and the screech owl recognized death as it wandered nearby.

Chapter 2
Tragedy

The morning's activities commenced the way they did every day of our journey. At dawn, small fires provided coffee and warmth. Mothers nursed babies and tended to their children. The men began packing the horses and organizing the march order for the day. Daddy moved through the camp, greeting each person, asking how each got along, providing guidance, and giving orders.

Some families stood ready to mount up when the sounds of a horse traveling fast through the woods and a man yelling *Indians! Indians!* reached our ears. Only later would I find out that the young horseman had earlier stolen a horse and other items from our camp, gathered deer hides the hunters had left hanging to dry, and sped off in the early morning hours, deserting our party. Now, he rode back into our camp shouting that one word that brought fear to every man, woman, and child's heart.

Daddy rushed forward and grabbed the man, pulling him from his horse, and belting out his request for information. Suddenly, I saw Daddy falter and step back. Uncle Squire steadied him and pulled Daddy into a hug. I saw Daddy's knees buckle and Squire's arms tighten, holding Daddy up. All around the camp, each person stood stunned, watching our leader. After only a minute or so, Daddy pulled himself together and turned to glance at Mama, before beginning to give orders once again.

Without another look toward the goings on, Mama gathered us all up, called for Israel, and told us to stay put beside her. Suzy and me grabbed up the baby and Daniel Morgan. For once, Viney and Becky stayed put, as Mama told them to. Again, all I could do was stare. Mama approached Daddy, and he whispered something to her while holding her tight against his broad chest. After a brief spell, Aunt Ann walked out to Mama and quietly led her back to us.

Within seconds, men began pushing families together, shouting orders, and building barricades using packs, felled logs, and brush in a nearby ravine. Still, Mama said nothing, her face blank, including her eyes, which had lost all their life, their joy, and I expect even their sense of being. All this ruckus scattered the livestock, but no one saw to rounding them up. Amid all this confusion, Mama pulled her two best linen sheets from a basket and carried them over to Uncle Squire. Even after Squire and several older, experienced men saddled up and rode away, Mama just stood there. Finally, Aunt Jane again led her back to our place within the hastily built fortification.

"Mama?" asked Suzy. "Be it James?"

"Yes, child," replied Aunt Jane, her voice breaking. "James' party was attacked. Your brother and the Mendinalls have been killed by Indians. Squire is leadin' a party to bury them. That's all we know for now."

The longest day of my life passed mostly in silence. James lay dead. James, who so resembled Daddy, a boy who said little, but listened and learned more intently than anyone I'd ever observed. James, who could read and write some. James, who protected us when Daddy traveled on long hunts. James, my brother, my oldest brother—gone.

Sometime during the day, men brought us water and wood for a fire we didn't really need. Aunt Jane passed baby Jesse to Mama to nurse when he fussed. Once time later that day, I saw she had to help Mama free her breast for the baby. Mama didn't utter one word all day. Her tears came only when Daddy would stop by, take her in his arms, and whisper to her softly. I do truly believe that's the first time I ever saw my Mama cry when not birthin' a babe. Aunt Jane saw to our needs.

All day, men stood guard and waited for the Indians to attack. Finally, Uncle Squire's party returned with Captain Russell and others alongside. All the men gathered together, simply ignoring the womenfolk and children, as they made the decision to turn back toward the settlements. First, it would be necessary to round up all the livestock, as they had scattered during the confusion. Uncle Squire and Russell had reported that the Indians had moved on, yet no one felt safe.

Two more days passed. Families decided where to go. Captain Russell urged us to return with him to his own home, and Captain Gass offered us an abandoned cabin near his home. We had nowhere else to go, so Daddy accepted. Uncle Squire decided to join us at Castle Woods. Only when all had turned back toward homes they had already deserted did Daddy lead us back toward the Clinch River.

It was a subdued journey, nothing like the days before when we had looked forward. Now we only looked backward. The weather turned harsh, and the days long until we reached the Clinch Valley. We unpacked into a borrowed cabin, amongst an unknown community, amongst strangers. Yet, those strangers did what people did at such times. The womenfolk thereabout brought food and stayed to help Mama and us girls clean the cabin and repair the chinking. Menfolk dropped by with fresh game and helped Daddy and Israel build a shelter and fencing for our livestock. They made sure we had life's necessities, fresh milk, firewood, and cornmeal. Captain Gass proved mighty generous. Uncle Squire and his family found another nearby cabin and settled in as well. Aunt Jane told Mama they planned to stay at least through the winter.

As the days and then weeks passed, Mama rarely spoke, and when she did her voice seemed each time to break with a pain unbearable, pounding in her soul and her heart. Daddy often hunted all day to provide us with meat, or maybe just to be alone with his thoughts and doubts about his decisions. Life became a series of days to exist, not to live.

I saw in my Daddy's face the look of defeat and sorrow. He took all the blame upon himself. Our party could have waited for Captains Russell and Gass to complete their business, meaning we would have been a larger, more protected party. Then James and the Mendinalls would not have been sent back as we would have started the journey with supplies aplenty. Others whispered these truths when they thought we weren't listening. Daddy's grief at losing James nearly tore us apart. I knew he cried when alone, as I had seen the evidence on his face.

Mama continued to be stoic. She carried out her daily routine, but rarely truly noticed us children. Suzy took over caring for the little ones, and I helped out with many chores and the cooking. Israel stepped up into James' shoes, hunting, trapping, and caring for our livestock. There was no laughter, no storytelling, no songs, no joy.

Life continued, if you want to call it life. We lived broken, defeated, and heart sore. Little by little, we learned more about that fateful evening into morning. As James' group bedded down, the wolves howling in the distance echoed through the hills thereabouts. Isaac Crabtree had chided James, Henry Russell, and the two slaves about their nervousness, telling them that *in Caintuck you'll hear wolves howlin' in the treetops*. During their slumber, fifteen Delaware, two Shawnee, and probably three Cherokee warriors observed them from the woods. These warriors were traveling home after attending a tribal gathering called to discuss white incursions into their lands. Just before dawn, they attacked, killing the Mendinalls immediately and wounding Crabtree and Drake, who both fled into the surrounding forest. One slave, a man named Adam, managed to hide in some thick undergrowth and espied the entire massacre. James and young Henry, both shot through the hips in the initial attack, could not flee. When I heard tell of this, my heart clenched in fear at the thought of James and Henry being unable to defend themselves. The witness told how at first the Indians ignored the wounded boys. Instead, they gathered up the camp's supplies, rifles, and horses. Yet, after a while one or two Indians started slashing at the boys with their knives, shouting and causing the boys to cry out in fear and pain.

As the Indians' rage grew, their actions intensified, fueled by hatred and resentment. James and Henry tried to fend off the attacks by grabbing at the knives, often clenching their hands around the razor-sharp blades. Soon each boys' hands were cut, mangled, and useless.

During this struggle James recognized Big Jim, a Shawnee who had often eaten at our table and been befriended by Daddy. James begged first for mercy, then for death. Big Jim reacted by pulling out James' and Henry's fingernails and toenails, causing them even greater agony.

Adam told Captain Russell and Daddy, when he wandered into camp some eleven days later, that James cried out to Henry that he believed his family must all be dead, massacred by these same Indians. Finally, Adam observed the moment their torment ended, as the Indians' tomahawks bashed in the boys' skulls. In one last vengeful fit, the Indians shot all the men's bodies full of arrows. Leaving the dead, the Indians gathered up all the items they wanted and the slave Charles, who had witnessed the whole event, and rode off. Others found Charles' body, with his skull cleaved in two, some forty miles away. Crabtree wandered into Castle Woods after about a week. I don't recollect Drake's whereabouts, though some say his body had been discovered years later. Poor Adam could never forget what he had witnessed; visions of violent death haunted his waking and sleeping hours. Many times in my life, I have wished I had never been privy to the tale. Perhaps some stories should remain untold.

I overheard Daddy and Captain Russell speak about their sons' burial some while later in the year. When Uncle Squire's party reached the massacre site, Captain Russell and Captain Gass stood shocked, surveying the brutal attack's results. Captain Russell, appalled at the violence heaped on his son and James, wept. They used one of Mama's linen sheets to wrap James and Henry together, and used the other for the Mendinalls. They buried them all together and covered the grave with logs to prevent wolves from tearing it open and getting at the bodies. Uncle Squire said prayers over the grave, the only service they would ever be given. The party searched briefly for the missing men before rushing back to help protect the living.

After we returned to the Clinch River settlements, the massacre story traveled quickly back east to Lord Dunmore, mostly because Captain Russell was such an important man. Lord Dunmore declared that those responsible must be punished and sent his Indian agent to the Cherokees. Only one, a man called No-ta-wa-gun, stood accused and received the death penalty. Indian upon white settlers and white upon Indian violence erupted across the frontier. Many others, white and Indian alike, died. The Shawnee felt the whites' encroachment the most, with settlers pushing west from Pennsylvania and from Virginia to the south.

As for us, us children, I mean, Suzy and me most often snuggled into a cold bed at night with Levina and Zek. Zek saved my heart, otherwise I believe, in those early months after James' death, it would have surely stopped beating. Tears flowed easily for us girls, but Israel, James' shadow for all his fourteen years, said almost nothing. He existed there in the cabin, did his chores, ate his meals, and lived, but not really. Late one night, after moon rise, I awoke to soft awful, sobbing cries and realized it was Israel. Not knowing what else to do, I helped Zek into the loft and we laid down with Israel. Zek, being Zek, snuggled into Israel's arms, while I put my arm over my brother and whispered *hush now, Israel, hush now*. Finally, he fell asleep, we both did. Mama and Daddy didn't ask why when I climbed down the loft ladder the next morning. Zek, with some help for me, for he couldn't climb into the loft on his own, took to joining Israel every night. I realized that just went right, as I had Suzy and Viney. Israel had only Daniel Morgan, who was useless being only four. Besides, he slept more soundly than a dead cat. Nothing woke Daniel Morgan.

⬤

In the spring, Daddy returned to the Powell Valley, aiming to hunt and to visit James' grave. When he returned to our little cabin, Captain Russell came calling to learn what Daddy had discovered. I overheard them speaking.

"Captain, sir, I visited our sons' graves as we'd planned. Some logs had been pulled or rolled away, and some varmint had dug down. I examined the bodies and found them undisturbed. I dug them in further and covered the whole of the thing with more logs and rocks. Reckon our boys will be safe now."

"Boone, I appreciate your doing this for my son as well as yours. I understand it was hard," Captain Russell replied, grabbing Daddy by the shoulder.

"Felt more miserable than I have in all my life."

"Did you encounter any trouble?" asked Russell, taking Daddy by the shoulder again to give him a moment of support.

"Well, I camped nearby to the graves and started a small fire. Later during the night, I heard Indians prowling about, so I loaded up and leaving the bell on my horse—so as they'd think me still in camp—and scampered into the forest while leading my horse. Guess that bell led them to believe I lay still in camp, for it gave me time for escape."

Their conversation continued as they discussed all the news from Caintuck. Captains Russell and Gass often received messages from militia commanders. They both read eastern newspapers and talked with those who traveled through the Clinch Valley toward the Cumberland Gap. We all knew how others, such as the McAfees, James Harrod, and Captain Bullitt now explored and surveyed lands in that beloved paradise. George Washington even traveled down the Ohio as far as Fishing Creek where George Rogers Clark had already built a cabin, giving thought to surveying land for himself. Simon Butler and his party worked daily to survey northern Kentucky, those lands along the Ohio. I knew Daddy resented these men,

men who had reached Caintuck and planned to settle there before he could accomplish his goal.

Yet, now was not the time to take a family into Caintuck's wilderness. All along the frontier, whites shot Indians on sight, while Indians attacked and killed any whites they encountered. The stories from that dark and bloody ground rang with violent deaths on both sides, as white hunters told the story about Henry Russell's death over campfires, often omitting my brother's name and the Mendinalls. You see, Captain Russell was a known and respected man. Few outside the Yadkin Valley knew the name Daniel Boone.

Chapter 3
Lord Dunmore's War

True spring arrived finally, and Suzy and I explored the community surrounding our borrowed home, now and then Viney tagged along. Something about spring lessened our grief. We met some new neighbors, including the large Cowan family, full of brothers and sisters, many married with children of their own. We spent time with Captain Gass' family and their many relatives, which included the Cowans and the Moores. Captain Gass was born in Pennsylvania just a few years before Daddy. Gass also talked constantly about moving his family to Caintuck. Some Scotts and Carrs also lived nearby. We visited with Uncle Squire's family, went to church meetings to listen as he preached the Gospel, and found some joys in life. Everyone except Mama.

Sometimes, news came from the east. In the early part of the year, we learned, through the Committees of Correspondence, about the Boston Tea Party that had taken place back on December sixteenth the previous year. All around us, settlers mostly worried about the Indian situation, yet they reveled in the events taking place along the eastern seaboard. Resentment simmered over Lord Dunmore's high taxes and his lack of militia support for the western settlements. A myriad of additional grievances filled conversations around the fort, over campfires, and in cabins. Even those as far removed as the Clinch River Valley, well beyond civilization, shared and followed the news of the rebellious acts in Boston and other towns and villages I'd never heard tell of.

Along the western frontier, the Indian trouble intensified. Lord Dunmore sent word to the colonists, especially those in the westernmost settlements, to prepare for war. I guess he didn't realize we'd been at war since last year when Henry, James, and the others were massacred. He called upon Captain Russell to send two experienced hunters into Caintuck to warn the many surveyors about the increasing danger. Everyone knew about those men now staking their claims to large land tracts west of the Appalachians. Daddy volunteered, as he had recently undertaken a commission to survey some 4,000 Caintuck acres for James Hickman. This gave him a dual reason for the journey. Gathering us all together, he spoke in that quiet voice I so much respected.

"Children, I be off to warn the surveyors in Caintuck about the increased Indian danger. I be plannin' to speak with Mike Stoner about joinin' up with me. There'll be just the two of us. 'Twill be a couple months, maybe a bit more 'til my return. Israel, you're the man of the house now, but do as your Mama says. Any trouble at all, you take the family to Captain Gass or Captain Russell. If you need a necessity, you ask Captain Gass, or send word to Captain Russell, you hear?"

"Yes, sir," Israel answered.

"Son, don't wander far in search of game. Hunt with one or two others if you can. Don't go out alone. Girls, stay near to this cabin and help your Mama."

After kissing us all on the cheek and holding each in a bear hug, Daddy took his leave pulling Mama outside the cabin for a private talk. She returned in tears. Mama cried more easily now, sometimes without any reason we could reckon.

Gathering the necessary supplies, Daddy walked off in search of his friend and hunting partner Mike Stoner. Only twenty years old and unmarried, Stoner was an awkward, short, stout man, who'd adapted his name from its original Holstiener. Daddy always said you could depend on Stoner. Yet his heavy German accent often made him seem a comic character, at least to us children. Daddy and Mike set off in late June for Caintuck after Daddy loaned Stoner a rifle, for he was without one at the time. Daddy had to rent a horse for the journey, for taking our one horse would leave us without transportation. Their instructions were to pass into Caintuck using the Sounding Gap, which lay north of the Cumberland Gap. Daddy had good directions for finding it from militia Colonel Andrew Lewis. By traveling through the less-used gap, they could avoid Indians, who more commonly used the easier Cumberland Gap.

—————————— ● ——————————

That same communication from Lord Dunmore instructed Captains Russell and Gass to build forts along the Clinch. Forts or stations made for a place of relative safety during an Indian attack. Under Russell and Gass' instructions, local men and the militia immediately felled trees to create green log walls for several forts. Seven or more forts, some small and some large, seemed to grow out from the earth overnight.

Nearest to us, they constructed Moore's Fort, a log stockade with two gates, one on the front and the other in the rear wall. People just commonly named most forts for whomever owned the land where they stood. Not far from Moore's front gate stood a limestone spring that furnished the fort with water and created a small pond. Suzy and I watched as some twenty families moved within the fort and additional militia men were employed to patrol the area for Indians. Some two miles away sat the much smaller Cowan's Fort, where only six or seven families lived.

We forted up several times when the militia scouts warned us about Indians in the vicinity. Most often, we had to stay for only a day or so. Other times we lived there for weeks on end. Our family suffered in the overcrowded, smelly fort, yet we understood that if Indians roamed the nearby forest, we were better off in the fort than at our cabin. Mama insisted we stay longer than necessary on several occasions, as she feared losing her remaining children to the evil that had taken our James.

She also would fret something awful about Israel's hunting. Sometimes we went without fresh meat just to keep her tears away. I could most often bring home fish to fry if allowed to go down to the river.

That same summer, while living in our cabin, a late afternoon thunderstorm rumbled in the distance. Storms usually came in from the west and blew down the Clinch River Valley, building to a frenzy after topping the Appalachians. As the wind began to move the heavy treetops surrounding our cabin, howling and crying out its force, we could hear the rain moving east toward us and smell the lightning even before we could hear thunder.

Suddenly, Mama grabbed her heavy shawl and rushed out into the still before the storm. Suzy and I gathered up the little ones, especially Daniel Morgan, who was terrified of storms, and set to distracting them with bits of hoecake and honey.

"Mima, you reckon Mama's okay?"

"Probably gone to the privy," I answered, distracted by Becky trying to drink Jesse's milk.

Several minutes passed, and the storm arrived with all its loud crashing glory, dropping rain in torrents about our cabin. While Suzy moved pots, kettles, and bowls underneath leaks, I covered bed clothes with hides to keep them dry. Israel climbed into the small loft to do the same. The rain intensified, lightning flashed, and thunder rolled. Daniel Morgan wailed, and Israel resorted to gathering him up in his arms, holding him tight, and pacing the floor. Finally, worried concern overtook us three, and I volunteered to go search for Mama.

Hurrying out to check the privy first, I found her sitting on a stump at the garden plot's edge looking out across a nearby meadow, laughing aloud, with tears of joy running down her face and mingling with the rain that drenched her more and more with every passing minute. I shouted to attract her attention, and when she saw me, she turned back and pointed toward the forest edge. There, amid the drenching rain stood a doe and her still-spotted fawn. As I watched, the doe ran around her fawn, kicking up her heels and throwing mud and wet grass into the air. Next, she sprinted toward her fawn, nudged her sharply, and took off running, often looking back to see if her little one followed. As we watched, she would stop and kick up her heels, jump high in the air, twisting this way and that. Finally, her fawn followed her example. Their dance of wild madcap joy continued as lightning lit the late afternoon sky and thunder rolled its percussive rhythm for their dance. Mama pulled me onto her lap, and we watched and giggled unabashed. Only as the storm passed, and the rain lessened, did the doe lead her fawn back into the surrounding forest.

Mama, soaked to the skin, but still shaking with glee, smiled at me and suggested, "Mima, I think the good Lord endeavored to remind me of life's joys, the joy of dancing in the rain, and the joy of my children." And with that pronouncement, Mama took my hand, and we skipped most ways back to the cabin. Our sudden appearance at the door shocked Suzy and Israel. Both rushed to Mama, asking if she was hurt or sick.

"Children, I believe I'll fry up some fruit pies," she declared, "just as soon as I be dry."

Then for the first time since James' death, Mama broke into song, singing in her lyrical alto voice an Irish ditty we more often heard in Daddy's baritone.

As I was goin' over

The Cork and Kerry Mountains

I saw Captain Farrell

And his money, he was countin'

I first produced my pistol

And then produced my rapier

I said, "Stand and deliver or the devil he may take ya"

I took all of his money

And it was a pretty penny

I took all of his money,

Yeah, and I brought it home to Molly

She swore that she loved me,

No, never would she leave me

But the devil take that woman,

Yeah, for you know she tricked me easy

Musha rain dum a doo, dum a da

Whack for my daddy, oh

Whack for my daddy, oh

There's whiskey in the jar, oh

Soon our little cabin filled with the smell of hot lard and fried pies, pear this time, as Captain Gass had a small orchard. As Mama sang, we feasted.

———— • ————

Daddy and Mike came home in late August, some sixty-one days after they departed, and regaled us with their adventures. My favorite story became one Daddy always told while imitating Stoner's thick German accent. Daddy recounted how he and Mike came to a small stream and a salt lick where the buffalo had licked a hole into a narrow ridge. Seeing the hole had been licked all the way through and a buffalo on the opposite side, Mike decided to have some fun and proceeded to take off his cap and wave it through the hole at the buffalo. The startled buffalo licking at the other side of the hole, instead of being frightened, charged the hole, wedging her head and neck all the way through immediately in front of Stoner. He fell back onto his backside yelling "Schoot her, gabtain! Schoot her." As Stoner was in no real danger of being trampled and finding the sight quite funny, Daddy described how he also fell to the ground writhing with laughter. Even Mike laughed when Daddy told the story in his presence. Now Daddy was not really a captain at this time, but as a matter of respect many men had called him such on our expedition the previous year. Mike continued to call him *gabtain* for the remainder of Daddy's life.

The home and life Daddy returned to had become much different than the one he left. Due to his bravery and daring on the rescue trip into Caintuck, and Mama's return to good humor, we met summer's dog days with joy in our hearts. I often saw Daddy pull Mama into an embrace and give her a quick kiss when he thought no one was looking. Captains Russell and Gass, along with Colonel Lewis, heaped praise on Daddy's head. Soon his name became recognized around the frontier by men such as Major Campbell and the returning Caintuck surveyors, who wrote to their sponsors about Daddy's diligence and service. Mike received his fair share of praise as well.

In late September, Daddy gathered up a small company under his direction and joined Colonel Lewis' campaign against the Shawnee and Mingo tribes. Only two days after they marched away, a messenger caught up with the militia forces and recalled Daddy to the valley. He'd received a lieutenant's commission from Lord Dunmore and was put in charge of three forts on the Clinch, including Moore's.

Autumn being the best time of the year to enjoy buffalo and turkey, Israel and others provided the meat while Mama and us womenfolk cooked up a feast to celebrate. Daddy's face shone with pride, and he carried that commission paper in his carry bag until after we reached Missouri, many, many years later.

Chapter 4
Moore's Fort

The autumn of 1774 brought more Indian raids and work for Daddy. He roamed between the three forts he commanded, making sure the militia consistently carried out their duties, that the walls were kept in good repair, and that they defended each fort as needed. Every so often, he got called to homesteads where families had been massacred or people, usually children, had been carried off. These were the worst for us back home. Daddy rarely told us of such raids, but as he had to put his actions and costs into formal reports, we would overhear him working late into the evening on his paperwork. Now Daddy's handwriting and spelling, until this time, must have been atrocious. Not that I could have told, not being able to read or write. So, Captain Gass suggested Daddy hire a local Irishman, William Hays, to help with his accounts. Many an evening Daddy and Will sat in our cabin working, until it was too dark to see well. Will ate at our table and read to us, him being more learned than us, including Daddy. He even owned several books, whereas Daddy just had the Bible and *Gulliver's Travels*, which he had read to us so many times we could practically recite it by heart.

"Susannah! Pay attention to your task," Mama chided.

"Yes, Mama."

"I do think, child, your mind be somewhere else these days."

"I know where, Mama. She's thinkin' on that Will Hays, I saw her lookin' at him with moony eyes," I answered, although my input had not been sought and was surely not welcomed by Suzy.

"And what if I am," replied my fourteen-year-old sister. "I be old enough to notice a man, if'in I wish."

"Jemima, go do your chores," Mama directed. "Suzy, you may be old enough to observe a man, but we'll have a lot less flirtin' if you want to keep in your Daddy's good standin'."

"But Mama, Daddy thinks kindly on Will."

"Susannah, your Daddy can like Will without wantin' him as a son-in-law. Now go on with your chores, but first change Jesse's nappy. He stinks worse than a polecat."

If'in you'd wanted to find a man more handsome than Will Hays, you'd have had to look a lot farther than Moore's Fort. Will's dark hair, blue eyes, and well-built stance made him stand out among the fort's men. With its strong Irish lilt, his voice often rang above the fort's everyday noises, singing the Irish fighting song *Follow Me Up to Carlow* or the lovely *Carraigdhoun,* one of Mama's favorites. While Mama liked Will a good deal, she was not yet ready for her oldest girl to be married off. Despite that, Suzy continued to moon after Will. Mama and Daddy watched as Suzy catered to Will's every need when he came to our table. She combed and re-braided her hair every time before his arrival, if'in we had warning. She always wore her best dress when Will showed up at the cabin. Wasn't long until Will took to looking back at Suzy.

Despite Mama's warning, I observed Suzy staring at Will several times one evening and smiling at him when Mama and Daddy didn't notice. In the weeks to come, Suzy often snuck off into the fort to find Will. She flirted with boys but seemed to enjoy more being around those several years older than herself. Suzy's frequent visits to the fort began to draw the attention of others, especially the womenfolk. While I kept my mouth sewn shut about such goings on, others talked.

In early autumn, Daddy had gone off to check on another fort under his command, and we had moved to the fort for safety. A beautiful clear day with warmer than usual weather sent the men from the fort, where they played ball games and ignored their duties. This had become commonplace when Daddy was absent. Some womenfolk, such as Mama and Mistress Samuel Scott, deemed this a real dereliction of duty. Now Mama, never one to shirk her own duties, took action to *put the men right*, as she would say.

"Jemima, round up as many women as are not busy. Then you and Suzy close and lock the front gate. Be quiet about it. Then you girls go load up your rifles with light loads, so as not to waste powder."

When we returned, Mama had taken the fort's womenfolk into her plan and several soon carried a lightly loaded weapon. Now, about six of us, led by Mama, slipped through the back gate and into the woods, where we quietly snuck around to the front of the fort. On Mama's whispered command, we fired in rapid succession, as Indians always did. Some of us reloaded and fired again. Two younger girls shouted out loud Indian war cries. Zek, whom we had left in the fort, barked and howled something awful. Oh, my, but did those men scatter and run for the gate. Some ran through the pond, others tried to scale the walls, and more pounded on the gate in fear for their lives. One young man even managed to scale the wall and fell into the fort's interior. He was only bruised some, not real hurt. Now, once those womenfolk left in the fort opened up the gate, we proceeded from the woods. The men commenced to shout obscenities at us!

"Mistress Boone, how dare you women pull such a stunt, you should all be horse whipped," one man demanded.

"I'll dare you to try," Mama answered, "seein' as us womenfolk have the rifles. As soon as Daniel returns, I'll be reportin' each and every man for leavin' this fort unprotected."

"Now, Mistress Boone, you don't want to be doin' that, now do you?"

"I consider it my wifely duty to do so," Mama replied and marched us toward our cabin within the fort, where we proceeded to have sassafras tea and honey cakes. We laughed and laughed about our little adventure.

* * *

Daddy now commanded fourteen militia rangers, and they moved up and down the valley, tracking Indians, checking on outlying homesteads, and reporting back to the more senior officers about attacks in the valley. The first serious attack on a fort came in late September of 1774, when the once-peaceful Mingo chief Logan led a party of Mingo and Shawnee warriors on a raid against Fort Blackmore. Blackmore sat some twenty miles downstream from Moore's Fort. Once named Talgayeeta, Logan had adopted English ways and befriended many white settlers. Now, he wanted to avenge a massacre against his own family led by a white man named Daniel Greathouse.

After capturing two slaves owned by families within the fort, Logan dared the owners to come out and recover their *bearskins*, an Indian name commonly used for Negroes. As no one was stupid enough to leave the fort, the Indians instead killed several cows and moved on to Moore's Fort. Daddy had returned by this time to Moore's, and on September twenty-ninth, Logan led his warriors against us. Despite knowing the danger that roamed the surrounding woods, John Duncan and two other men left the fort to check on their traps. Suddenly, the Indians attacked. Daddy and several others ran from the fort, returning fire, and helping the men back to safety. Unable to act in time, Daddy watched as a war-painted warrior scalped one man. While the warriors did not press the attack, the next day, a child discovered a war club at the spring outside the front gate.

It all happened so quickly we didn't really have time to be frightened. Besides, I then had my own rifle and was an excellent shot.

Forted up, our family tried to make the best of the situation. We kept our rifles loaded and only left the fort to carry water from the spring. As the women and children went to fetch water, the men would stand nearby to protect them from surprise attacks. Each family seemed to have a different way of coping with the fear; the knowing Indians might attack at any time. In our cabin within the fort, Mama made sure we were kept busy with chores and such. She allowed us to visit with only a few other families, otherwise we had to stay close by. Despite all her precautions, we still heard the talk—the talk of attacks on other forts, of atrocities carried out by Indians, and even the story of Chief Logan's family being massacred.

On my way back from the fort's privy one day, I spied Daddy walking around checking the stoutness of the log walls and how the lookouts faired. Approaching him, I asked, "Daddy, I've heard tell about how Chief Logan's family got massacred, including how a white man killed his sister-in-law and cut her baby from her womb and stuck it on a stake. How could any white man do that?"

"Mima, oh, child, I wish you hadn't overheard that story. The evils perpetrated by both natives and settlers are horribly cruel. To most folks' way of thinking, only Indians are cruel and kill for no reason, but white men do the same. Some white men shoot any Indian they espy. Now, as you know, some Indians are my friends, but as with any man, white or red, my opinion can change based on how they treat others."

"But Daddy, why? Why is it this way?"

"Mima, throughout the history of man, there have been wars, mostly fought over land and other resources. Seems to me, men and women seek new territory when an area gets too crowded. Right now, here in Virginia, the Indians are fightin' to protect the land they see as theirs— it's the same in Caintuck, and all the land west of the mountains. White men fight back because they believe they have a right to settle on that land as well. If'in each could see clear, they might realize both parties might enjoy and live on the land. 'Twill be many more fights before this is all settled. I do believe, some awful happenin's will come to pass before that time."

"Daddy, did you ever kill an Indian? Do you want to kill Big Jim?" I asked, thinking back on how a man once a friend had betrayed us.

"Well, Mima. I reckon I've killed an Indian, don't know for sure. But I've shot at many in troubled times, and most say I'm a right fair shot. Doubt I missed all those times. As for Big Jim. I be rightly confused. Big Jim sat at our table and broke bread with us. I welcomed him to my fire whenst we'd meet up. Still, Big Jim and the others carried out cruel deeds upon James and Henry. Mighty cruel deeds. . ." Daddy stopped talking and thought for a while. Then he asked, "Mima, you be planning' on killin' Big Jim yourself?"

"No, sir. I reckon that's not my place, but Israel, well. . ."

"Spit it out, child. What does Israel say?"

"Well, Daddy. He plans to sneak off next spring and go hunt down Big Jim and kill him," I blurted, hating I had revealed Israel's confidence. Also relieved that I had.

"Jemima, you're a true sister. I'll talk with Israel; don't you worry yourself none. Looks as if I need to tend to my family a bit more than I've been doing."

"What'll we do Daddy? Stay here? Fight? Give up and go back to North Carolina?"

"I reckon we'll fight. Don't see as there is right or wrong on either side, just the way of it. War is comin' to North Carolina, war against the British unless I'm much mistaken. No sense goin' into a different war than the one we be fightin' here. Now, go on back to the cabin, daughter, and try not to dwell on others' evil deeds."

As it happened, I'd find plenty of time to dwell on those events while even more attacks occurred up and down the Clinch River, including another attack on Blackmore's that sent Daddy and Captain Daniel Smith with some thirty others to that fort's relief. Finally, on October tenth, forces under Colonel Andrew Lewis' command defeated the Shawnee in a lengthy battle at Point Pleasant on the Kanawha River. Chief Cornstalk, a lover of peace, surrendered his men and agreed to a treaty. Lord Dunmore's War came to an end. Daddy's actions led to his promotion to captain. Chief Logan went home and later had a letter written on his behalf to Lord Dunmore. Will read us the letter that had been printed in a newspaper back east.

Colonel Cresap, the last spring, in cold blood and unprovoked, murdered all the relatives of Logan, not even sparing my women and children. There runs not a drop of my blood in the veins of any living creature. This called on me for revenge. I have sought it. I have killed many. I have fully gutted my vengeance.

For my country, I rejoice at the beams of peace: but do not harbor the thought that mine is the joy of fear. Logan never felt fear. He will not turn on his own heel to save his life.

Who is there to mourn for Logan? Not one.

As we listened, I thought back on that conversation with Daddy. So many on both sides lost all—family, home, and even their lives. Some died horrible, suffering deaths. Others survived while their family members perished. Seemed as no family continued unscathed.

Chapter 5
Boone's Trace

Daddy's vision of Caintuck came back into focus with the war's end and peace restored. Mine too. Each day I longed to leave this valley and follow the hunters and surveyors headed west. Things had not changed considerably from our days in the Yadkin district. Our family lived in a borrowed cabin and had run up debts over the previous months—more than Daddy's militia pay could ever cover. Sometime late that autumn, or maybe even into early winter, Daddy corresponded with Judge Richard Henderson of North Carolina, a powerful, wealthy man. He commissioned Daddy to undertake two tasks. In return, Henderson planned to pay for another venture to settle Caintuck. We learned all this firsthand, as Will and Daddy read aloud the letters from Henderson and penned Daddy's replies.

Daddy's first task centered on visiting with the Cherokee leaders and convincing them to meet up with Henderson and others near the Watauga Settlement at Sycamore Shoals in March of 1775. Officers of Henderson's Louisa Company, named for the river in Caintuck where we planned to settle, wanted to negotiate with the Cherokee for land in central Caintuck. Henderson later changed the company's name to the Transylvania Company. Transylvania means *across the forest*. Henderson said he desired to announce more clearly its purpose *to settle beyond the mountains*.

Daddy's second task required him to hire and lead men to hack and mark a trail into Caintuck. This newly marked trail over the mountains of western Virginia, through the Cumberland Gap, would break through canebrakes, across meadows, and ford streams and rivers to allow settlers, hunters, and traders alike easier movement into that promised land.

Just before Daddy left for the Watauga River, family matters captured his attention, and not in a good way. A man from Moore's pulled him aside for a private conversation.

"Captain Boone, don't wish to be the one sayin' this, but that oldest daughter of yours is likely to get herself in the family way. She be considered the biggest flirt in all the settlement. Others deem her to be fast. Some women refused to let their daughters associate with her," he stated quickly, as though wishing to get it said as fast as possible.

"Thank you, kindly, for presentin' me with this information," Daddy answered soberly. Thinking but a moment, Daddy then asked, "Be there any one man in particular?"

"Not wantin' to cause any trouble, Captain, but as you asked directly, I be tellin' you. It's that Will Hays, what's been with her the most."

I believe Daddy thought on this news for a few hours before talking it over with Mama. I saw them step from the cabin and carry on a right serious conversation. This time it was Israel who overheard Daddy tell Mama what the man had said about Suzy. Myself figuring Suzy be the person being discussed in their conversation, I glanced about and noticed she was once again absent from the cabin. When Daddy and Mama returned and asked her whereabouts, I dreaded telling them she was most decidedly at the fort. Sure enough, Daddy gathered up his rifle, as he ventured nowhere, near or far, without it, even in these times of peace, and left the cabin. Not much riled Daddy, but he expected us to be upstanding and righteous. Daddy may have no longer been a Quaker, but some of those teachings still ran deep in his blood.

Daddy was barely out of sight when Israel pulled me outside and whispered what Daddy had told Mama. We understood how seriously such matters were taken by both our parents. I'd always figured Susy's behavior would someday come to be her comeuppance.

Not long afterward, Daddy returned with Suzy in tow. They sat all alone outside on the bench and talked together quietly. Daddy never once raised his voice. Mama occasionally glanced in their direction, but it seemed to me she thought Daddy might have more influence than her in this particular situation. Finally, father and daughter walked into the cabin. Suzy hung up her shawl and Daddy his rifle. I itched dreadfully to ask questions but knew better than to.

Several hours later, Will Hays showed up at the cabin and asked to speak with Daddy. Suzy glanced at Will as he stood at the door, giving him a great big ol' smile. Daddy and Mama stepped into the cooling evening to speak with Will. Now, Will may not have expected Mama to have a say, but being as she'd practically raised us, with Daddy being absent so often, she felt it was her right. Thank the good Lord for Israel, for once again he overheard their conversation being as he had just returned from feeding our livestock.

"Captain, Mistress Boone, I've given our previous conversation a good deal of thought, sir, and I've come to ask for your permission to marry up with Susannah," Will stated firmly.

"Oh, have ye now, Will Hays," Mama snapped back. "I do hear tell from Daniel that you've been takin' liberties with Suzy. I don't take kindly to such, her bein' barely fourteen years old. I'll not ask if it is true, I know my daughter. Still, just how do you expect to support our Suzy? Don't know as you own any land or a cabin, not much to speak of can you claim as your own, far as I can see?"

Israel said he could tell Mama was riled something terrible, but she never raised her voice. While Daddy rarely showed his, Mama had a temper that often boiled over in times such as this. Poor Will.

"Mistress Boone, I'm a weaver, a good hunter, and have already signed on for Captain Boone's trail-blazing expedition into Caintuck. As an educated man, I could teach school, if necessary. I may not be rich, but she'll not go hungry."

"That's all well and good, but do you love her, Will? Can you stand by her? She's an awful flirt with a soiled reputation. I don't expect our Suzy'll stop flirtin' once she's married," asked Daddy.

"I rightly do, Captain Boone," Will answered with a smile. "As to the flirtin', well, ... I don't see any harm in Suzy's flirtin', as long as it goes no further."

I guess Daddy and Mama believed him, for he was given permission to ask Suzy for her hand in marriage. I already knew her answer before he even asked. Suzy'd been on the hunt to marry Will Hays since last fall. Soon Daddy announced their engagement and asked Uncle Squire to perform the ceremony.

Daddy and Squire planned a quiet ceremony here at the cabin. And before I truly realized how it had happened, my sister had gone and married. Daddy and Mama did the best they could for her. Suzy had a new dress and shoes. Mama even gave her a fur-lined cloak. Suzy and Will took a cabin in the fort, where I guess they were happy. Will seemed to dote on her and her on him. I felt a bit abandoned but stepped up to help Mama with the little ones.

———— • ————

Days later, Daddy rode off again, leaving us behind. Mama carried yet another baby, and we waited. Months would pass before we would learn the whole story of those months spent breaking a clear trail to the Louisa. Even Uncle Squire left us, taking his family back to the Yadkin Valley for a visit while he traipsed off with Daddy on the road-building crew. Squire managed to convince a few Yadkin Valley men to join up.

Daddy told us before he left how Judge Henderson believed purchasing the land from the Cherokee and building a fort on the Louisa River at the mouth of Otter Creek would provide all the safety the settlers would need. Henderson promised to fund a more numerous migration, which would include our family and any relatives that wished to go west. For breaking the trail, Daddy would receive two thousand acres on the Louisa, or nearby. Many men from the fort and Yadkin signed on to the road-building crew, including ones we knew such as Mike Stoner and Will Hays. In total, about thirty men formed Daddy's crew. Each received some ten pounds and ten shillings in pay. They had to bring their own tools. Suzy argued long and hard, and finally Daddy allowed as she could go along as the company's cook. A Virginian, Richard Callaway signed on at Sycamore Shoals and brought along a female slave to help Suzy. They were the only two women on the crew.

From others we heard about the happenings at Sycamore Shoals, where Henderson, called *Carolina Dick* by the Cherokees, had negotiated with the Cherokee leaders and achieved an agreement for the Holston River area, the Cumberland Gap, and the land between the Cumberland and Louisa rivers, that so called Great Meadow of Caintuck. Yet, not all the Cherokee agreed.

A younger chief named Dragging Canoe told those in attendance that *there was a dark cloud over that Country.*

The Great Chief Attakullakulla pulled Daddy aside just before he left and said, "We have given you a fine land, but I believe you will have much trouble in settling it."

------------ ● ------------

Weeks passed, and with each traveler we learned more and more about the road builders' progress. Daddy instructed the men to chop trees, saplings, brush, briers, and vines along the route he marked each day. They hauled large rocks from the path and searched for shallow places to ford streams and rivers. The men struggled day by day, carrying out backbreaking work. Daddy rode in front, marked the trail to be cleared, and shot game for the company to eat. Their favorite was sweet, tender bear meat, but deer and smaller game furnished most of their meals. Late snows and ice came with freezing temperatures. The men kept brush fires burning all day to warm their hands and feet. They crossed the Cumberland Gap and turned north into the Pine Valley Gap, then turned northeast toward the Louisa. Finally, they reached the Rockcastle River and, after hacking their way through miles of thickets, reached that view they all desired, Caintuck's Great Meadow.

Talk of this Wilderness Trail into Caintuck, being created by Daddy and the road builders, swarmed about the fort and even appeared in newspapers back east. Some called it the Cumberland Road, while others used the name Boone's Trace. That one was my favorite, since I believed wholeheartedly that Daddy should get the credit for opening the way into Caintuck. Why, Daddy's crew cleared over 200 miles of wilderness from the Holston River, north through Moccasin Gap of the Clinch Mountain, crossed the Clinch River, and through the Powell River valley to the Cumberland Gap. All territory west for many miles was considered Caintuck. The trail continued on to about where Crab Orchard is today, near Dick's River.

On the first day of April, Will helped Daddy pen a letter to Judge Henderson, telling him about their first true calamity. The letter's deliverer shared with us the contents as he passed up the valley. Seems that on March twenty-fifth, Indians attacked the trail blazers and killed Mr. Twitty and his Negro. Felix Walker received a severe wound to his thigh. While hunting for game, some two days later, Daddy and Squire met up with Samuel Tate's son, who told of their camp being attacked. Daddy and Squire rode to Tate's camp and found two men murdered and scalped. Daddy sent a man to warn all the companies in the area, and for them to gather at the mouth of Otter Creek on the Louisa. Daddy's letter requested that Henderson join up with them as soon as possible, as his men had become uneasy about the Indians. Some men turned back. Seems the new treaty had not ensured their safety after all.

On Daddy's return, he told us how the road builders had constructed a rough, barely roofed cabin, aptly named Twitty's Fort for the man who had lost his life at that spot. There Daddy nursed Felix Walker back to health. While they waited for Walker to recover some, the men speculated about which Indians had attacked them. Some said it was Shawnee; others said Cherokee under Dragging Canoe's command. Some even said Mingo. After a few days, Daddy re-gathered his men and forged on. They rigged up a litter between two horses and carried Walker to the river. I once heard Walker tell of reaching the Great Meadow, where the men surprised several hundred buffalo at a nearby salt lick. He described what he called the romantic sight of those huge, shaggy beasts running away, splashing through little streams, throwing up grass from their hooves, and thundering off into the far distance. Oh my, how I wished I had been there.

Daddy's men began building the fort Henderson had planned. Slowly, due to bad weather, Henderson moved forward with his larger party of men and supply wagons, but most every day met one or two men fleeing from the Indian violence in Caintuck. Most were from various surveying parties, and not associated with Daddy's trail blazers. Poor man. Henderson had believed his treaty with the Cherokee would provide them with safety. However, he had not treated with the Shawnee, Delaware, Iroquois, or Mingo. Even some Cherokees remained agitated and extracted vengeance upon any white man or party they happened across in Caintuck.

Henderson's group inched along, bringing supplies in by wagon and cart on Daddy's new trail. Due to his slow rate of travel, Henderson became afraid the men would all abandon the fort's site and return across the Gap, signaling his Transylvania Company's demise. Promising ten thousand acres of Caintuck land, Henderson convinced Captain William Cocke to ride to Otter Creek and let Daddy know he was on his way with reinforcements and supplies. Cocke arrived on April fourteenth, just after yet another attack. Daddy asked, and Mike Stoner agreed to ride east to guide Henderson's party. Finally welcomed by a volley of guns, Henderson's group reached the fort some six days later. Henderson found a crude structure barely under construction. Despite his gratitude to Daddy, Henderson was a tight-fisted man and offered my father no more land than the original two thousand. Daddy resented Cocke's ten thousand, earned for only a four-day ride along a newly constructed pike.

Daddy's men had dubbed their construction *Fort Boone*. Henderson wanted a more civilized name and changed it to *Boonesborough*. He also decided on what he thought was a *better* place for the fort's construction. Civilization and cooperation proved hard. Henderson planned a large fort with two-story corner blockhouses, cabins along the wall, an internal clearing, and two gates. Instead of building his dream, he found Daddy's remaining men busy clearing fields for corn crops, lazing about, hunting, collecting hides, and working to establish their own homesteads. None of the road builders were carpenters, nor did any have the skills for construction of a fort. Daddy cajoled, urged, begged, and threatened the men in order to make progress on the fort. He agreed with Henderson in the belief this fort would become essential to their protection. In addition to the walls, cabins, and blockhouses, they needed to dig a well within the fort and build a walkway along the walls so that men could see to fire over while under attack. A powder magazine was needed to protect their precious gunpowder store.

While Henderson held little regard for the men at Boonesborough, Daddy, being a woodsman like them, understood their dislike of governmental control and their desire for independence. He also knew the men would come together in a time of need and work for the betterment of all. Henderson, being wealthy and feeling privileged, expected these backwoods hunters and farmers to bow down to his every command.

Daddy later told us how Henderson seemed overwhelmed with the entirety of the situation. He could not understand the men's desire to clear land and plant crops such as potatoes, squash, beans, and of course, corn. Despite their lack of progress, Henderson called a meeting in late May, urging all the leaders of the various new settlements in Caintuck to come to Boonesborough. By this time, James Harrod had begun constructing a fort at Harrodsburg and a station at Boiling Spring. Benjamin Logan and other men settled at St. Asaph, later called Logan's Station. Henderson wanted to institute a governmental system and land registration for Caintuck. Daddy and Squire attended, along with many, many others. Henderson proposed a militia to respond to Indian attacks, restrictions on the wanton killing of game, and a sergeant-at-arms to help settle disputes. Immediately, militia Colonel Richard Callaway urged the convention to bring up John Gass on charges he had insulted Callaway. This was dismissed. Most men in attendance found Callaway to be a pompous pain in the backside. Uncle Squire told us how his brother, my Daddy, had proposed a bill to improve the breed of horses at the fort, for they both knew how important horseflesh was to Caintuck's settlement.

On May twenty-ninth, just after Henderson's meeting of the new Transylvania settlements, news from back east reached Boonesborough telling them about the battles of Lexington and Concord, fought in mid-April. Henderson now applied to the Continental Congress to be recognized as a separate province. Thomas Jefferson and Patrick Henry led the action to deny his request. For Boonesborough's men, nothing much changed.

<hr>

Spring turned to summer. Food supplies ran low, and more and more men gave up their thoughts of settling in Caintuck. Land disputes grew common as poorly recorded surveyed tracts caused claims to be shingled, one partially on top of the next. The men at Boonesborough resented Henderson's constant hounding about the work to be done as he himself rarely raised a hand to any type work. As a rich member of the gentry, he owned a slave named Dan, who cared for Henderson's every need, to include fishing, raising a garden, carrying water, washing his clothes and so forth. Back in Virginia, we listened to the news of how Henderson's Transylvania Company was declared illegal by the newly instituted Continental Congress, perhaps simply because Henderson had refused to allow rich, influential men such as Thomas Jefferson and Patrick Henry to invest in his venture.

More news about the company and the events in Boston, New York, and Philadelphia arrived every week. Daddy left Boonesborough on June thirteenth, accompanied by several settlers who wished to return east of the mountains, to the settlements.

The first half of 1775, while so much happened in our world, Israel and I worked to keep our family fed and safe, while Daddy stayed absent once again. To make matters worse in my mind, Suzy, who never wanted to go to Caintuck, went there before me. I'd watched all spring as Mama, normally a strong woman, struggled with her ninth pregnancy. Many days, Mama lay sick in her bed, unable to do much more than eat a bit now and then. Viney and I cared for the little ones and kept food on the table. We put in a garden, made soap and candles, washed clothes, churned butter, and carried firewood. Israel kept us in meat and cared for our livestock. We didn't starve, but at times we ran low on necessities. We were often lonely and wished for family, as Uncle Squire had taken Jane and the children back to the Yadkin before he left to help build the Wilderness Trail.

A midwife from the fort visited often and came immediately to help Mama the day my new brother presented himself to the family, July twentieth, if'in I remember correctly. Since his return, Daddy'd wandered off now and then to recruit others for settlement at Boonesborough, but he arrived back in time for the birth.

Mama suffered mightily giving birth to a poorly baby boy, named William Bryan Boone. Little Willy lived only a short while. Grieving, Mama and Daddy buried him in the cemetery outside Moore's Fort. While once a fieldstone and a wooden cross marked his grave, I doubt anyone could find it now after all these years.

As Mama slowly regained her strength, Daddy made preparations for our journey. This was not the grief we felt following James' death, as we didn't know little Willy. Still, again, we left a brother buried all alone, in a grave far from family.

Only three families decided to make the journey, although seventeen young married and unmarried men signed on. Many were from the Boone, Bryan, Morgan, and Callaway families. Besides ours, only Hugh McGary and one other man brought his family. Daddy organized the party, which included a fair number of riflemen, and we set forth for Caintuck. It's often been said that Mama and I were the first white women in Caintuck, even Daddy has said it! In all truth, Susannah Boone Hays arrived there several months before us. Why, back in 1755, Mary Ingles escaped from her Indian captivity at Big Bone Lick in Caintuck. But, shucks, Mary may not have even known she was in Caintuck, but Suzy sure did and was right smart on pointing that out to Daddy and anyone else. She often disputed Daddy's claim about Mama and me, stating *every Kentuckian ought to try my gait, since I was the first white woman in Caintuck.*

Unlike our previous trip, we traveled fast, being as there were fewer families and a cleared trail. We left about mid-August and arrived at Boonesborough on September eighth. First, we stayed in a poorly built cabin, but Daddy built us a new one nearby to the fort. Far enough for privacy and near enough to take shelter in times of trouble. Our new cabin had puncheon floors—Mama insisted—and real glass windows from Judge Henderson's personal supply. Why, our cabin even had an attached indoor stall for our horses. Daddy purchased about one hundred yards of linen for Mama to make bed linens, curtains, and new clothes for us children. Will and Suzy, already settled in a cabin at the fort, helped us make the place our home.

Daddy had already cleared and planted a field near our cabin with corn, and we soon had milk corn and other vegetables from the garden. Just as he had predicted, the soil yielded a great quantity and became more productive with every crop, if one took care to plant properly.

Some days, when time allowed, I stood before our cabin, facing the Louisa River and watched and listened. I saw deer and buffalo aplenty. We caught and ate huge catfish from the river; coated in cornmeal and fried up in lard, 'twern't nothin' better. Daddy and Israel brought home bear and deer meat quite regularly. I shot rabbits in the meadow and squirrels in the large oaks. I gathered chestnuts and other nuts from the trees that surrounded our encampment. That autumn we feasted on turkey whenever we wanted. It seemed like Caintuck's bounty surprised us every day. We lived and ate much as kings and queens in a land of milk and honey. I thought God had delivered us to his promised land or the garden of Eden, yet I knew His wilderness masterpiece to be called *Caintuck.*

Chapter 6
A Home in Caintuck

Daddy always despised neighbors. He didn't like living near other families, yet soon we lived in a small community, some even called our new home a settlement. Every week during the autumn of 1775, more and more men and some families arrived at Boonesborough. Some stayed while others moved on to outlying stations or Fort Harrod. Hugh and Mary McGary took her sons on to Fort Harrod, along with the other family that came over the trace with us. I think Daddy missed Hugh, though he was a rough, violent man. Many say it was marrying the widow Mary what tamed him and made him into a likable person, except when his Irish temper got riled.

Most other families that came built a cabin that would one day be enclosed with the fort. Other families built nearby on scattered homesteads. Although the log walls stood incomplete, we deemed our situation secure. Soon, a new supervisor for the Transylvania Company, Col. John Williams arrived. He supervised the surveying and recording of land, sold land, claimed any revenue from gold, silver, lead, copper, or sulfur mines. There 'twern't any. Daddy received yet another promise of more land—an additional two thousand acres for his work arranging the meeting with the Cherokees, building Boone's Trace, and holding the men together at Boonesborough until Henderson arrived.

To our great delight, Squire and Jane arrived with all their little Boones in late September, along with Richard Callaway and his family, among several others. We Boones enjoyed celebrating little Sarah's first birthday on the twenty-sixth of that month. Sarah was Squire and Jane's second daughter, though little Jane had died not long after birth.

Our settlement now seemed crowded with women and children. Us six and Uncle Squire's four made ten Boone children. Richard Callaway and his second wife Elizabeth brought along five children from his first marriage. The other nine remained in the eastern settlements, since most were married and on their own. Already fifteen, Betsy immediately became my best friend, and her twelve-year-old sister Fanny often tagged along on our adventures. We did chores together and repeated gossip we'd overheard. Us three looked over the young men of the fort, knowing one of them might be our future mate.

Like Mama, Elizabeth Callaway had given birth only a short time before leaving for Caintuck. Baby John was only two months old when they reached Boonesborough. I often noticed Mama holding John and cooing over him. I'm sure he made her think of our Willy.

Flanders Isham Callaway, Richard's twenty-two-year-old nephew and his younger brothers, James and Micajah, had traveled to Caintuck with our party despite their family's strong objections. Their father, James, had passed many years earlier and their mother, Sarah, only two years earlier. I remember well the Callaway boys since Flanders stared at me everytime we encountered each other on the journey. His brothers teased him something awful for doing so. I, more often than not, just stuck out my tongue at him, when Mama wasn't looking.

Men came and men went from the fort constantly that autumn. I was visiting with Suzy one late day when we took to making soap, as both Mama and Suzy need soap. Occupied with our task, we didn't notice him until a tall man, well over six feet in height with long reddish-blond hair tied in a queue, which hung most ways down his back, strolled up.

"Good day, ladies," he stated, doffing his felt hat, "might I bother you for directions to Captain Daniel Boone of hereabouts."

I could hardly speak for staring. "Yes, sir," I finally replied, "I'll take you to Daddy straight away."

"Oh, so you are one of the Captain's daughters?"

"We both are," answered Suzy. "I'm Susannah Hays, and this is my little sister Jemima. Perhaps we can both walk you over."

Having noticed Suzy beginning to flirt with the young man, I scrambled to drop my leather apron and grab the stranger's arm. "Right this way, I'll show you while Suzy stirs her soap."

After taking but a few steps, the young man stopped and said, "Excuse me, but I believe I have failed to introduce myself properly. I'm Simon Butler, early on of Virginia and now of the Limestone Creek settlement."

"Oh, have you family there?"

"No, just myself and my huntin' partner Thomas Williams."

We walked the short distance to our cabin, where I discovered Daddy had gone off to the fort's blockhouse. "I could show you the way, Mr. Butler," I suggested.

"No, I've taken enough of your time, and I suppose that imposin' two-story blockhouse is where I should go," Simon replied, bowed in my direction, and walked away.

"Mima, if you can quit starin' at that young man, I suggest you go back and help your sister," Mama whispered.

Later, Daddy brought Simon to our cabin for the evening meal. Over fresh venison stew and roasted turkey, Simon told us some of his adventures and how he'd spent the summer guiding families from Limestone Creek up on the Ohio to various settlements like Hinkston's, Martin's, McClelland's and Ruddle's stations. Simon, barely twenty years old, often traveled from station to station, warning each of approaching trouble after watching Indians cross the Ohio in large numbers.

"Simon, do you have family back in Virginia?" Mama asked.

"Yes, ma'am, I reckon I do." Simon stated politely before changing the subject. "Captain Boone, have you yet met George Rogers Clark?"

"Yes, Simon, I met him at Harrod's. I believe he may one day be the savin' grace of Caintuck. He seems like a worthy man to follow. Have you, yourself had reason to meet with him?"

"Only briefly, last time I visited Harrod's."

Their conversation continued well into the night. Us girls, Levina, Becky, and myself, finally crawled into the loft and bedded down for the night. Mama kept Daniel Morgan and Jesse with her, but both had long before fallen asleep. Israel often slept on a pallet in the blockhouse, having decided our cabin was much too full of giggling girls. The next morning, I awoke early and found Simon, sound asleep, curled in a deerskin, in front of our hearth. I walked quietly out to the privy, and when I returned, he was gone.

———— • ————

Winter came early and cold. We now rushed back and forth to the spring for water and often had to break an ice skim before filling our buckets. I watched, just four days before Christmas, as Judge Henderson gathered men from the various settlements for yet another meeting about the Transylvania Company. Daddy attended the meetings but spoke little to us about what was said. Then on the twenty-third, disaster struck. Colonel Arthur Campbell, a newly arrived company official, and two others left the fort and crossed the river. They had planned to survey some land. Their party split up with the lads, William McQuinney and Samuel Saunders, going one direction, although they were not armed, and Campbell going the opposite. Only a short time later, men in the fort heard shots and Campbell's cries of distress. Taking the lone remaining canoe, they crossed the river and found Campbell running toward the river, wearing only one shoe. Immediately, the fort's men gathered and searched for the two lads. While Daddy found numerous moccasin tracks, neither Will nor Sam could be found. Several days later, Will's dead and scalped body was found in a cornfield some three or so miles from the fort. No one ever saw Sam again. Most thought the Shawnee had taken him captive.

As more Shawnee raids occurred, additional settlers left Caintuck and returned east to the settlements. We stayed, never once talking of leaving, but more often than not lived within the fort, as we had a small cabin there as well. By spring, only about two hundred folks remained in Caintuck, few of them women and children. These hardy souls now mostly gathered at Fort Harrod, Logan's Station at the head of the Dix River, or Boonesborough. Soon, at each settlement, the families began to plan their spring planting using their hoard of seeds carried from Virginia and North Carolina the year before. Daddy and Squire returned from a surveying trip to explore the Ohio River all the way to the famous falls, just when it should have been time to plant.

Yet, winter hung around much too long. We ran short of all supplies, particularly food. Problems seemed to arise most every day. Then came the heavy and continual spring rains. The Louisa rose almost to our cabin door before the rains stopped.

Good news arrived from Fort Harrod, where Mistress Hugh Wilson had given birth to a baby boy, they named Harrod, in the early winter. Suzy'd hoped to birth the first white child in Caintuck but was the losing tortoise in that race.

Good news arrived when some of Mama's Bryan relatives from the Yadkin came by the fort. We had a grand ol' party, as they brought gifts of flour, meal, and such. The brothers Morgan, James, William, and Joseph didn't stay at Boonesborough, but built Bryan's Station on Elkhorn Creek. We were pleased to have them nearby.

I enjoyed that spring, listening to the mockingbird that perched on top of the nearest blockhouse each morning to sing his many stolen songs. He could entertain a girl for hours. I heard several of the men whistling replies as they moved about the common. In the evenings, the first whippoorwill, as it lay hidden among the undergrowth, cried out from the Louisa's banks. Another answered from somewhere along the river, or from the sycamore hollow. Their replies sang me to sleep each evening. I watched eagles and hawks in the meadow beside the fort. I saw a killdeer nesting in a small depression, defending with her broken-wing dance her nest full of small eggs. Turkeys marched by in flocks and tiny fawns scampered after their mothers to the river to drink.

I believed we had truly found paradise.

Seems like just when life begins to turn right ways, problems arise to turn it upside down once again. This time it was family. Suzy, now heavily pregnant, and Will lived just a few cabins away. Will hunted, stood his post when needed, and put in a large crop of corn that spring on land he had claimed. Then in late May, a neighbor arrived about dusk and asked for Daddy. They stepped outside, and after only a few seconds, Daddy threw open the door and asked Mama to step out with him. I took over stirring the pot and watched as they both stalked off into the coming darkness. Daddy returned some while later, but not Mama.

"Daddy, where's Mama. Is it Suzy's time?" Israel asked.

"No, son. Never you mind. Jemima, put the food on the table," Daddy replied stonily.

We ate in silence, and after listening to Daddy read from the Bible, crept to our beds. All of us knew enough not to ask questions. I carried Daniel Morgan up the ladder with us girls. Jesse already lay sleeping in the old cradle beside Mama's bed. As I lay there, unable to sleep, worried about Suzy and Mama, I remembered the verse Pa had searched out. It read, "For husbands, this means love your wives, just as Christ loved the church. He gave up his life for her." Daddy had found it in Ephesians.

The next morning, Mama came in early and called to me. "Mima, go stay with your sister and help out wherever needed."

I rose, dressed, and gathered my shawl against the early morning chill. As I turned to leave, Mama handed me fresh hoe cakes and fried bear bacon wrapped in a linen towel.

"Mima, Will is family. Still, if he comes to their cabin, don't let him in. Stay with Suzy and call out if'in we're needed. Daddy or I will be listenin'."

I found Suzy bundled into her bed. Daddy walked out as I walked in, saying, "Bar the door, daughter."

I nursed Suzy's sore body, cooked, cleaned, and worried for two days. Mama came often, so did Aunt Jane. We all knew what had happened. Some of last year's corn crop had been distilled into hard liquor. Will drank, quite often too much. Despite all his learning and refined manners, William Hays turned out to be a harsh, violent man with an extraordinary Irish temper. Suzy never told me what set him off that evening, but she couldn't hide the two black eyes, the swollen jaw, and the bruises across her arms and legs. Mama despaired the babe would arrive too soon. So, we kept her to bed.

Israel and Daddy brought firewood and meat. Nothing was said of Will. Over a week passed before Suzy felt like moving from her bed and taking up her chores. The next day, Will Hays stood beside Daddy at their cabin door. Daddy sent me home. Worried, I lingered beside their door even after it shut.

"Will, Suzy is my daughter. I expect you to treat her with respect. Suzy, honor your husband and stop flirtin' with every man you see."

With that Daddy opened the door and left. He saw me standing, listening. "Mima, when you marry, child, please make sure he's a gentle man."

Many times, over the coming years, Daddy or Israel, or others, would have to stop Will from beating Suzy to death.

In mid-June, Suzy sent for Mama and Aunt Jane. I listened as she birthed a baby girl, on the twelfth. They named her Elizabeth; I believe in honor of Will's mother. Finally, we had a new baby at Boonesborough. All the men, married and unmarried, begged to hold her in the weeks that followed. Many had tears in their eyes, especially Daddy. Suzy may not have birthed the first white baby in Caintuck, but she sure 'nough had the first one at Boonesborough.

Chapter 7
July 14th, 1776

Caintuck might be the most beautiful place on earth, but in the middle of the summer, I do believe, it is the hottest and sticky-est. That Sunday, we attended church services out in the common area of the fort. Uncle Squire led the service, and him being a Calvinistic Baptist, the women sat apart from the men, and except for singing and such, we took almost no part in the service. Thank the good Lord, Uncle Squire also suffered from the heat and humidity of the day and didn't preach a long-winded service. Besides, Uncle Squire and Aunt Jane planned to ride for Fort Harrod that day. Recently he had surveyed and recorded some land thereabouts, and they planned to build a cabin. Jane wanted to help pick out where they built. In the meantime, they'd live in Fort Harrod.

Now Betsy and Fanny Callaway and I'd concocted a plan. Using my sore foot as an excuse—I'd stepped on a cane stob earlier in the week—we begged and begged until Daddy let us take one of the fort's canoes out on the river. Without changing from our Sunday best, we took a canoe and pushed off from the bank. No one else was out on the river. We floated back and forth, below the fort, keeping it in sight, like we had promised Daddy. I lazed about with my sore foot dangling in the water, and we talked.

"Betsy's in love with Sam Henderson," Fanny stated, giggling. I glanced over to see Betsy blushing below her bonnet brim.

"Truly, Betsy. Who would have guessed given the way your eyes follow him everywhere?" I teased.

"Well, Jemima Boone, at least I've got a fiancé, and yes he notices me. That Simon Butler scarcely ever talks with you. You should be lookin' toward the fort's men, instead of that wanderer. Besides, my Pa says he's much too quiet about his family back east."

"Oh, my Mama says the same thing. But Simon's a respectful man, and Daddy says that means he was raised right. Perhaps he *is* hidin' somethin', but many of the men here in Caintuck had trouble with the law back in Virginia or North Carolina," I retorted.

"Includin' your own Daddy, says my father," retorted Betsy.

"Betsy Callaway, you know well my Daddy paid off all his debts last time he went back east. Everyone knows that."

"Oh, stop arguin', you're ruinin' a perfectly fine canoe ride," demanded Fanny. "Besides, if you'll pay more mind to where we are, you'll realize we cannot see the fort at all!"

Betsy picked up the oars and tried to steer our canoe toward the south shore and back to the fort, but eddies carried us closer and closer to the north bank, just where her father and mine had told us not to go. Everyone in the fort called this side the *Indian bank* for good reason. At first, struggling to guide us away from the north bank, Betsy relented and instead suggested we gather some flowers growing along the bank to take back. She even tried rowing closer to shore.

Suddenly, someone dove into the water from the north bank, and Fanny, thinking it was a friend from the fort, yelled, *Law! Simon, how you scared me!* In that instance, she realized it was an Indian and not Simon. As more warriors appeared on the bank, Fanny began beating the man over the head with her paddle, which started the other Indians to laughing at him. Suddenly Fanny took one hard swing and her paddle broke right over the man's head with one end flying off into the water, leaving Fanny sitting holding only a small piece of the handle. Betsy and I now screamed for help. Betsy, remembering she also had a paddle, soon followed Fanny's defensive action. The other warriors jumped into the river and pulled the canoe toward the *Indian bank*. As the canoe reached the shore, they pulled each one of us onto land and let the canoe drift away. One warrior grabbed my long braids and threatened to slit my throat and scalp me. Instantly, we girls all hushed. Some of our captors spoke good English, and they threatened us to keep quiet. Fanny sobbed quietly, while Betsy and I, although terrified, silently allowed ourselves to be led away from the river and home.

Three warriors tied each one of us—Fanny, Betsy, and me—to one of them by leather thongs around our wrists. Without discussing it, each of us realized we had to do our best to slow our rate of progress. So, I complained loudly about my sore foot, and took to falling and yelling out something horrible at every opportunity. Fanny and I didn't even have shoes, and Betsy had on her Sunday best with little wooden heels. She took to digging them in as often as possible, marking a clear trail. Fanny and I helped out by tearing off bits of our petticoats and dropping them off or tying them to the undergrowth. That is, until the Indians caught on. With sharp words, they threatened us again, but laid not one hand on us in punishment. We continued to mark the trail when possible, but with much more caution.

Hanging Maw, one of the two Cherokee men, spoke some English and had visited our family back at the Watauga settlement. I could tell he recognized me. "You Boone's daughter?" he asked.

"Yes, Daddy will be comin' for us."

"These your sisters?"

"YES!" I felt it better to lie, as we all knew the Indians respected Daddy and would be proud to take us back to their village if we were all his daughters.

"Ah, we done pretty well for Old Boone this time!" he replied laughingly.

At dark, we stopped, and the two Cherokee and three Shawnee warriors talked among themselves. Then, one approached us each with a knife and cut off the bottom of our dresses and petticoats and cut the heels off Betsy's shoes. They gave Fanny and me moccasins and tied us tightly together and to one of the warriors before making a cold camp. They offered us neither water nor food. Exhausted, hungry, thirsty, and terrified, we spent a horrible night tugging at our restraints and praying for deliverance. I had a small penknife in my pocket but couldn't reach it. I tried all night. Several times Fanny sobbed fresh tears, shaking with fear. Betsy took to shushing her, afraid her sobs would bring us all to greater harm.

Back at the fort, people relaxed and enjoyed a day of freedom. Most everyone followed the Good Book's teachings and took Sunday as a day of rest. Daddy lazed on his bed, taking a nap, still dressed in his Sunday best. Betsy's beau, Sam Henderson, who shaved only once a week, had decided that chore needed to be accomplished as he planned to kiss Betsy later in the day. He lathered his face, completed one side, and turned to start the other, glancing at his reflection in the small hand mirror. Two other young men, Nathan Reid and John Floyd, dressed to the nines in their Sunday best, sat complaining that the only girls to court were off canoeing on the river. Children played, and the women talked and shared the latest news.

Abruptly, the alarm was raised. "The savages have the girls," screamed one of Betsy's younger brothers after hearing our cries of alarm and running toward the cabins for help.

Immediately, men and women appeared in cabin doors, including Daddy. Dressed in his Sunday breeches and still barefoot, he ran for the river, calling for others to follow him. Betsy and Fanny's father, Dick Callaway loaded his gun as he ran, followed by Sam Henderson with shaving soap still covering half of his face. Each stood and stared at the empty canoe, now floating on the far side of the river. While Callaway, his nephew Flanders, and others mounted horses and rode hard toward a ford about a mile down river, twelve-year-old John Gass started stripping off his best clothes.

"John, what are you about?" shouted Daddy.

"Sir, Captain Boone, I can swim over and get the canoe. I've swum this river many a day," he shouted before diving in. Pulling a long stroke, he crossed the river in no time.

Minutes later, several men joined Daddy as they crossed in the canoe to discover the course of the fleeing Indians. The men split into two parties. One headed upstream, and Daddy's headed downstream. Quickly, he met up with the horsemen. Daddy, believing the Indians took us north toward the Licking River, sent the horsemen on ahead to cut them off. His own small party proceeded upstream. Meanwhile, the other party of men had discovered our trail and moved on after us girls. Finally, after about five miles and not long before dusk, the two parties converged. Almost instantly, they heard a dog barking, and believing it was the Indians' camp, crept forward only to discover a new settler's cabin under construction. Here, Daddy found his old friend, Will Bush. As the sun was already setting, the party decided to camp for the night and to send a volunteer back to Boonesborough for supplies, including proper clothing and foot gear.

"I can go, sir," volunteered young John yet again. "I'm a fast runner and know the way, even in the dark."

"Well, John, remember all the items we need. Borrow a horse for the return trip and be careful," Daddy instructed.

John made the journey back to our fort and returned on horseback with the needed supplies just before daylight. Now prepared for the rigorous task that lay ahead, the men departed, taking the three cabin builders with them.

"John, step over here a minute," Daddy asked politely, speaking just before they moved out. "Young John, you've proved yourself twice now. We acknowledge your bravery and skill, but you haven't slept, and we need to move fast. I'd like you to return home and reassure the womenfolk that we'll find the girls. Besides, we need you to help protect the fort with all of us gone. Can you do that for me? Can I depend on you?

"Yes, sir, Captain Boone. You rightly can,"

As John rode off toward the fort, Daddy turned and began to move quickly along the well-known Warrior's Path.

The next day intensified our fear as the warriors pushed and pulled us girls harder and faster. We broke small branches off bushes and shrubs, pulled up vines, and dropped anything possible to leave a trail. Late in the morning, one warrior saw what we were about and threatened us each with his knife. Still, I continued to hobble about on my sore foot. In midafternoon, they allowed us to rest against a tree and offered us water. We could hardly move, we were so tired. A short time later, one of the Indians came back with a horse led by a leather tug. He forced us each on its back after we pretended not to know how to mount a horse! Now all three of us were splendid horsewomen and could ride like the wind. Yet, silently we'd again made a pact—act like you cannot ride.

The one of us riding in the rear fell off the back of the horse time and time again, landing on our rumps and screaming out in fear and pain. When none of our captors were looking, we kicked the horse or pinched it to make it rear up and bare its teeth at us. It even bit Becky on the arm. All five warriors found it extremely funny that Boone's daughters didn't know how to ride! One of them demonstrated how to ride before putting us each back on the horse. We didn't get any better after his lesson, and finally they abandoned the animal and made us walk once again. That may not have been one of our smarter ideas, but it did slow us down considerably and gave our rescuers more time to catch up and a clearer trail to follow. Our first full day of captivity ended the same as the one before, with us all tied together and no fire. This time they did bring us water and jerked buffalo tongue. Nasty stuff that none of us would eat. Bone-weary, we slept huddled together in great fear of never being found. Yet, down deep in my soul, I felt sure Daddy would come.

The Boonesborough pursuers, after a rough day of following a barely recognizable trail, began losing heart. All except Daddy.

"Men, I do believe they will cross the Licking at the Upper Blue Licks. As they are makin' tracks faster than we can follow them, I suggest we move ahead to the Licks," Daddy stated. And with little discussion, our rescuers turned off our trail and headed directly for the crossing. Later in the second day of pursuit, they once again crossed our path, assuring one and all of Daddy's correct assumption and ultimate knowledge of Indian ways.

The morning of the third day, Daddy's party crossed Hinkston Creek just above where we had crossed only an hour or so before. Not long afterward, Daddy led the men across our trail once more. Daddy realized the warriors now followed a buffalo trace that paralleled the well-known Warrior's Path. Late in the day, they found a buffalo calf carcass, partially butchered, with blood still running freely. Then an almost dead snake lay wiggling in the trail, knife wounds along his body.

"They'll stop and cook at the first water they come to, 'tis their habit," Daddy informed the others.

Despite his great skill at tracking, Daddy then lost the trail and had to divide the searchers, sending each off in a different direction to look for signs. He warned each man to be extremely quiet and not to make a move if they discovered our whereabouts until all were organized and ready. Daddy knew the Indians would tomahawk us to death if they were not taken totally by surprise. It was Billy Smith who discovered us sitting in a small glen where we had stopped. He waved both groups together to prepare to plan a rescue.

Oh, my, oh my, by late afternoon, I didn't think I was able to take another step when we halted. One of the warriors built a fire and began roasting a large piece of buffalo meat. Another kept tugging at Betsy's hair as she warmed her hands by the fire. Betsy, always one to react quickly, picked up some hot coals with a piece of bark and dumped the contents on the Indian's moccasin. As he hopped about howling like a wolf, Hanging Maw pointed at Betsy and declared her a "mighty fine squaw." I think these words and the fear they brought sank all our spirits instantly. Betsy dropped down against a large tree, and soon Fanny and I had our heads in her lap. Fanny softly murmured for her mother, while Betsy pulled twigs and other rubbish from our hair.

Each of us was old enough and had heard the stories of what happened to white girls captured by Indians. Fear of that life, of rape, of torture if we resisted, created visions in our minds and intensified the fear in our hearts. We knew the farther we traveled from home the more likely we would not be rescued.

As we sat motionless and worried, our captives paid us little mind. One stood watch a ways off on a small rise, while another rested on the ground. Two tended the fire and gathered firewood. Hanging Maw walked away to get water. They seemed to have little regard for their own safety, and I realized they no longer feared being found. I watched as their sentinel leaned his gun against a tree and walked to the fire to light his pipe. He and I both noticed the slight sound of a twig breaking in the nearby woods, and while I searched for the source of the sound, the warrior simply went on about his business after a quick glance about. As I scoured the bushes and trees, I spotted Daddy, on all fours, creeping up on the camp. Our eyes met, and I knew first and foremost, I had to remain quiet.

Within seconds, the man tending the fire toppled forward with a spray of blood from his chest, then I heard the rifle blast as the sound broke through the camp. Just as quickly, the wounded warrior jumped up and ran off clutching his wound. As I yelled "Daddy" and fell to the ground, I pulled Fanny with me. Daddy yelled *"get down, get down."* Instead Betsy jumped to her feet and barely missed being hit by a warrior's war club. Daddy and the other rescuers fired into the camp and then reloaded on the run. Betsy ran toward one of them who, mistaking her for an Indian, almost clubbed her with his gun.

"For God's sake, don't kill her when we've traveled so far to save her," Daddy cried out just in time.

Our captors fled, and quickly our rescuers had us cradled in their arms. Daddy thought only one of the Indians had been killed outright and another wounded. When his men searched the area later and set a guard, they found the wounded man dead. Daddy pulled blankets from their packs and wrapped us all up. I can still remember his arms, like a vice, squeezing all his love back into my body.

"Thank Almighty Providence, boys, for we have the girls safe. Let's all sit down by them now and have a hearty cry," Daddy declared, noticing there was already not a dry eye in the bunch.

The loudest sobs came from the man who had almost clubbed Betsy to death.

Chapter 8
Rescued

I sat in Daddy's lap and leaned against his shoulder, snuggling in as close as possible, "Are you hurt, Mima?" he whispered.

"No, Daddy, other than makin' us walk and not havin' any food and little water, they treated us well. Hanging Maw was one of them, did you see him?"

"No, child. I suspect he recognized you?"

"Yes, I told him we were all *your* daughters," I rushed on. "He thought that was mighty funny and bragged about what fine squaws we would make. He treated me well, patted me on the head, played with my hair, and called me *pretty squaw*. He even made me fix his hair and look for lice. He made sure the others treated us well. There were only the five, but they spoke of meeting up with others at the Licking. They were traveling home from a war council and claimed they'd planned an attack on the Watauga settlement."

We continued to talk, just the two of us. I remember thinking back on how I had disobeyed Daddy by going so near the *Indian bank*. I promised myself right then and there, I would never again disobey my Daddy. Also, I would always stay with him, no matter what. For in this land of beauty, death lurked around each corner. Yet Daddy's presence nearby always made me feel safe.

After all the excitement of our rescue, I noticed Sam holding Betsy and her examining his half-shaved face. One of the other men, whom I knew to be a bachelor, held Fanny, as her father was with the riders. He talked to her and smoothed her hair as they whispered together.

She had stopped crying and even smiled shyly at him as I watched.

Daddy sent word to the riders of our rescue and told them to ride for the fort. The rescue party had left the fort with too few men for protection. Betsy, Fanny, and I were exhausted, hungry, and relieved, but determined to begin our return home. The men cooked enough of the meat to feed us, and afterward packed the rest for our return trip. We had to walk yet again but met up with that same ol' tired horse as we moved south toward the fort. Each of us rode, sometimes all three, and none of us fell off, not even once. We told the story of how we'd pretended not to know how to ride, and everyone had a good laugh. Sam often carried Betsy on his back for long stretches of the journey—now that he could hold her again, he claimed she would never again be out of his sight. The men teased him about such a ridiculous notion. We spent one more night in the forest, safely guarded by Daddy and the men of Boonesborough. As safe as I felt, I could not help looking for warriors behind every tree.

I first saw Mama's face from across the Louisa River, as the men used the few canoes to ferry us over. Mama grabbed me in her arms and cried and laughed at the same time, as I had seen her do so often. Zek barked and ran about frantically. Soon Levina, Becky, and Daniel Morgan joined in the celebration. Israel, helping with the canoes, approached me next.

"So, Duck, you left to go canoein' on the river and got yourself captured by Indians!" he declared loudly, pulling me into his arms. "Are you well, Sister?" he whispered into my ear.

"Yes, Brother, we are all well and safe."

"I'm glad. I missed you." And with one more hug, he walked away, tears brimming over.

Mama grabbed me back from Israel and held me tight against her and declared I needed a bath and feeding up. Seemed she could not stand to let me free of her arms, as over and over she pulled me in against her body and held me tight. Next thing I knew I was standing in my shift in front of the fort's only tub as Israel carried in water from the spring, and Suzy added hot water. Over on Mama's bed, little Elizabeth slept soundly while three-year-old Jesse tried his best to wake her when no one was looking. Mama pulled out her lineament and doctored all my cuts and scrapes. She threw my shift into the rag pile along with my Sunday dress and petticoats, each now thoroughly ruined. As I soaked, Suzy washed my long hair and combed out all the tangles. Mama continued to cry and laugh, bending to hug me at unexpected moments, until I finally rose from the bath, dressed, and collapsed into my bed. I wanted to sleep for days.

When I awoke, I found a celebration being planned for the following Sunday. I also learned from Israel a bit of news.

"Mima, did you hear about Nathaniel Hart's place?" he asked over dinner.

"No, what happened?"

"While you were needin' rescuin', Indians burned his cabin, crops, and all of his apple trees. Luckily, he was with the riders headed to the Lickin' and 'twas not at home. Daddy says they'd most likely have killed him. That's one reason we're workin' so hard to finish puttin' up the fort's walls. Soon all twenty-six cabins will be enclosed in one solid picket wall. Daddy says Harrod's and Logan's are also laborin' on their fortifications. No one feels safe."

"Mima, there's other news," Viney said smiling. "Betsy and Sam have set a date for their weddin'! Sam says he's taking no chances on Betsy gettin' away."

"With Uncle Squire gone, who's going to marry them?" I asked.

"Oh, Daddy is," answered Israel laughing, "and Dick Callaway is mad as a wet hen. He says he's not sure Daddy's appointment as *magistrate of Transylvania* makes him suitable to conduct his daughter's weddin' and plans to have Sam sign a bond promisin' to re-marry Betsy as soon as a *higher authority* is available."

"Sam says he don't care what he has to sign as long as they get hitched," Viney added.

Despite these good tidings, my mind constantly drifted back to our capture, the dangers we three girls faced, and what our lives would have been if not rescued. Fear invaded my dreams and I often woke screaming and crying out. A couple of days later, Mama and Aunt Jane ushered me into Squire's cabin, handed me a rare cup of tea, real tea, and asked about my feelings.

"Mima," Aunt Jane started, "how are you dealin' with your adventure?"

"Oh, Mama, Aunt Jane, I betrayed Daddy!" With those words, tears burst from my eyes—the tears I had held back since my return. As I sobbed, Aunt Jane pulled me into a hug, while Mama found one of the baby's nappies and wiped my face with its softness.

It took several minutes for me to regain myself, to wipe my eyes, to find my voice—mostly to give my heart permission to tell Mama of my fear. Finding words had never been so hard.

"Mama, Aunt Jane, I am so sorry. I know Daddy is disappointed in me for placin' myself and my friends in danger. I knew the danger *of* the *Indian bank*. I understood his warnin's; we all did. I failed him. I doubt he'll ever trust me again."

"Oh, Mima, is that your worry? Oh, child, your Daddy forgave you the minute he heard you were in danger. He puts none of the blame on you, instead it rests now, and will forever, completely on his shoulders. He's afraid you now have so much fear, such intense fear, you can never feel safe here again. He recognizes how close he came to losin' another child to his dreams of livin' in this wilderness. He sent us to find out if you wish to return to the settlements and live with family?"

"Mama, never! I'm afraid, yes, but my fear is one tempered by knowledge. I understand now so much how the beauty of this place can lure you into believin' it is truly paradise. My greatest fear is that I have lost Daddy's respect. I know I have his love, but I want to have his respect as well." Once again, my tears began to flow.

Aunt Jane slipped quietly out while Mama held me tight but kept silent. I believe Jane and Mama knew I had to hear Daddy's words from him and not words of reassurance from her.

A few minutes later, I heard him step into the cabin. Mama and Aunt Jane stepped outside, leaving us alone. I glanced toward him to see tears running down his face as he gathered me into his arms.

"Daddy, oh Daddy, I am so sorry for disobeyin' you. Please don't send me away. I can be trusted, truly I can."

"Jemima, little Duck, you always will have my love, my trust, and my respect. Caintuck offers up more dangers than I imagined possible, yet you and your mother, brothers, and sisters have flourished here. There have been no complaints except those of everyday life. If there is any regret, it is how I failed you. I failed to provide you with the knowledge you needed to survive here."

"Oh, Daddy, you never did. Without your teachin' us children how to survive, to mark a trail, to be strong, I think we would have disappeared across the Ohio long ago."

"Now, now, Mima, I would never let that happen. Believe me, I'll sacrifice all for my children, if possible. Still, you need to understand how we all make mistakes at times. Why, how many times have the Shawnee snuck up on Squire and me? Never believe I am all-knowin'. I am just a man tryin' to do what's best for his family."

We sat in our silent hug for several long minutes before he spoke again, "Now do you want to go back to the settlements, maybe just for a while? You can stay with Hannah or your uncles George or Neddie?"

"No, Daddy, I'll be fine right here in my home with you and Mama. I love Caintuck. Like you once told me, we have as much right to be here as do the Shawnee and other Indians. We just need to find a way toward peace."

We talked awhile more, often laughed, always remembering the fear we both held hidden in our hearts, but mostly learning how to express what we felt. As evening came and I thought back on that conversation, I realized I grew up so much in those few hours. And yet, when we parted, each going back to his own chores, I understood one thing more clearly than ever before. I would never desert my father, for I knew he would give all for me.

So, on the seventh of August, we all enjoyed the first wedding at Boonesborough when Samuel Henderson married Elizabeth Callaway. A fabulous feast followed, crowned by our enjoyment of Kentucky's first crop of watermelons. They'd been chilled in the spring. Why, now I think on it, it must have been the first white wedding in Caintuck.

The folks at Boonesborough pestered any newcomer with news of the conflict back east. Most enjoyed a spirit of revolution, and at Fort Harrod in June, the men had created our own Committee of Safety. As leaders of our various settlements, these men wrote to the Virginia Committee to offer their aid in any *laudable cause of American freedom.* George Rogers Clark and John Gabriel Jones stood as our representatives.

Along with the lure of cheap land, most every man and woman came to Caintuck seeking relief from taxes, oppressive government intervention, and opportunities for self-rule and freedom from British rule. So when, in early

August, a new settler presented us with a copy of the *Virginia Gazette* containing the Declaration of Independence, we celebrated yet again.

Those who could read, read it off to others. People gathered to listen to the words on that scrap of newsprint, over and over again. Men and women alike debated its effects on our own situation. Daddy, Simon, and Israel talked of war between the colonists, now called the Patriots, and the British Redcoats. Some men even talked of going back east to join up in the fight. A letter arrived from Mama's family telling her how her Bryan family had split, some for freedom and some who held strong with England. Most everyone recognized Bryan's Station, located only twenty or so miles away, as a Tory stronghold. Two of Mama's brothers returned to North Carolina to serve as officers in the Tory militia.

Indian troubles continued to be an important topic of conversation. Word came about the Cherokee attacking the Watauga settlement back on the twentieth of July. The settlement held and defeated the Cherokee on the following day. Chief Attakullakulla and other more peaceful Cherokee chiefs gained control after the defeat and ended most of the attacks by their people. Still, the northern tribes caused trouble in Caintuck, especially for those settlements directly along the Ohio River.

Sporadic attacks occurred at isolated homesteads and some smaller stations and forts. While more settlers left, even more continued to come across the mountains. Caintuck still held the reputation of being a rich land possessed of unfettered freedom lying just over the mountains—there for the taking for those willing to risk their lives.

We gathered our first crops that autumn and laid aside supplies for the winter. Men gathered firewood, women smoked meat and made jerky, ground corn, and prepared hides for coats, warm moccasins—which most of us wore, as shoes were impossible to come by—bedclothes, and even window coverings, as few of the cabins had glass windows. Even those with glass had hide curtains to help keep out the cold. Mothers tasked their younger children with filling the cracks between logs with mud daub to keep out the coming cold and wet weather. Men and boys repaired roofs. We thought we were prepared. Then winter commenced. In came the cold, the sleet, the ice, and, within days, the snow. Inches and inches fell in soft wet flakes. Weeks passed with not a day above freezing.

Simon Butler came and went throughout the winter, often warning us of large Indian parties having crossed the Ohio River. He shared news from other settlements and told Daddy how George Rogers Clark and John Gabriel Jones had gone east to beg the Virginia Assembly for assistance. Still staying with our family on most visits, Simon presented me with a well-cured buffalo robe for my bed.

"Jemima, I hope this will keep you warm this winter," he stated so as only I could hear, while handing me the carefully folded and tied bundle. "I thought it might ease your nightmares."

I guessed Mama or Daddy had let slip how sometimes during the night I woke, calling out for Daddy and shaking with fear. "I thank you kindly, Simon. I've heard tell how some settlers name their buffalo hides. How about I call this one *Simon*?" I teased.

Now, I'd rarely seen Simon blush, but there he stood, his face almost as red as his hair.

"Don't rightly know how Daniel will take to you doin' so. Perhaps you'd better pick another name."

"Oh, like. . . Butler maybe," I continued to tease.

"Jemima Boone," snapped Mama, "thank that young man properly and quit teasin' him."

"Yes, ma'am." And I stood on my tiptoes and kissed his cheek. "Thank you, Simon, I'll treasure it. I'm sure it will keep out the chill."

"Uh, I need to go to the blockhouse, 'cuse me Mistress Boone, Jemima." And he practically disappeared in an instant.

Later, Daddy, grinning like a possum, returned to our cabin. "Mima, what did you say to poor Simon? He came into the blockhouse all flustered and embarrassed."

"Nothing much. He gave me a buffalo robe, and I thanked him kindly."

Mama cleared her throat and gave me a look. "Go on, tell your Daddy how you embarrassed the poor man."

"Oh, Mama, all I said was I would name my new hide *Simon,* and he turned all red and ran out."

"Daughters! You girls will be the death of me yet. Well, maybe he'll get himself over his unease and show up for supper after all." Daddy laughed, shook his head, and lit the grease lamp.

"It'll be my guess his stomach will override his head, and he'll be here," I answered.

Sure enough, Simon knocked several minutes later. He kissed Mama on the cheek and settled down with his pipe. He didn't glance, not even one time, in my direction. He and Daddy instead discussed one of the recent immigrants.

After our meal, while Mama and I helped Viney clear the table, a knock came at the door. Daddy stood and looked out the window, before stepping over to the door. "Good evenin', Flanders. Is somethin' amiss?"

"No, sir, Captain Boone. All's quiet, I just checked the sentries and figure we're all in for the night. Actually, I was wonderin' if I could speak with Jemima a moment?"

"Jemima? . . . . Oh, my daughter. You mean the one standin' there lookin' mighty puzzled. Well. . ., I rightly think you can, Flanders."

"Alone sir, we'll stay right near your cabin, and I'll have her back in a spell," Flanders promised.

I nodded to Daddy, grabbed my shawl to cover my head, and my heavy cloak. When I stepped outside, Flanders smiled and took my arm, real gentlemanly like. I think we both overheard Daddy's comment as I closed the door.

"Well, Rebecca, what do you make of that? Two suitors in one day!"

I didn't know until later Simon had replied, "Well, Daniel, you have a beautiful, spirited, brave daughter. She will make some man a splendid wife." Israel repeated Simon's words to me later and said, "Daddy sat reading his Bible and nodding. Mama laughed."

Flanders and Simon courted me, so to speak, all winter. Not that we could do much stepping out together with the weather being so cold and miserable. We managed to skate on the river a few times in early February, staying close to the bank. We used wooden sleds built by one of the men to slide down a nearby hill on other occasions. And once or twice each month, our fiddler would tune up and someone would call dances in the blockhouse. As there were fewer girls and women than men, we often made up squares of three men and one female. I danced each night until my feet could take no more. Often beside me, Fanny danced almost exclusively with John Holder. He, like Flanders, had been one of the riders during our rescue. As the winter progressed, Israel told me that all around the fort, men placed bets on who would win out, Simon or Flanders. He also mentioned several other young men who wished I'd chose neither.

Both of my suitors stood taller than most men, including Daddy, who's not especially tall. Simon reached well over six feet with broad shoulders, while Flanders stood about six feet with a wiry, quick athletic body. Of course, both had proven themselves to be excellent hunters. I think I've said, Simon's hair glowed reddish blond, while Flanders' hair tended to be dark blond with streaks of almost white in the summer. Most important of all, Daddy respected both men; Mama not so much. She still wondered about Simon's background, while Flanders' quiet manners impressed her and overshadowed her worries about him being Dick Callaway's nephew. Mr. Callaway, on occasion, proved himself an arrogant fool.

All winter, my fifteenth, I only smiled when asked which one I favored. I knew which one, but for the moment it was fun to have two suitors.

⎯⎯⎯⎯⎯◆⎯⎯⎯⎯⎯

On a later trip that winter, Simon told us how George Rogers Clark had arrived at McClelland's Station and reported receiving five hundred pounds of powder and lead from the Virginia Assembly to be used in defense of Caintuck. Clark had ferried the supplies down the Ohio as far as Three Islands, where he and his party hid the powder and shot in three different caches, for the Shawnee seemed to know what they carried and heavily pursued their canoes. The increased Indian activity forced Simon and Clark to travel to Fort Harrod to round up enough men to retrieve the much-needed supplies. By the time they returned, McClelland's had already come under attack from the Shawnee and Mohawk. John McClelland and Mohawk Chief Pluggy soon lay dead. Pluggy's death caused the warriors to withdraw. Simon followed the natives all the way back to the Ohio and watched them crossed the river. Finally thinking it safe enough, Simon led a large party of men to the islands to retrieve the powder and lead.

All the settlers of McClelland's Station left. Some came to Boonesborough and others continued on to Fort Harrod. Even more returned east of the Appalachians. Clark and Simon distributed the much-needed lead and powder to each of the stations and forts.

Soon, word came from back east that changed so many things. On the last day of December 1776, the Virginia Assembly established the County of Kentucky, encompassing what we knew as Caintuck. They appointed Clark to head the Kentucky militia with the rank of major.

Major Clark appointed Simon Butler and Thomas Brooks as scouts for Boonesborough and tasked them with patrolling the woods between our home and the Ohio and warning us of imminent attacks. Many a morning, I awoke to find either Simon or Thomas speaking with Daddy or enjoying breakfast at our table.

Only three forts held sufficient men to protect their occupants if attacked. Major George Rogers Clark commanded all the militia men from his headquarters at Fort Harrod, where Captains John Todd and James Harrod were second in command. At Boonesborough, Daddy's previous British militia appointment and his reputation granted him a new appointment as a captain in the Kentucky militia. Benjamin Logan received the appointment at Logan's Station.

In early March of 1777, a roster listed one-hundred-twenty men to protect two-hundred-eighty settlers in the new County of Kentucky. Fort Harrod had forty families and eighty-four men. Boonesborough's strength was listed at twenty-two men and ten to fifteen families, including about a dozen women, and ten to fifteen slaves. Logan's Station held only fifteen men, with few families. Theirs was a perilous position if attacked.

⟵ ● ⟶

Although our now perilous position in Kentucky often occupied my mind, another problem also haunted my thoughts and dreams. I acknowledged how I would soon need to make a decision concerning my two beaus, I took to using various means to judge how I felt about each one. I could, of course, try to determine which one would be the more skillful provider, the more upright father, and the more skillful husband and lover. Yet, they seemed pert near equal in each regard, excepting I knew Simon, like Daddy, was a wanderer.

Still, there was one contest that had me downright stumped, for each of my beaus sure knew how to kiss. As winter had moved into spring, I figured a bit more trial with each would be needed before I could decide which kiss I wanted to look forward to for the rest of my life.

Chapter 9
Our Lives in Danger

A necessity of life when one lives off the land is farming. Without crops at each of Kentucky's settlements, starvation would arrive, taking first the elderly, the children, and the ill and wounded. So as early spring arrived, and just after the militia muster, our men left the fort and journeyed forth to their individual land holdings to clear land and prepare the soil for planting. Some even started building cabins on their land, planning to live on their land instead of in the fort. Many built rough three-sided lean-tos so they could stay overnight and work longer hours each day.

Since such work requires concentration and strenuous labor, the men would often lay aside their weapons. You can't clear land or pull stumps while holding a rifle. On a beautiful spring day, the seventh of March, the fort's sentry heard shots and cries for help from two men working in a nearby field. In a surprise attack, Shawnee warriors had killed a Negro slave and severely wounded his master. Sounding a horn of danger, the sentry called in all the fort's occupants. Daddy and others rode out and recovered the wounded man and returned him to the fort. Yet, no Indians appeared outside our walls.

Feeling the necessity for caution, Daddy split the men into two groups each day. Women could work with the farmers as long as they understood and accepted the risk. Each group of farmers now had other men holding rifles to help protect them from random attacks.

Within days, news arrived from Fort Harrod about an almost simultaneous attack there. "Daniel, a group of men left the fort to continue boilin' maple sap to make sugar when attacked. No one knew of any trouble until they failed to return that evenin'," Simon stated.

"How many were killed?"

"Three includin' one of Hugh McGary's stepsons, William Ray. His brother, James, outran the Indians and hid. Will Coomes managed to hide in a downed tree and watched them mutilate William's body. He said they danced about and drank maple syrup from the kettles.

"I wasn't with the men who found the bodies, but others said William's body was so mutilated that Hugh became ill and almost swooned off his horse when the rescue party arrived. Hugh was one of thirty or so men who rode off to find them when they didn't return. Hugh's wife's in a bad way. She took the news hard and has not left her bed. Some say she hasn't spoken a word, doesn't even cry. She stares at somethin' none of us can see."

"Oh, poor Mary, poor Mary. We traveled to Kentucky together. Did you know that, Simon?" asked Mama.

"No, ma'am, I didn't. I like Mary. She's always been kind to me. She raised two fine sons long before she married Hugh," Simon replied.

All stayed quiet with their own thoughts on love of a parent and death of a child. Seems few families had not lost at least one member to the dangers of Kentucky. Mostly to Indians, but some to snakebite or accidents and illnesses.

"Any other sightin's?" Daddy asked after a while.

"Yes, sir, the next mornin', Shawnee warriors began burnin' those few cabins lyin' outside the fort's wall. McGary and a few others rushed out and attacked them. Hugh and another man were slightly wounded, but McGary killed a warrior wearin' his stepson's hunting shirt. Daniel, the man's gone mad. He cut up the warrior's body and fed it to his dogs. He says his stepson, wrapped in a burial sheet, comes and talks to him about vengeance."

"Hugh's always been a rough man, and I understand how the loss of a son in such a manner can drive one . . ., well, a bit insane," Daddy replied. 'Twas one of the only times I can recollect him speaking openly about James' death.

"But Daniel, I don't believe you've ever taken such actions, even against those that kidnapped Jemima," Simon stated.

"No, no, I haven't and never will. I guess it's all those years of Quaker teachin's. I believe in life, in peaceful livin'. Now, I'd take a life if need be to protect and defend and have done. Yet, I take no joy in killin' a man, white or Indian. 'Tis against the good Lord's commandments. I have great respect for the Cherokee, Shawnee, and all the other tribes. No, vengeance belongs to the good Lord, not to man. I'm sorry to hear about Hugh and his troubles. You and Thomas plannin' to stay around for a while? We could use some men to help guard those tendin' crops."

"Yes, sir, Thomas is still recoverin' from his latest round of fisticuffs. You recall how that man does love to fight! Reckon we'll be here a while, as he needs to heal. Be glad to help in any way needed. Still, we'll need to scout around occasionally."

<hr>

The next attack came without warning on the twenty-fourth of April. I remember it well, as Mama, Susie, and me was planning to finish up the last seams on my new Sunday dress. Daddy had purchased for me several lengths of a soft chintz dotted with flowers. Mama'd promised me a new dress when Spring came. Secretly, I planned to wear it for my wedding.

After a while, I wandered out of our cabin to fetch water, and at the gate found some men trying to get the cows to leave the fort for the nearby pasture. This was a morning ritual, and usually the cows would just mosey on out. That day, their loud bawling and moving about—the cows, not the men—had created a blockade of sorts at the gate, so I had to wait to walk out to the spring. Daddy sent two men out to investigate the area. We all saw them returning and shouting of finding no Indians, when shots rang out. The two men ran for the gate, being as they had about seventy yards to go. Yet they were overtaken. Daniel Goodman fell to rifle fire before Indians surrounded him and lifted his scalp. One warrior held his trophy high and let out a tremendous war cry.

I could only stand and watch, as others ran for their rifles. Women gathered up children, their own or any that stood nearby, and fled to the blockhouse. Men began moving to close the large gates.

Simon ran toward the downed man. In anger, he stopped, raised his rifle, and shot the warrior dead. As the Shawnee scattered and Simon reloaded, Daddy, Thomas Brooks, Mike Stoner, Willy Bush, and a dozen others rushed from the gate to protect the other man. Again, shots rang out, and Mike fell as one ball passed through his wrist and another into his hip. I watched as our men gathered around Mike to protect him and help him toward the gate. That's when I saw other warriors, who had been hiding in the nearby sycamore hollow, rush toward the gate, putting themselves between our men and the fort's gate.

Daddy saw them at the same instance and cried out, "Boys, we have to fight! Sell your lives as dear as possible."

While I helped several women move to close the gates, others ran for rifles to defend the fort. I watched in horror as our men turned and raced for the gate, firing and reloading when they could, and otherwise using their rifles as clubs. Some pulled knives to defend themselves. Chaos reigned. As our men fought vicious battles one on one, our women screamed. Indians uttered heart-shattering war cries. Daddy and Simon called out warnings. The sounds seemed to echo within the fort. Finally, our fighting men broke through the melee, though a number had received wounds.

Then I saw Daddy sprawled on the ground with an Indian astride his body, knife raised to lift his scalp. Before I could scream, Simon raised his rifle and fired, just as another warrior, knife at the ready, ran up to scalp Daddy. Simon swung his rifle and crushed the warrior's skull in one swift move. As Daddy had been shot in the ankle and could not walk or run, Simon hefted him over his shoulders and ran for the fort. Bullets continued to hit the walls as Simon drew closer and closer. Daddy said later he could hear and feel the bullets passing by his head.

Though aware of the danger and despite Mama's cries to stop, I ran out to help Simon with Daddy. Mama and Suzy screamed for me to get back in the fort. Nearby, Willy Bush helped Mike return to safety. With Willy's support, Mike somehow managed to walk despite his injured hip. As Willy stopped to reload once again, Mike called out "Tem gottam yellow rascals vill schoot us, ve are too pig a mark, Pilly Push." So, Willy turned as if he *had* reloaded and stood the warriors down while continuing to rapidly back toward the fort's gates, all the time still supporting Mike. Others rushed out and grabbed Mike, carrying him to safety. Once Willy realized he was the only white man still outside the gates, he turned and ran, expecting to be shot at any second. Miraculously, all the bullets missed him completely. Willy had helped rescue Mike, Isaac Hite, and John Todd. It seems many of our men became heroes that day.

All around us, men took up positions along the walls, expecting an imminent attack. Yet none came. Some women began gathering up their children, many counting heads to see that all were present. Younger boys and girls gathered the livestock into their pen. All about, other womenfolk grabbed our rifles, shot, and powder horns, preparing to join the battle. Some ran to treat the wounded.

Simon carried Daddy to our cabin and placed him on the bed. Mama rushed to his side and saw his ankle wound still held the ball. The bone was shattered. As we had no doctor, several men came to help. First, she cleaned the wound with some corn liquor, and Daddy, though not really being a drinking man, swallowed some down to ease the pain. Next, the men held him still while Mama removed the ball and set his ankle. Suzy and I had gathered up the little ones and carried them off to her cabin.

Flanders, now standing on one of the wall platforms, saw me leave our cabin and jumped to the ground, leaving his rifle with a friend. As we came together, he grabbed me and shook me hard.

"Why, Jemima, why did you go out there? You could have been killed," he whispered, pulling me in against his chest.

"'Twas Daddy about to be scalped, and Simon tryin' to carry him all alone. I couldn't risk them not makin' it back. I'd planned to take Simon's rifle and defend him and Daddy," I answered, half crying and still shaking with fear.

"Oh, so Simon and your Daddy meant more to you than me?" he asked, pushing me away and holding me at arm's length.

"No, Flanders, not Simon, he's only a friend. But. . . Daddy does. . . I mean I love you both, but he's my Daddy. He saved me and well, I. . . " I cried and blubbered.

"I rode out to try and save you as well. Have you forgotten that? I almost died of fear seein' you run out that gate. I love you Jemima Boone and mean to marry you," Flanders asserted. "Of course, not right now, as right now I need to get back to my post," he answered and, kissing me on the cheek, walked back to the ladder and climbed to his position.

I stood stunned for several minutes, wondering if I had just received Flanders' proposal.

Just as I turned to see where I was needed, Flanders once more jumped down from his defensive position and ran across the common to me. Then he grabbed me up and kissed me senseless! Men and boys began to wolf whistle. Many urging him on. At length, Flanders quietly placed my feet back on the ground, smothered out my shawl, and smiled.

"You're mine, Jemima Boone, mine. We'll be married soon and I won't take no for an answer," he whispered.

As he sauntered back to the wall, a big grin on his face, his brother Micajah called out, "Well, did she say yes, little brother?"

"It be none of your business, but yes, she'll be marrying me. Better get your best clothes ready, if'in you want to stand up with me."

Still a bit stunned, I just turned and walked off, back to our cabin, a smile lit my face. I may not have made up my mind that day but at least I knew that Flanders knew how to kiss.

⸻ ● ⸻

Others tended to Mike, Isaac, and John. No one left the fort for hours, not even Simon and Thomas. Much later in the day, Simon came by to check on Daddy and to report on the situation around the fort.

"Daniel, sir, looks like they've gone. They carried off all their dead and wounded, as usual. We estimate killin' at least twenty warriors but lost only Goodman. We'll keep a constant watch. Thomas went out to scout the area," Simon concluded.

"Well, Simon, you have behaved like a man today; indeed, you are a fine fellow."

The rest of us had many more thankful words to heap on Simon, especially Mama. Israel came by and shook his hand, and in his usual quiet way, let Simon know how grateful we all were. I kissed him on the cheek and thanked him kindly.

As Simon left our cabin, he pulled me outside for a private word. "Jemima, while I applaud your brave actions comin' to my aid today, I'd prefer you stayed safely out of harm, as I like my women alive when I court them."

"Simon Butler, I guess you'd better stay out of the way of Indians then, as I also prefer my beaus alive and in one piece," I stammered. "Besides, I was savin' my Daddy, not your worthless hide," I shouted. Thinking I'd ended this conversation, I'd turned toward Suzy's cabin when Simon whirled me around and kissed me thoroughly. That man did know how to kiss a girl.

"Jemima Boone," shouted Suzy several days later, "will you answer me?"

"No, sister, I likely will not. You have no right, not one, to ask me why I chose to marry Flanders. You, who married a man who beat you to within an inch of your life and still hits you on occasion. Why, you even lie about it! You tell Mama and Daddy you fell. I'd be ashamed. First of lyin' and then allowin' that man to beat you." I screamed back, just as I glanced up to see the tears in Suzy's eyes.

"I thought people believed me," she whispered. "Mima, does everyone know?"

"Yes, Suzy, everyone knows he hits you. Israel has threatened to kill him. Mike Stoner even says he's plannin' to beat Will the next time he hurts you."

"Oh, no, they mustn't. I love Will, truly I do. It's only when he drinks, not at other times. Most times, he's a gentle, lovin' man, Mima. I promise."

"Well, sister, you better hope he doesn't drink." In my heart, I believed Suzy, but we all knew Will would drink. He loved his corn liquor.

We sat quietly for a while, hemming a linen sheet for my trousseau, before Suzy asked again, "So Mima, why Flanders? That Simon Butler is a good man."

"Yes, he is, Suzy. Simon's a strong, brave man, and he says he loves me. Yet, he's likely goin' a get himself killed one of these days. Flanders, well Flanders makes me smile and laugh and makes me happy to face each day when I awaken. He *really* loves me. He told me he knew for sure the day I was taken by the Indians. He's a good provider, a good Baptist, and not at all like his Uncle Dick. What can I tell you, Suzy? He's the one I want to spend my life with. Daddy likes him fine. Mama does too."

So, one Friday morning in early May—Fridays being considered luckier for a wedding than other days—I rose and bathed, while around me my family made the last preparations for my wedding. Flanders' Uncle Dick Callaway, using his authority as a Virginia justice of the peace, now that we were a county of that colony, would marry me and Flanders, and his daughter Fanny to John Holder.

Daddy watched all the goings on from his place on the bed. He had been appointed a justice of the peace for Kentucky County, but being unable to stand didn't feel it was right to marry us while sitting down. Still in great pain at times from his ankle, he had agreed we should go ahead with the wedding despite all the Indian troubles. Daddy, like most of us, didn't believe in putting off our lives because of a few threats from Indians.

Our families agreed to work together for one big celebration. The fort's menfolk brought in catfish from the river, and lots of small game like rabbits and squirrels, as venison was very lean at this time of year. We even had a buffalo haunch to roast. Mr. Callaway killed one of his hogs and roasted it over an open fire. He made his slaves turn the spit and keep the fires burning all night. We could smell the delicious aromas all around the fort. Mama and Elizabeth Callaway had combined their stores of white wheat flour and sugar to bake us a cake. We had plenty of walnuts to add, and maple sugar to make a topping of sorts. The portions would be small, but each resident would get a taste of our wedding cake. We baked the few sweet potatoes left from last year's harvest. Spring greens had been gathered, washed, and dressed with bacon drippings.

Under the watchful eyes of their brothers, Viney, Becky, and Fanny's sisters, Lydia, Theo, and Keziah, gathered spring flowers, including white and yellow bloodroot, Virginia bluebells, and yellow trout lilies for our bouquets and decorations. The day dawned clear and warm with a slight breeze, so we held the ceremony and celebration on the fort's common.

While the girls decorated, Suzy helped me dress my hair with ribbons and flowers. Tiny yellow and white flowers and green ribbons soon trailed throughout my black tresses. I would wear my hair down, as an unmarried maiden, to my wedding. After today, my hair would always be braided and worn up under my cap or bonnet, except in the privacy of our cabin.

Daddy called me over and asked me to turn and show him my hair when we had finished.

"Sit, daughter, and talk with me a spell."

As I sat softly on the side of his bed, so as not to increase his pain, I smiled on my father, knowing he would always be there when needed.

"Are you sure, Mima? You be still young, only fourteen if I remember correctly. I still think on you as that small girl, sittin' on my lap, beggin' to hear more about Caintuck. My little Duck, playin' in the creek and comin' to home drenched from head to toe. Are you sure you love Flanders?" he asked, smiling over at Mama, who now fiddled with her own long black hair, braiding it into long plaits, wrapping each around her head, and securing them with combs, before reaching for her cap.

"Yes, Daddy. I love him very much. Besides, I'm only goin' next door. Our cabin's right beside yours. I'm not leavin' you."

"Oh, child, yes you are. 'Tis now you'll be his, his to hold, to love, to care for. You'll be a Callaway, think on that, Mima, you'll be a Callaway, not a Boone any longer."

"Oh, silly man. I'll always be a Boone, now let's get you out to my weddin'," I stated firmly while bending to kiss his cheek.

A large oak in the common stood in as our altar. I watched from our window as Flanders Isham Callaway, dressed in his Sunday best breeches and coat over a white linen shirt, moved to stand beside John. Both looked as nervous as I felt.

Mama handed Suzy a threaded needle and said, "Here, put in the last stitch for good luck, and I'll help the men get your Daddy settled."

As Suzy sewed the last stitch in my wedding dress, I stood nervously and anxiously waiting. Two men arrived with a borrowed armchair and, respectfully placing him carefully upon the seat, carried Captain Boone up under the shade of the oak. Mama went to stand beside him, carrying a small stool to prop his injured foot. I took Israel's arm. My brother now stood an inch or so taller than Daddy, and at seventeen was a handsome young man.

"Are you sure, Mima, really sure?" Israel asked, taking my arm.

"For heaven's sake. Daddy just now asked me the same thing. Have you ever known me to be unsure of any decision I've made in my entire life?"

"No, Mima, you always seem to know your own mind and heart."

Our fort's fiddler, Uncle Monk, as we called him, arrived shaking his fiddle back and forth for all to hear the rattlesnake tail within. As I stepped out the door, he started his tune, *Red is the Rose*, leading me first and then Fanny to the altar to stand hand in hand with our beaus. Some might think it strange to have a Negro slave play at your wedding. Yet Uncle Monk, who belonged to the Estill family, was recognized as our best fiddle player, an outstanding shot, and an excellent hunter. He even knew how to make gunpowder and had taught Daddy. Seems he always had a batch of the black gooey mixture drying in the sun.

As I walked in rhythm to the tune, I glanced toward the gates. Both stood closed and locked. On each parapet, a sentry stood, keeping watch. Daddy had promised that no Indians would disturb my wedding or our celebration. What a strange way to live—where men and women could not carry out their daily chores or special occasions without guards. I whispered my daily prayer for peace.

I barely remember saying my vows. Flanders held my hands in his and soon Mr. Callaway declared us man and wife. With fiddles tuning up and cowbells being rung, we kissed once in front of all those Boonesborough folks. I saw Daddy wipe away a few tears, but Mama stood laughing at him before placing a big kiss on his lips. All afternoon, we danced and ate and celebrated. Fanny and I danced the wreath dance together. The wreaths stood for our maidenheads. Keeping us within their circle, all the married women protected us until they grew "tired" of fighting off the young bachelors, who finally broke into the circle and stole the wreaths. Next, the women bound up our hair and placed our matron's caps upon our heads. All in great fun, each of the fort's men, married and unmarried, begged for dances from Fanny and me. But first, they had to pay a price, slipping a coin into a small bag we carried for this purpose.

As the sun began to set and the evening chill crept up on us all, Flanders and I slipped away to our cabin. I found my new nightgown lying across the foot of our bed. Mistress Callaway had given us a beautiful quilt and beside the bed, folded on a stool, lay Simon's buffalo robe, in case the night turned cold. Soon the sounds of the Shivaree rang loud as our wedding guests gathered outside banging pots and pans, ringing cow bells, and shooting off rifles. They begged us to come out and join the fun once more.

"Jemima, I don't care if every Shawnee in the world attacks this fort, tonight I plan to be here with you and you alone," Flanders whispered, pulling me into his arms. After a long kiss, he pulled off my cap, removed my hair combs, and let my black tresses fall to my knees. Needless to say, we didn't leave the cabin until late the next day, and only then because the chamber pot needed emptying, and food and fresh water became a necessity.

I could still hear the echo of Uncle Monk playing *The Walls of Liscarrol* the following morning as I carried out my chores with a skip in my step and a song in my heart.

Chapter 10
Indian Troubles

Troubles continued at all the Kentucky settlements. We learned how, only five days after the attack here, some seventy Shawnee ambushed two Fort Harrod men out practicin' their marksmanship. Francis McConnell was shot and killed immediately, but James Ray, Hugh McGary's remainin' stepson, ran for the gate. It was closed and locked, so he hid behind a large stump. He stayed pinned down for hours before yelling "For God's sake, dig a hole under the cabin wall and take me in!" They did, and James crawled through to safety. I knew and liked James and was happy he had escaped the fate of his brother.

Indians wounded poor Mike Stoner again in mid-May. Daddy's friend had barely recovered from his last injuries. Likewise, Daddy hobbled about with a crutch and tried to keep up the fort's defenses. The Shawnee schemed up a surprise attack on the men out planting crops on nearby Hackberry Ridge. Luckily, one of our guards saw the reflection of sunlight on a rifle and warned our farmers. This time they fled back to the fort safely, with not one injury. For two days we forted up, besieged. During each night, the warriors tried unsuccessfully to set fire to the fort. From almost constant rifle fire by our attackers, three men received minor wounds. A more serious loss occurred to our cattle, as the Indians butchered them before they departed on the twenty-fifth of May. During the attack, Will Bailey Smith volunteered to slip out and go to the Yadkin settlements to ask for help.

Inside the fort, fear dwelt within everyone's mind. Little else could we think of. I huddled beside Flanders, in those few hours here and there when he came to our cabin to rest. My heart and mind wondering if it would be our last such time together. During the daylight hours I did my chores, helped the other women, and even stood guard, as many knew I was an excellent shot. We all rejoiced on the morning the Indians had gone. Still, we knew they would return.

A short time later, we learned the Shawnee had attacked Logan's Station on the same day. Running low on shot, the fort's women melted down their pewter tableware and cast balls of pewter instead of lead. Each being an excellent shot, Esther Whitley and Jane Menifee took up rifles and fired on their attackers from the fort's loopholes alongside Logan's male defenders.

One evening Simon arrived with news and immediately began his tale of recent happenings at Fort Harrod. *"Boone, come up!"* one of his companions cried out. He said he turned toward the voice, and yet another cry from the opposite direction rang out, again shoutin' his name, *'Boone!'* just as the shot hit, pushin' him backward and shatterin' one of his ribs.

"I asked him *'Why were you outside the fort? You all knew the Indian snipers were still around.'* He answered me with a wry smile, *'Oh, arrogant fools we were. Thought we might sneak up on them and end their little game. Instead, I went and got myself shot. I guess you'll go back and tell Daniel what a fool I am.'* I told him, *'No, Squire, I'll tell Daniel how lucky his brother is!'* Simon concluded his tale with a laugh.

"So has Squire recovered?" Mama asked while Daddy snickered.

"Oh, yes, ma'am, from that wound. But he was ambushed while tendin' his corn crop before he completely recovered. The man workin' beside him fell dead, just as Squire squatted in the tall grass, readyin' himself to return fire. The warrior who shot his companion came in to claim the scalp, not seein' Squire beside the body. Squire pulled that sword he carries and swung at the warrior, who pulled his war club and fought back, cuttin' a deep gash in

Squire's forehead. Now barely able to see for all the blood pourin' in his eyes, Squire grabbed the warrior and, as they fought, he ran his sword completely through the Indian's body. Squire says they fought on, reachin' for each other's weapons for several minutes before the warrior collapsed. When the man fell, he broke the tip off Squire's sword. As your brother tells the tale, *it was the best little Indian fight I ever was in as we men both stood and fought so well.*"

"My uncle should move back to Boonesborough. Fort Harrod seems like a dangerous place," I stated.

"Well, Mistress Callaway," Simon began. . .

"Since when am I *Mistress Callaway* to you, Simon Butler?" I demanded.

"Well, ma'am, since you up and married my good friend Flanders. I rightly know you to be a married woman now, I saw the weddin' and danced with the brides, so Mistress Callaway it is."

As everyone around the table, especially Flanders, laughed, I scowled. How dare he forget we had once courted? I may have married Flanders but I still counted Simon as among my closest friends.

⸺ ● ⸺

Now I've been scared quite a few times in my life, but Flanders Callaway gave me one of the worst. We'd not been married past six months when I sat tending to a tear in Flanders' best linen shirt, well his only linen shirt, if the truth be told. Suddenly, I heard a ruckus in the common and dropped my sewing to scamper out to see what mischief the men had gotten themselves into. I seemed always a curious sort, and mostly wanted to know about any goings on.

The morning still being early, I suspected someone had spotted a warrior or two. Sure enough, several of the younger boys, including one of the Callaways, had been sent for firewood and came back in a rush claiming to have seen Indians near the corner fence at the river. As many of our menfolk and several of our women were headed to that particular corn field to gather the rest of the crop, Flanders and his brother, James were assigned guard duty. Our sentry dismissed the children's claims, saying he had seen nothing at all from his vantage point.

As the workers prepared to leave the fort, Flanders said quietly, "Boys, go on about your chores. Go over by that hickory stand nearer the fort to gather firewood, and I'll keep my eyes out for our enemies."

I moseyed back into the cabin, feeling a big fuss had been made over some boys not wanting to gather firewood. I picked up the shirt, stirred the morning's mush, and pulled my stool into the autumn sun to finish the job. The field workers left, others took the cattle to pasture, women hurried back and forth to the spring for water, and Suzy hung her wash just outside her door.

Suddenly a shot rang out. I heard it hit a timber close to where our sentry stood guard. I dropped that shirt right in the dirt and ran for the gate. In the cornfield, I saw men and women dropping their baskets and running for the fort. Well, most dropped their baskets, a few tried to run while carrying their load. I saw Flanders running and helping others along the way. Then suddenly he stopped and yelled, "Where's my gun? I'm in a pretty fix, with no gun." I heard him plain as if he'd been standing right beside me. The other guard stopped beside Flanders, and they talked briefly and then ran back toward the cornfield.

Only after they returned to the fort would I learn that Flanders and James had laid down their guns and shot bags to help with the harvest, being confident that those boys had not seen any Indians earlier that morning. Now all I could do was watch as they both ran back into danger. Almost instantly shots rang out, and people scattered for the gate. Inside the walls, some ran for their rifles, while others just stood and stared as the drama unfolded in that early Kentucky morning haze.

Flanders and James grabbed their rifles and gear and hotfooted it for the gate. Balls pounded the dirt beside each as they ran, and just as Flanders reached the gate, he fell. Someone cried out, "Flanders Callaway is killed!"

Up he jumped, answering back, "I'm not hurt," while hopping about on one foot. "I just stubbed my blame toe on the bottom timber."

No one had time to laugh as we closed the gates and took up our positions. Daddy already stood nearby, shouting commands. After a few more shots, the warriors disappeared into the forest. Later in the day, under heavy guard, our menfolk proceeded out to gather the corn.

I waited and waited. I'd said nothing, not one word, to Flanders since the morning's incident. Yet, my temper boiled. Finally, near dark, he returned home. I listened as he washed up in the basin outside the door. I'd planned all I wanted to say. I'd thought it through. So, when he opened the door, I turned to give him more than a piece of my mind. I'd planned to give him a full load.

Instead, I ran into his arms and blubbered and cried like a baby. Not ever having seen me cry before, Flanders had no notion of what to do or even what possessed me to cry. So, after a few minutes, he gathered me into his arms and carried me next door to Mama.

Now for him to do that turned out to be the worst decision of his life. Mama began scolding him for being a fool to lay down his rifle and then to go back for it after the Indians had begun firing on the harvesters. She told him how scared we all had been while watching the attack. She then proceeded to inform him, and I'll never forget her words, "Flanders Callaway, the worst happenin' a married woman faces is the loss of her husband. While I've not suffered it myself, I suffered with her as Daniel's sister Hannah grieved for John. Today, Jemima stood at that gate watchin', while her husband acted like a fool, exposin' himself and his brother to the danger of being shot and scalped. And yet *you,* young man can't figure out why Mima is crying?"

As I now quietly sobbed against Flanders' shoulder, he turned to Daddy, "Daniel, do you have anything to add to my scoldin'?"

"No, Flanders. It appears Rebecca covered all the points that needed to be said."

"I think I'll take her home then, a fine evenin' to you both."

Once we reached our cabin, Flanders placed me on the bed, brushed back my hair from my face, and lay down beside me. He held me tight for a long time. I never once said a word about his foolishness that morning. I knew he had learned a valuable lesson. Besides, Mama'd said all I'd thought to say.

Chapter 11
The Salt Boilers

Sure enough, Uncle Squire and Jane moved their family back to Boonesborough in late September. Squire had about recovered from all of his injuries, though the scar across his forehead would be noticeable for the remainder of his life. Not long afterward, on the sixteenth of October, Jane gave birth to little Enoch Morgan Boone.

While the large Shawnee raiding parties stopped, small groups of warriors continued to harry travelers and outlying cabins and settlements. A few more families left for the east and the rest of us settled in for the coming winter. About that time, Simon and Thomas had arrived back at Boonesborough after scouting all the way to the Ohio, bringing with them the news of various settlements and the war.

"I'm hopin' some relief is headed our way. I hear tell Captain Charles Gwatkin and fifty, or so, volunteers are headed this way from Virginia. Some say another fifty from the Yadkin are comin' as well. These men will provide additional protection for each fort and some stations. They bring supplies, powder, and shot," Thomas reported.

"Without Henderson's store, I can see a demand for other necessities," replied Mama. "I hope they bring more than just powder and shot."

"Yes, ma'am, I believe 'twill be a hard winter," Simon answered. "With all the Indian trouble on the Ohio, few flatboats are makin' it down safely. Those bringin' in supplies seem to be the ones the Shawnee attack the most. I agree, a hard winter for all will be had without some relief. I believe it will be a hard winter indeed after seein' the abundance of silk on this year's corn."

"The men have finished the harvest, and we have little corn for the winter, since those scoundrels burned most of our crops," Daddy said. "Luckily, they can't burn the roots, so we have some onions, potatoes, and turnips. We took out baskets and collected all the nuts in the immediate surrounds; we even found some muscadines and scuppernongs. You know all those pigs we brought in back in 1775, well, them and their offsprin' now run wild in the forest. So, I tasked young Will Cradlebaugh to hunt the wild boar in the area and bring the meat in to me. We've smoked the hams and preserved what we can for all to share when foodstuffs get low. What we need is a shipment of corn. Oh, and salt, I forgot about salt. We are almost out of that precious substance. I've sent letters back east askin' for shipments of necessities, but fear with the comin' of winter and the war, none will be able to bring us corn or salt, and other goods."

"Daniel, do you think the Indian danger is less in winter?" Thomas asked. "If so, a group of men might go to the salt lick up on the Lickin' and boil off some salt."

Now that Thomas' brothers, William and Samuel, lived at Boonesborough, we saw him much more often. Also, they tended to keep him out of fights.

"I reckon so, Thomas," Daddy replied. "Shawnee don't travel much in the dead of winter. I'd thought on that some and don't want to leave the fort unprotected. I figure if some men arrived from the east, we might make up a party of salt boilers. We'd rotate men every month to give each a chance to get warm and rested up. Keepin' those kettles boilin' and the fires going is hard work. A few men would need to hunt for game, and others would need to bring the salt back to the fort on a regular basis. Guess it could be done, if'in we have enough men. I'll think on it some more." Each of us could see Daddy was already lost in thought about the dangers and needs of such a proposition.

I stood silently by as Daddy led a party of thirty men and pack horses out the fort's gate on the eighth day of 1778. They were headed for the Lower Blue Licks and had with them several large iron pots for boiling the water to get out the salt. Daddy, Flanders, and Thomas Brooks planned to supply the camp with game. Thomas' brothers, William and Samuel, and Flanders' brothers, Micajah and James, numbered among the salt boilers. After thirty days, these men would return, and others would go out to take up the work. Daddy planned to stay the entire time.

"Promise me you'll come home in a month, Flanders," I begged.

"No promises, Mima. We all need to pitch in and do our duty. Daniel gave Thomas and me the easy job. I can't imagine workin' all day cuttin' firewood to keep those fires a burnin'." He gave me a big wet long kiss, which entertained the entire salt party, many making wolf calls and such, just before he mounted up.

The days passed slowly. Mostly we kept to the fort. Women, those who knew how to shoot well, and the remaining men stood sentry duty. Not having a baby to tend, I often took the night posts. Winter snows and cold crept up on us. At night I wrapped in Simon's buffalo hide and anything else I could find, as I no longer had Flanders to keep me warm. Food became scarce, salt even more so. We rationed what little salt we had, and boiled salt pork in most everything to add at least some seasoning. As the temperatures dropped even lower, I took to wearing one of Flanders' doeskin hunting shirts and a pair of his breeches under my skirt, as they proved warmer than my own clothing.

Finally, in the second week of February, the next party of salt boilers, including Simon Butler, left for the Licking River and the Little Blue Licks. I expected Flanders home in a few days and set about making the cabin neat and clean. I watched from the blockhouse most of each day, hoping to spot him riding in, only to go to bed for several nights alone and discouraged, even a bit mad at him for staying away so long.

Instead of Flanders and the first party of salt boilers returning alone, we saw almost the whole party of replacement boilers riding for the fort. As soon as they entered the gate, Flanders called for the gates to be shut and men to take up a post.

Mama and I stood, side by side, stunned, so aware of the meaning of these actions. Finally, Flanders began to speak to the wives and those few men left at the fort.

"Mistress Boone, Jemima," Flanders began, nodding toward Mama and me, "Thomas and I arrived with fresh game at the licks after an absence of three days, as we had to journey far from the camp to find enough game. The camp lay deserted. Salt scattered and what few kettles remained, overturned."

Sobs of fear passed from one to another among the female listeners as realization of our men's plight, and our own, rose to the forefront of our consciousness.

"We found no bodies, not one drop of blood, but plenty of sign. It appears our men have been taken by the Shawnee. We believe Daniel, who had also been out huntin', had returned to camp and was captured along with our men. The relief party arrived not long after we did. Simon agreed with our judgment and has gone off to follow their trail. We figure twenty-seven men and Daniel were taken, includin' my brothers and Thomas' brothers."

By now, many of the women cried aloud, other sobbed quietly. The older children huddled nearby and talked while the younger ones hung on their mother's skirts, hiding, perhaps from the fear and sorrow felt by all. We now had just forty or so men left to help defend the fort. All our supplies were dangerously low. Day after day, only the bravest of men left the fort to hunt, and we kept our cattle, hogs, and chickens, those few left, inside the fort. The commons soon became a field of offal and manure. The fort's privy trough overflowed. We had little clean water.

Clothes and bodies stayed dirty. The stench overwhelmed us all and we often covered our noses with soft, damp cloths soaked in water with whatever good-smelling herbs we had remaining.

To make matters worse, the men of the fort argued among themselves as to who should be in command, with the militia officers being the worst. Our own residents resented the outsiders' intrusion into our lives and our safety, as most of them had little experience in Indian fighting or living in the backwoods. In mid-March, more militia rangers arrived from Virginia, though their supplies brought us little joy. With more mouths to feed, the entire fort suffered, for now we had not even the meat the hunters had once provided. That's when one of the militia men shot Dick Callaway's largest steer. Dick reacted in the way we all expected him to—he pulled his rifle and threatened to shoot anyone who killed any of his stock.

"Mima," Flanders warned, as we witnessed Uncle Dick's rage. "Hold your tongue. You know he blames Daniel for all our troubles."

"Well, there he stands, threatenin' women and children while many starve. Look at poor Suzy, her in the family way, barely able to stand she is so weak and thin. And the children, why, he will not even share the milk from his cows! 'Tis not right."

"No, it is not. I've been discussin' it with others, and well, David Gass and I have a plan. Help guard the fort, and we'll be back soon," he reassured me, grabbing up his rifle and coat.

David stood waiting, and they convinced several of the rangers to join them on a trip up Otter Creek to hunt David's hogs that ran wild in the forest on his parcel. Soon they returned with five fat ones, which we roasted for the whole fort to enjoy. Many resented sharing with Dick and his family. Yet share we did. We could not punish his wife and children for his stinginess.

Despite all I did and said, Mama believed all the stories about our men being carried off and murdered. Her own nephew, Daniel Boone Bryan, had heard the story from other Kentuckians at Moccasin Gap, and rushed back to the Yadkin to share the news. Letters came from Mama's family, urging us to return to the safety of the settlements. Before long, Mama made up her mind to go. She planned to take all us with her.

"Mima, please, please, won't you and Flanders come back to North Carolina with us? There be nothin' for you here except starvation and death. Suzy and Will are goin'. So is Israel," Mama begged.

"Israel is only goin' to help protect you and the children. He doesn't trust those rangers, who are desertin' their posts to go home, to protect you if there be trouble. Besides, I don't believe our men are all dead. Simon would have found the bodies."

"No, I feel it, Jemima. Daniel is gone. None of the men have returned, not any. I always expected some of the younger ones to return, like Thomas' brothers, William and Samuel, or Flanders' brothers, Micajah and James. We must carry on, but no longer in this awful place, this place of death."

"Uncle Squire and I don't believe Daddy's dead. Squire and Jane plan to stay. This is my home. I'll not go back to North Carolina!" I stated emphatically. "Mama, you be takin' our family back to a land filled with war, how do you see they will be safer there?

"Mima, they may not be safer, and I worry about Israel's talk of joinin' the Patriots. Still, we'll have food and clothin' and our Boone and Bryan families. Please, daughter, I can't imagine leavin' you here all on your own."

"Mama, I won't be alone. I'm a married woman. Flanders and I have decided to stay. I have family, and I don't count Dick Callaway's family, except maybe Betsy and Fanny. I have Uncle Squire and Jane and their children. Besides, Flanders wishes to wait for his brothers' return."

Days later, I stood silently sobbing and staring straight ahead as Mama, Israel, Levina, Becky, Daniel

Morgan, and Jesse rode off in May for North Carolina. Suzy and Will, with my tiny niece tied to Suzy's breast, mounted up and left with Mama's party. I busied myself with cleaning our cabin. I found Mama's old cat in their now empty cabin and tried to get her to move in with us. Instead, I ended up taking the occasional bowl of milk and leaving it on Mama's table for her. I kept their cabin cleaned and scrubbed. Flanders and I might have moved into their more spacious one, but I felt it needed to stay empty for Daddy's return.

Some days, I visited with Betsy and her daughter Frances, now a year old. I watched little Fanny learn to walk. On other days, I worked beside Aunt Jane and helped with little Enoch. I found joy in living as spring arrived. We planted crops and gathered greens to add to our diet. A couple of parties brought in supplies to sell. I purchased enough wool cloth for a new dress, as my everyday bodice and skirt had worn plum out. A weaver at Fort Harrod sent over some wool cloth, and I made a new petticoat and a jacket. I still wore Flanders' deerskin shirt on cooler days.

Not long after Mama's departure for North Carolina, the first word came of what had occurred at the salt lick. Andy Johnson had arrived at Fort Harrod after escaping from the Shawnee village called Chillicothe at the end of April. The story did not reach us immediately, as few traveled between the forts and stations that winter and spring. The story told to us, relayed how Andy, an excellent woodsman, had pretended to be a fool and crazy after their capture. The Shawnee had adopted him and named him *Pequolly*, it meant *the fool* in Shawnee. One night in late April, Andy stole a rifle, ammunition, and a blanket coat, and escaped. Although the Shawnee had searched and searched, his tracks led them in circles before they gave up. Then he made his escape along the Little Miami down to the Ohio, where he rafted across and finally made it on foot to Harrod's. There he claimed Daniel had sold them all off to the Shawnee, and being a Tory all along, had taken an oath of allegiance to the British at Detroit. He told how Daddy lived peacefully among the Shawnee, never trying to escape, and had been adopted by Blackfish and given the Shawnee name of *Sheltowee*, or Big Turtle.

Uncle Squire and I saw in Andy's story the probable truth, that Daddy simply waited to find a time for escape. Andy told Thomas Brooks the news of how his brother Samuel had died of a broken arm and other injuries during the march to Detroit. His other brother, Will, was adopted into a Shawnee family, before angering them by trying to drown the women assigned to clean him for the adoption ceremony. Will, like Sam, had then been marched to Detroit. There he was sold to the British and held as a virtual slave.

While Thomas mourned Sam, he kept up hope for Will's eventual return. Many, many an evening we spent talking over what might have happened and what should be done on their behalf. Squire wrote a letter to Mama and sent it with the next man headed to the settlements. At least it would give her hope.

Likewise, Flanders and I often discussed the various rumors about Daddy and the fate of our men. Never once did my belief that Daddy still lived waver. I somehow knew he would return to me, to us. I had Uncle Squire write a letter for me, telling Mama and my family of how Flanders and I fared. I urged them to return to us. Yet, I received no answer. Things became hard for us Boones, as so many believed the lies told concerning Daddy's actions. We especially avoided Dick Callaway, although Elizabeth, Betsy, and Fanny continued to be friendly toward us when Dick was out of sight. Uncle Squire and Aunt Jane even considered moving back to Fort Harrod, but discovered they were no more welcome there than they were here. Seems the Boones and any associated with them were now despised by most of Kentucky's settlers. Only a few stood with us.

While there had been some minor attacks, yet most of the spring and early summer remained quiet. Men and women planted crops, gardens, and even began to build cabins on their parcels of land. Flanders surveyed out a portion for us. Some days, I worked to help him clear a plot for corn, the most valuable commodity in Kentucky, as we had learned last winter.

Other days, we hunted together. Flanders taught me how to track game, how to recognize Indian sign, and how to hide, if need be. One afternoon we sat beside a small flat-bottom creek on our parcel of land where we dangled our feet in its cool water. We talked of his fears for his brothers and those of Simon Butler.

"Mima, I feel guilty for being here safe with you. I should have been with the salt boilers, but Daniel gave me the easier tasks."

"Flanders Callaway, you earned the right to be a hunter. It was not a gift because we're married. Everyone in Boonesborough knows you to be one of the best at findin' and bringin' home game. You kept those men fed, wanderin' here and there in the cold instead of being warm like those in the camp," I reminded him.

"Now wife, can't say it was warm in the camp, but one could stay toasted on one side next to those kettle fires. Still, I feel guilty. 'Twasn't right that I am here and not sufferin' like the rest."

"I for one don't feel that way. Seems to me it 'twas the good Lord's plan for you to be here and them to be there. We're not meant to understand, just to recognize and accept His will over ours, or so Uncle Squire says, being as I can't read the good word for myself. Yes, I worry about and pray for all those men and their families. But I have lost enough without having my new husband taken by savages as well."

We passed the remainder of the afternoon wading and splashing in that creek until we were both soaked. Afterward, we risked a small fire, roasted a rabbit, and allowed our clothes to dry. I recollect the peace of that afternoon. How at times we forgot our worries, our cares, and those who were far away. I do believe the beauty of Kentucky can take away anyone's cares and woes if only they'll take the time to be still and look about.

Too soon, we had to return to the fort. Otherwise, someone would notice our absence and the alarm would be raised. I knew Aunt Jane would already be watching the gate for our return.

Chapter 12
One Man Returns

Rumors abounded and bounced from settler to settler, running amuck into summer. Soon we listened as the tale of how Andy Johnson led a party of Harrod's men north to raid the Shawnee village at Chillicothe was repeated incessantly. The men had dressed like the Shawnee and even painted their faces. Seeing real Shawnee warriors in the village's vicinity, Andy's party instead stole horses and escaped back across the river after only a brief exchange of fire. The warriors recognized Pequolly and reported to Blackfish about him leading the raiders.

I clearly remember how, on June twentieth, men working near the river listened carefully to a voice calling to be recognized. Raising their rifles in alarm, they saw what they believed to be a Shawnee warrior. Yet, the man spoke good English, calling again and again "hello, Boonesborough" while naming out several men.

"Bless your soul, Daniel, welcome home," replied one; however, Daddy later told us how the others stood with rifles aimed at his heart, with sullen looks and scowls. At the gate, most stood in silence, staring when the men walked him back to the fort.

"Can you tell Rebecca I'm home?" ask Daniel.

"She put into the settlements long ago, packed her belongings, and was off to the old man's in Carolina," one replied gruffly.

"Daddy, Daddy, oh, praise the good Lord you're alive and home," I cried, collapsing at his feet and smiling up into his face. That's how Flanders, Squire, and Jane found us minutes later.

With their help, I doctored Daddy's sore feet, found him clean clothing, and prepared a meal fit for a king. We talked of the rumors and listened to his story, one he had to tell repeatedly for several days. Some fort occupants believed him immediately. Others continued to hold on to those rumors of his treachery.

We learned how he had been captured first while out hunting. He'd learned from Blackfish that the warriors planned to attack the fort. So, he led them instead to the salt makers and guaranteed their surrender. He told Blackfish he would lead the warriors back to Boonesborough in the coming year and surrender all the fort's occupants to the Shawnee, where they would be welcomed as tribal members and taken back across the river to live with the Shawnee people. He had also bargained for the salt boilers to be well treated and not to have to run the gauntlet. We heard about their long, cold march back to the Shawnee villages north of the Ohio, and finally off to Detroit. He told us of meeting Governor Hamilton and refusing to take the British loyalty oath.

He relayed news of Sam Brooks' painful death, and the others sold to the British at Detroit. We learned that Flanders' brother, James was among those now held in Detroit, while Micajah had been adopted by the Shawnee. Daddy tried to name every man and tell us where he was held.

Daddy relayed his plan, how he had survived, and escaped. He told how he convinced Blackfish of his loyalty to the Shawnee and allowed himself to be adopted. He told about slowly gaining their trust and quietly and secretly hiding away shot and powder. Daddy had taken great care to prove himself a good gunsmith, so they had allowed him to repair broken rifles. This gave him the chance to squirrel away bits and pieces, including a rifle barrel and lock.

"After Andy Johnson's raid on their village, Blackfish realized the Kentuckians now knew how to find their homes and advanced their plans to raid into Kentucky and defeat Boonesborough. That's when I knew I had to escape and warn you. I slipped away early one morning when I had been left with my Shawnee mother and the other women on our way to boil water for salt. As the men rode off after a flock of turkeys, I told my Shawnee mother, *I'm off to see my squaw and children.* She begged me not to go and said I would be hunted down and killed. Ignoring her words, I ran. I headed for the Ohio, disguising my trail. Once there, I floated across using a log to keep my powder dry. The current carried me much farther down river than I had planned. The following morning, I awoke to the pain of scalded feet from my long run. I could barely walk, so I made an oak sap poultice and rested. As I sat, I cut down a sapling with my knife and whittled out a stock for my rifle. I used the hemp strings of my pack to tie it on. Moving on south after my rest, I used my rifle to take down a buffalo and feasted on his hump. I even smoked the tongue to bring home to Daniel Morgan, knowing it was his favorite. That was the first food I'd had in two days."

"Oh, Daddy, we tried. Squire and I tried to convince Mama you yet lived. I'm sorry she's not here, her or Daniel Morgan or Israel. Israel would love to know your story. Did I tell you Suzy is in the family way again? She should be delivered most any day now," I answered in a rush, my heart breaking at Daddy's suffering. Only now did I know what dangers and hardships my father had endured. Yet, he had overcome each, survived, and returned to us. As my heart just about broke in half hearing of his and the other captives' ordeals, I envisioned his suffering, his longing for us, and his bravery to escape.

Daddy interrupted my mind's wandering when he said, "Best they are not here, daughter, for Blackfish and his warriors will be soon. We must prepare."

In the days to come, Dick Callaway and others railed against Daddy. After hearing his story, some didn't believe him and continued to trust in the old rumors. Instead of trying to convince them, Daddy instead had met directly with Captain William Bailey Smith and the other Boonesborough militia men. With Squire and Flanders at his side, he finally convinced Will of his sincerity and the need for preparations. Once again, Daddy took charge at the fort, and, as Captain Boone, organized the fort's defenses, beginning with the strengthening of its palisade and blockhouses. They replaced rotten timbers, built a stronger gate, and completed the two corner blockhouses that had stood unfinished since we arrived in 1775. The men collected gunpowder and shot while the women gathered provisions, molded bullets, and made bandages. The more experienced women collected and prepared various medicinal herbs and plants. Older children worked to clear brush and debris from around the fort's walls.

Billy Smith sent off messengers to forts Harrod and Logan for reinforcements, and to tell them about the threat against all Kentuckians. Daddy insisted the African slaves be armed as well. While Mr. Estill agreed, Dick Callaway argued against such a measure. Squire, the fort's leading gunsmith, worked tirelessly to repair rifles and built several more, including smaller ones for the boys and women. I, of course, had my own, made by Squire many years before. Mama had finally given in to my begging, not long before we came to Kentucky.

Within weeks, news reached North Carolina of Daddy's return, and Will Hays arrived without Suzy, as she had recently delivered a baby girl they named Jemima. I felt so honored. I even hugged Will, partly for the new baby and more so for coming to help in our time of dire need. Everyone old enough to hold a rifle found themselves preparing to help defend our lives and assigned to a position along the wall. Some older women, and those with small children, Daddy assigned to take turns cooking, caring for the babies and children, and helping load rifles for the better marksmen.

Then the waiting began. We continued to plant our crops and go about our daily routine. And waited. Men took the livestock to pasture. Women and girls carried water from the spring. Men hunted for game to fill our pots and stood guard over the farmers. Life continued as usual as we waited. The fort's occupants felt a sense of urgency and fear in every action, every chore, and every minute of life. No one seemed to be able to rest, to relax, for we waited for an attack. Uncle Monk tried quieting our fears with his fiddle. While it worked on the younger ones, everyone else moved about with anticipation of that first war cry, that first shot to ring in our ears, followed immediately by the call to arms.

⸺ ● ⸺

Weeks passed. Still, we waited. News from Fort Harrod and the many stations reported no Shawnee activity. Our anxiety lessened when no Shawnee appeared outside our walls. Men stopped working on the palisade and gave up digging a well within the fort. The summer heat overtook all ambition to accomplish a task. Rain didn't come, and the grass turned brown and crops withered before our eyes. Even the Louisa seemed to be going dry. A pebble beach could now be walked upon without wetting your feet. Scouts and other travelers reported in, relaying that no one had encountered any Indians of any tribe. Those old rumors of Daddy's treachery crept into many men's minds yet again.

Besides our immediate family, only Simon and a few others continued to believe that danger lay only miles beyond the Ohio and probably stood hiding beyond the forest's edge beyond our walls. With some sense of hope of reinforcements, in late August we gathered the fresh corn from the fields and any other crops ready for harvest. We filled every available container with water from the spring every morning.

The waiting fueled the men's desire for action, to know what was coming and when. So, Daddy and Simon decided to lead a large group of our men north to scout for Indian activity. They also planned to raid one Shawnee village and steal horses. Daddy and Simon knew this would alarm the Shawnee as to their own safety. Dick Callaway raised his voice in anger and shouted to all who would listen that Daddy and Simon were leaving the fort undefended by taking so many men. He told how this was Daddy's plan, to let the Shawnee take us all. He screamed about how the men were leaving us doomed to death or captivity. Still, some thirty men rode out for what they thought would be a glorious raid on an Indian village.

As our men rode out, Callaway attempted to take over the fort's command, but many occupants despised the man still for his pettiness the previous winter and his manner toward all except his immediate family. Even Flanders, his own nephew, had received the benefit of his bitter tongue for deciding to ride out with Daddy. At the Blue Licks, worried for their families' safety, most married men turned for home and rode back into the fort the following day. Some still held a lingering belief about Daddy being a traitor.

Dressed as warriors with painted faces in the style of Johnson's raid, the remaining men moved north across the Ohio. Simon reconnoitered the village and found no men and no horses, only women and children. Upon hearing this news, Daddy realized the Shawnee warriors were headed south. Daddy turned his remaining men toward home. Along the way, they encountered warriors moving south to join Blackfish's war party. After a brief skirmish, and leaving behind Simon and Alexander Montgomery as scouts, Daddy and our men rode day and night in a wide arc around the Shawnee army to return in time to defend our home.

The next morning after their return, September seventh, we awoke unaware that Blackfish had led his warriors across the ford about a half mile downstream. Us women and many of the girls went about our morning ritual of going to the spring to fetch fresh, cold water. The day was clear and warm, a true Indian summer day, with blue skies and no clouds, yet the birds and squirrels remained quiet. Daddy and some men patrolled around the edges of the fort's clearing. Daddy spotted the warriors first as they appeared in the trees near the fort's rear wall. I heard him yell for Moses and Isaiah to run for the fort. Squire's sons' usual morning chore was watering the stock. Both boys took off at a full run. Turns out the boys had seen the warriors approaching, but seeing flags flying thought it was some militia coming from Virginia to help in our defense. All those outside the fort ran back inside, and we closed and locked the gates. Our days of waiting had ended.

Soon Blackfish's army swarmed into the clearing and occupied the nearby peach orchard, so carefully planted only three years earlier. With Blackfish were Tory militia officers with flags. They built an arbor of sorts in the orchard to provide shade for their headquarters. We watched all this from our defensive positions. Everyone remained quiet, although whispered commands occasionally rose from our commanders.

Hours later, a large black man, carrying a flag of truce, walked toward the fort and called out, "Captain Daniel Boone."

When Daddy answered, Pompey, a former slave captured by the Shawnee years before, relayed the message, "Chief Blackfish has come to accept your surrender."

Inside our fort, voices called out in anger, many, once again, believing Daddy planned to surrender us all into captivity. Our enemies' next action added to their distrust, when we heard a Shawnee voice call out *Sheltowee, Sheltowee.*

Daddy turned and spoke with Billy Smith and others, assuring them he had no intention of surrendering the fort, but would meet Blackfish outside the fort for a discussion. I watched, trembling with fear, as my Daddy walked out the gate, unarmed, and approached the old chief, who pulled him into a hug and loudly, for all to hear, called him *son.* Several other chiefs came forward. They settled themselves some sixty or seventy feet from the fort, where they spread a blanket and talked.

I stood and listened to the hatred now issuing forth from almost every mouth within the walls. Each one angered at how Daddy had betrayed them after all. Flanders, Squire, and I watched in silence as Chief Blackfish cried about Daddy leaving them, calling out, "My son, what made you leave me?" On the other hand, Chief Moluntha showed great anger toward Daddy and demanded to know why Daddy'd killed his son a few days earlier. Daddy told us later how, when hearing this news, it took him a minute or so to remember the men had taken one or two Shawnee lives during that raid north of the Ohio.

As we watched, Blackfish handed Daddy a letter from Governor Hamilton. After giving Daddy time to read the letter, he produced a colorful, glass-beaded belt and handed it to Daddy. This wampum belt, strung with three colors of beads, red for war, black for death, and white for peace, would be used in Daddy's answer, for one end represented Boonesborough and the other Detroit. The path between the two indicated by the three colors of beads. Finally, with great ceremony, he presented Daddy with seven smoked buffalo tongues, announcing them to be for *your women.* Next, they smoked a pipe together. Blackfish demanded Daddy's reply, but he forestalled any decision, telling his Shawnee father, "I was so long from my home that others are now in command of the fort. I must speak with them before a decision can be made."

When Daddy returned to the fort, several men rushed toward him in anger, meaning him violence. Billy and Squire stepped in front of Daddy, armed and ready, to make the men step back and allow him to speak. Slowly, he relayed all he had discussed with Blackfish and Moluntha. We listened as he read the letter aloud—Hamilton's own words about how Daddy had promised to surrender the fort in return for pardons and safe conduct for all to Detroit. The pardons would be for our Patriot actions against the King. Hamilton promised all our officers would receive equivalent ranks in the British army. As the King's subjects, we would be compensated for our loss of land and property.

With everyone trying to talk at once, few could be understood. While some ranted and raved against Daddy, others talked quietly among themselves. Dick Callaway insisted the buffalo tongues were poisoned, but one brave man cut off a big hunk, chewed, swallowed, and declared the meat to be safe and delicious. Finally, some of our leaders restored calm. We listened to how Blackfish had stated that if we did not surrender, we would all be slaughtered, except for the young women, who would be taken as squaws. I could hear several women and girls crying at the gathering's edge. Aunt Jane stood stony-faced, watching Squire and Daddy. Betsy, Fanny, and I trembled in fear, having faced this threat once before. Once Captain Smith restored order, a vote was taken. Only our men could vote—to fight or to surrender—only two choices.

Dick Callaway called out in vicious anger, "I will kill the first man who proposes surrender."

Captain Billy Smith gave a brief speech, stating his firm opinion that we should fight.

"I'll fight to the death," shouted Squire, smiling at Daddy.

When all had voted, except Daddy, the decision was, to a man, to fight. No one asked my opinion or that of the other women. I knew not one would voluntarily surrender, for in our hearts we knew the outcome of such a decision.

"Well, I'll die with the rest," Daddy said.

Billy, Daddy, Squire, and others agreed to try to delay giving our answer while we strengthened our defenses. Also, we held out some small hope of help arriving from Virginia. So, they arranged to meet and parley later in the afternoon. Daddy and Billy were chosen to speak for us.

Flanders gathered me in his arms and whispered that all would be fine. "Trust in your father and Captain Smith to lead us through this troubling time. Your father has never yet failed to keep us safe from harm."

Later in the day, we climbed to his post along the wall to watch as Daddy and Billy slipped out the gate as other men stood rifles at the ready, expecting treachery. Flanders and I both had our rifles loaded and cocked. While Daddy remained dressed in his only clothing, his hunting shirt and doeskin leggings, Captain Smith had donned his militia officer's uniform with its red tunic and plumed hat. After making a show of spreading a panther hide upon the ground, they settled themselves and the talking began.

As agreed, Captain Smith first stressed that even more officers and commanders waited inside the fort, and how each would have a say in any decision. He stressed how, if they surrendered, the trip all the way to Detroit would be hard on the women, children, and old folks.

"I have brought forty horses—mares for the old people and women and children to ride." Blackfish answered, demonstrating his caring attitude toward our people.

Daddy thanked him for his kindness, and they agreed, once again, to talk over the chief's proposal with the fort's officers. Before Daddy and Captain Smith departed, the two parties established another meeting time and rules for the negotiations. The rules stated no Indians would come within thirty yards of the fort, and the settlers would not carry their arms outside the walls. Also, the Indians could help themselves to corn and cattle, but should not waste either. Our women would be allowed to go safely to and from the spring to carry water.

Billy announced all this upon their return to the fort. He assigned some men to take up the long-abandoned task of digging a well. He recognized siege conditions might leave us without sufficient water. Sentries were checked and last-minute arrangements for the first night of siege were made.

As Flanders and I lay together that night. I wondered, even feared, if it would be our last together. Daddy, Squire, Jane, Flanders, and I had discussed, over our evening meal, what to do if we were overrun. Jane had turned and looked at little Enoch, not yet a year old, settled and asleep in his crib beside her bed. Her older boys had already climbed to their pallets in the loft, and little Sarah sat sound asleep cuddled in my lap, sucking her thumb. We had so little here in Kentucky, yet we had so much to cherish and hold dear.

Only now was I happy that Mama and my siblings were in North Carolina.

Chapter 13
The Siege

"I'll not let my wife parade around in breeches," Flanders declared, staring at my limbs, outlined by his best wool pantaloons. I also wore his extra hunting shirt and a cap I had found in Daddy's cabin. I believe Israel had left it behind.

"Don't think I asked your permission, Flanders Callaway. I'm acting under orders from Captain Boone and Captain Smith. For they wish as many women and girls that are able and willing are to dress as men and parade about inside the fort and on the walls. We'll make it appear we have more men than we do. Would you have me defy the militia captains? Well, would you?" I snapped.

"But Jemima, it's indecent, the men will look at you and besides, you're setting yourself up as a target. You know that their scouts on the *Indian bank* are observing movements within the fort. They might start shooting at any minute."

"Flanders, I've already paraded myself back and forth to the spring carrying water three times this morning. I see that as much more dangerous than parading around in breeches carrying a rifle. Besides, men look at me all the time. Some even venture to speak to me during the day," I said, taunting his jealousy.

So, all morning, I walked around, back and forth, carrying my rifle and pretending to be a man. So did several other younger married women like Betsy and Fanny, and a few older girls. We would stop and talk. Spit and scratch ourselves. We made quite a show of being *men.*

About midday, we once again heard Pompey call out. "Boone, Boone, Blackfish wants to see your beautiful daughter and wife. Send them out and have them let down their hair for all to see."

"No, since my daughter's capture by the Shawnee, she and my wife are afraid of the Shawnee," Daddy answered, not wanting it known that Mama was not in the fort.

"They only need stand just outside the gate, and none will approach," Pompey answered.

Daddy called me over, along with Betsy, Fanny, and Aunt Jane. "Ladies, are you willing to do this? It might give us a few more hours before the attack."

I could see how Betsy and Fanny were terribly upset at the idea. Truthfully, so was I, but in the end we three agreed, as did Aunt Jane, who would pretend to be Mama.

Daddy and Flanders both talked with me while I changed, Daddy assuring me of his protection, and Flanders of his love.

So, dressed in our own clothes, us four women stepped outside the gate, each followed closely by a man holding a loaded rifle. The rest of our men stood ready at their posts, attentive to any hint of threat.

"Let down your hair," Pompey yelled again.

We each released our combs and let our long hair flow down over our shoulders. Each shook our heads to let it fall, all four had hair that reached well past our backsides. Blackfish, Pompey, and a small group of warriors looked on from one hundred or so feet away.

"Pretty squaws, Boone," Blackfish called out. Others shouted out their approval, nodding with pleasure.

We quietly returned to the fort and slipped away to shake off the nerves and fear of standing so exposed before over four hundred Indians. Daddy had identified Shawnees, Chippewas, Wyandotts, Cherokees, and Ottawas. Also, in the war party were twelve Frenchmen under Lieutenant Antoine DeQuindre's command. Hamilton had hired these mercenaries and provided the shot, powder, horses, and other supplies for the raid.

Within the fort, Callaway and a few others raged against Pompey's attitude and threatened to shoot him if he again approached the fort. They resented a Negro demanding the fort's attention and issuing orders to white men.

Aunt Jane returned to her cabin, Betsy to her baby, and Fanny and I again took to our men's clothing.

Much later in the afternoon, Pompey called out that Blackfish awaited Boone's answer. Daddy and Captain Smith, along with several others, once again left the fort and approaching Blackfish, Billy announced, "The people have determined to resist surrender as long as there is a man living."

Daddy told us later he saw anger in Blackfish's eyes. With expectations of violence, they stood, prepared to run, and after a minute the old chief proposed more discussion the following day. Again, playing for time, they agreed.

The following morning, I worked with the fort's women to prepare a fabulous feast featuring venison and buffalo tongue accompanied by corn and other fresh vegetables. We worked in almost total silence, each engrossed in our own thoughts and fears. We made fresh bread and chilled all the milk available. We pulled out our reserve stores of cheese, honey, and fruit preserves. Our menfolk carried the fort's tables, chairs, and stools out to the clearing before the fort's gate. We collected all the pewter ware and wood table wares and invited the Indian leaders and their allies to a feast. Daddy and Billy said this would demonstrate our abundant resources within the fort.

Some of our menfolk joined the chief and Frenchmen at the table. After they finished, our leaders walked with them to the shade of the giant elm near the sycamore hollow. The fort's remaining men helped carry everything back inside as Captain Smith, Dick Callaway, Flanders, Squire, Isaac Crabtree, Will Buchanan, Edward Bradley, John South, and Daddy once again took up negotiations for peace. Daddy had left explicit instructions to his best marksmen stationed along the wall, "At the first sign of trouble, do not hesitate for fear of hurting your own people. Shoot without one moment's delay."

I stationed myself at the gate, being one of several women ready to close the gates immediately upon our men's return or any treachery. From my position, I watched most of the activities and even overheard bits and pieces of their discussions.

Captain Smith introduced each one of our leaders, our chiefs. Then Daddy complained to Blackfish about so many warriors just standing around. "Father, we brought only our captains to this meeting, are not these warriors not chiefs."

So, some were sent away, yet more Shawnee remained than did our men. We learned later that Blackfish now proposed to leave for six weeks and then to return for our surrender. Captain Smith refused this proposal immediately, angering Blackfish, who began to complain loudly about white men and families taking possession of their lands, their hunting grounds. Going on and on for a while about white men's treachery, Blackfish then argued for a new boundary line—the Ohio. He suggested the whites might stay in Kentucky peacefully. The Shawnee would trade and hunt south of the river and all would be friendly, if only the whites would declare their allegiance to the King. Still playing the delaying game, our men agreed. The English officers wrote out the agreement and great ceremony was made of them signing it.

Then, Blackfish declared his need to explain the treaty to his warriors. He told our men, "My warriors have come here to take home prisoners, not to leave in peace. I must explain how this will benefit us all."

Blackfish addressed his followers in Shawnee. While Daddy said he understood some words the great chief said, he was not warned of what came next. For when Blackfish finished, he turned back and demanded that all shake hands, to conclude this great peace treaty. Suddenly each American found themselves surrounded by at least two Shawnee warriors who grabbed their hands and tried pulling them away. Dick Callaway immediately began to struggle with those who attempted to embrace him. He jerked away. Someone in the fort, seeing the struggle, fired into the melee.

Blackfish had stationed snipers in the sycamore hollow, and they rushed to help capture our men. I beheld all as Daddy pushed Blackfish to the ground right as another warrior swung a calumet at my father and hit him solidly across the back. He staggered. Our other men, all large men, managed to pull themselves free and run for the gate. I tried to observe Flanders, Daddy, and Squire as the mad rush occurred. Within the fort, men aimed and fired and reloaded time and time again. Women screamed while grabbing their children and retreating to cabins and the blockhouses. Those of us at the gate urged our men loudly. "Run, run," we screamed.

I watched as several warriors fell from gunfire while others, believing Blackfish had been shot, rushed to his aid. It looked like our men would reach the gate safely, then Uncle Squire suddenly fell to the ground, blood shooting from his shoulder. I heard one of his sons scream out from the wall. Squire immediately sprang to his feet and rushed inside the gate, just before we closed it and dropped the bar.

Organized chaos reigned. Everything seemed to happen at once. The warriors fired on the fort. Our men took careful aim, using every precious bit of shot and powder to take down one of our enemies. I saw one chief fall dead and listened with dread as the warriors cried out in anger. From across the river, on the *Indian bank's* high ground, snipers fired on Ambrose Coffee, who had positioned himself prone on the bastion's upper edge. Suddenly, he tumbled to the ground. Several men ran to his aid, only to discover fourteen bullet holes in his clothing but not one mark on his body. Thereafter, Ambrose found a safer place to be.

Dogs barked as horses and cattle ran around in the fort, panicking from all the noise. Children and babies cried, women screamed, and men called out orders. I climbed down and went to help Aunt Jane. I knew she would have her hands full with three small children and Uncle Squire. Captain Smith had posted their oldest son, Jonathan to help reload rifles within a blockhouse. Moses carried supplies to various men but was ordered to also stay within the relative safety of the blockhouse. We didn't put children on the wall platforms, but some women volunteered to stand beside their men and load an extra rifle. With this tactic, the fort's sixty men could fire as rapidly as one hundred and twenty.

I ran toward Squire's cabin, watching as Elizabeth Callaway beat Matthais Prock with a broom as he ran out her cabin's door. "Coward, coward," she screamed before turning and telling me, "I found the coward hiding under my bed." Matthais, being a potter and not even owning a gun, jumped into the unfinished well and shouted about how he was not made to be a soldier, yelling over and over again, "I ish potter" from his hiding place.

Running from cabin door to cabin door, staying close to the walls to avoid the snipers, I finally reached Squire's cabin. Jane had him settled on their bed and had examined the wound. "I believe he was only grazed, but he keeps complaining about the pain," she told me as I gathered up Sarah and tried to comfort her.

Soon, the warrior's first frenzied attack settled into a lull, and Daddy came by to check on his brother. After a quick examination, he declared, "Jane, I believe the ball is still in there, probably in the bone. We'll need to get it out."

So, I took Sarah, Enoch, and Isaiah and slipped them quietly back to my cabin. Daddy called for a few men to help and dug the ball from Squire's shoulder with the tip of his hunting knife. He never once screamed out. I guess, after all his previous injuries, he knew how to deal with the pain. Later, Daddy came by to tell me Squire was resting peacefully and to take the children back to their cabin. Seems I was needed elsewhere.

Fanny, Betsy, and I, along with any woman free and willing to help, carried water, food, and ammunition to our fighting men. All around, the older boys and some girls helped load rifles. Yet this work and any movement in the fort's yard became dangerous due to the snipers on the opposite bank. Several of our cattle and horses were shot and had to be butchered for meat. I was returning to our cabin when I felt what I thought was someone slapping me on the backside. As I spun around to confront my assailant, I realized I had been shot, and anxiously pulled at my dress and petticoat, causing the ball to fall to the ground. I asked Fanny to look, not being able to see my own backside, and we discovered the ball had not even torn through my petticoat or flesh but had left a dark red mark upon my flesh. Daddy says the bullet was spent. It had reached the end of its velocity. I didn't care if it was spent, I had an awful bruise on my backside and could barely sit for almost a week. Not that I had much time for sitting.

Only darkness brought quiet. We had lost no men, only one wounded, Uncle Squire—not counting my backside.

Chapter 14
Squire's Cannon

After a restless night of sporadic gunfire and mounting fear for the coming day, Thursday morning brought more of the same. The men stood guard and fired at any approaching targets. We withstood the siege's second day, confronted our fear, and held dear to our lives and our loved ones.

Daddy and Billy came by while Flanders and I ate a late meal together. "Well, Mistress Callaway, seems like the Boone family will survive to fight another day. Squire now has an ax by his bed for protection, in case we are overrun, and your Daddy told me about your wound," he continued, snickering.

"Don't find it so funny myself, Billy," answered Flanders, standing up and confronting our militia captain. "My wife might have been killed."

"Flanders, we are well aware of how close Mima came to being severely wounded. We are taking steps to lessen our visibility within the commons. Several men are already using axes to cut holes in the walls between cabins. That way our women and children can move about more safely. I expect they'll be by here shortly."

As Flanders calmed himself, I changed the subject by asking, "Daddy, Captain Billy, do you think they have cannons?"

"No, Billy and I believed before today that Hamilton had supplied them with artillery. Yet, as they didn't fire them yesterday or today, it seems unlikely."

Suddenly, voices rang out, calling for Captains Boone and Smith.

Flanders and I followed them out, only to see flickering flames outside one end of the stockade.

"Captain Boone, those rascals set fire to the flax drying outside the wall. John Holder done slipped out the gate to put it out!" someone called.

Flanders and I climbed to his post and kept guard while others called out Holder's movements.

"He's throwing water on the flames and trying to rake the flax away from the wall."

"Keep up a steady fire over his head, men," called Captain Smith.

All within, and I imagine outside, the fort heard Holder shouting loud curses at the Indians while he worked. The loud thud of balls striking the wall all around where Holder toiled to keep the fire from the stockade walls echoed within. Finally, exhausted and still cursing, the fire now out and flax pulled away from the walls, John returned to the fort, slipping in through the gate. Fanny ran out to embrace her husband, but Elizabeth Callaway scolded him loudly.

"John Holder, it would be more becoming to pray than to swear!"

"I've no time to pray, goddammit!" John thundered back.

I do believe we all took to our beds snickering that evening. Well, maybe not Elizabeth Callaway, who did not believe in the power of curse words to keep one safe during dangerous times.

<hr>

Friday morning. We all seemed to have fallen into the routine of siege warfare. Most had slept little, and tempers often raged. Children cried more often, and many women had dark circles under their eyes from spending the night calming little ones back to sleep. It was mid-morning when one sentry noticed mud flowing downstream from a spot along the river that lay directly behind the fort. Daddy and Billy soon investigated the sound of chopping and digging. The Indians were attempting to dig a tunnel under our wall from the riverbank. With the river being so low, they had found a place that offered them shelter from rifle fire.

As the word spread, terror did as well. It increased with nightfall, as two or three warriors at a time, carrying burning torches, would run toward our walls and hurl their torches over. They created their long well-constructed torches from loose hickory bark and flax coated with dampened powder. Once set aflame, they burned long and hot. Our men shot many, as a man carrying a burning torch makes for an easy target in the dark. Some torches landed on roofs, which us women swept off with long poles, pulling burning shingles off and leaving holes. No real worry, as the weather stayed dry and warm.

Uncle Squire, now up and about, improvised some rifle barrels to shoot water. They worked well if the fire was still small. Yet, using our water supply to put out fires was not something we could afford to do. Of course, we couldn't let them burn either.

During the night, our first man fell to enemy fire. A small fence outside one cabin's rear wall had been set ablaze. Several men dug under the wall, fearing it would burn through if not put out. An African slave, London, whose master was away in the settlements, crawled out the hole and pushed the burning fence away. No one ordered him to do this, he volunteered, for he, like us, knew the consequences of failure to defend ourselves. While outside the wall, London, seeing a Shawnee warrior hidden nearby, asked for a rifle to be passed out to him. Unfortunately, the rifle misfired twice, the second time illuminating London as the powder flashed. A shot rang out and London fell dead.

Seems most every woman and many men shed a few tears that night, for many thought kindly of London. London, neither black nor white that evening, had given his life for ours.

The following day, Uncle Squire convinced Daddy and Captain Smith to let him use his other invention. He had worked for days to build a cannon by attaching two black gum tree halves together with iron straps he had scavenged from a broken wagon wheel. Squire insisted that black gum, being a straight-growing tough tree, was the perfect choice.

"All I need, Daniel, is just for you to open the gates halfway, just as the Indians make their next approach. As soon as I fire my cannon, close the gates," Squire instructed.

"But will it work, Squire, or will you blow us all to kingdom come?" Captain Billy asked, not being as aware as us Boones of Squire's intelligence and ingenuity.

"'Twill work," Squire snorted, "just you get ready to open and close the gates on my command."

So, at the sound of the next attack, several men pulled open the gates and Squire lit the fuse. It felt like minutes before the blast shook the entire fort and the ball flew out toward the charging Shawnee.

Flanders observed from the wall and took aim on the foremost men in the charge. He said the warriors practically fell over themselves trying to retreat. He didn't think the large cannon ball actually hit any them, but it threw up dirt and debris as it hit the ground. Then a rousing cheer rose from the fort's occupants. Yet, the warriors reformed and charged again.

Again, our men opened the gates, and Squire fired his cannon. This time disaster struck as the two halves burst apart and black gum tree fragments flew in every direction. Squire and others dropped to the ground and covered their heads while Daddy and Billy screamed for the men to close the gate. Miraculously, no one received even a scratch from the flying debris.

For the rest of the day, the Indians jeered Squire, asking, "Why don't you fire your damned cannon again?"

For two more days, the pattern of our lives remained the same. Sleep a little, eat a little, and guard the fort with our lives. For if we did not, our lives and those we held dearest would be forfeited to the enemy outside our walls. The Indians continued to dig, and we began digging a cross tunnel that would hopefully allow us to fire on those digging or emerging from their tunnel before they reached the fort's interior. Other men dug in the well, hoping to find water, as each day our supply dwindled.

Everyone stank, even more than usual, from not being able to wash as we needed to use our water wisely. Babies' nappies and the privy trench created the worst smells, along with rotting animal carcasses we'd needed to butcher and the manure of those still living within the fort.

I saw men carrying the stones we dug up, to the wall's top and throwing them over toward where the warriors dug. Soon came the cry, "Come out and fight like men and not try to kill with stones like children."

One older grandmother, hearing the warriors cry, admonished our men with, "For God's sake, don't throw stones, it might hurt some of the Indians, and they will be mad and take revenge."

Unable to contain their laughter or glee at such a silly statement, our men began throwing baskets filled with rocks, dirt, and various waste materials over the wall toward the tunnel diggers, while chanting *"Don't throw stones. Don't throw stones."*

The shouting between the two parties of men continued all day, with the Indians using foul language as often as our men. I must say our men used much more inventive curses. Perhaps they had been taking lessons from John Holder.

Several times our men watched as one warrior climbed a tree some ways out, about a quarter mile, turned his back on the fort, and greeted us with his backside. He continued to carry out his actions until one man, infuriated with this insult, loaded a large bore rifle with a heavy load, steadied his aim through a loophole, and fired. The boom rang out just after the warrior tumbled from the tree. We saw him no more. As Indians always carry off their dead and wounded, we had not one thought, from day to day, how many enemy warriors lay dead or wounded, just beyond our sight line.

It was the next day when Daddy, running across the yard, took a shot to the upper shoulder from one of the snipers we had come so to despise. I ran toward him and helped him into our cabin. Sitting Daddy down, I began to remove his stock, already soaked in blood. Blood shot from the wound, across my apron and dress. Panicked, I used my apron's hem to stanch the flow. It soon lessened, and I was able to bandage Daddy's wound. It was not deep and would heal well, if it didn't turn putrid.

I said a prayer to the good Lord for his healing and then begged, "Daddy, please rest, I'll let Billy and Flanders know your condition."

Well, Daddy did rest for a while, but the constant shouting between our men, and some women, and our enemies changed its direction. Seems the sniper that had shot Daddy and others outside the fort realized they could no longer hear Daddy's voice calling out commands. They took up a new call, "We've killed Boone, we've killed Boone!"

Daddy, unable and unwilling to resist the taunt, left our cabin to answer back, "No you haven't. I'm here, ready for you yellow rascals."

Insults, jabs, and jeers continued to ring about the fort and from without. A yelled taunt usually brought rifle fire back toward the taunter. Also, when a rifleman fired through one of the fort's many loopholes, he then had to draw back behind the walls and resist looking to see if his shot had struck his intended target.

On Friday evening, David Bundrin made just such a mistake and took a rifle ball to the forehead. Despite his horrible wound, he managed to live for several hours as his brains seeped out through the crack in his skull. Shocked,

I listened as his wife kept saying how lucky he was that the ball didn't hit him in the eye. I guess, in her horror and grief, she coped with his loss in this ridiculous way.

Finally, Dave passed. The men carried him to the blockhouse's ground floor and wrapped his body in a sheet. His burial, and London's, would have to wait. Dave's wife sat by his body until some women forced her to return to her cabin where she grieved alone, as they had no children. One or more of us stopped by to be with her when time allowed. Her grief infected us all with dread, afraid we would be next to lose a loved one or friend.

Our enemies lost Pompey about this same time. His black face often appeared, popping up from behind logs and even from where the warriors dug toward the fort's walls. Tired of his taunts and resentful of his race, our men often made a sport of trying to shoot Pompey. Raising up from his hiding space to answer a well-aimed taunt, a rifle ball took him square in the face.

Our men continued to chide our enemies, calling, "Where's Pompey? Where's Pompey?" The Shawnee first answered "Pompey ne-pan." *Pompey sleeping.* Soon tired of our men's questioning, one warrior answered, "Pompey ne-poo." *Pompey dead.*

⸺ ● ⸺

Eleven days, eleven days. Can you imagine our horror, our fear, our dread? We had been captive in our own homes for eleven days while our enemies tormented us day and night. Foodstuffs now ran low. Captain Smith rationed our water. At night, women, boys, and girls would use knives to dig balls from the fort and cabin walls. We melted these and formed new balls for use in our defense.

Exhausted, our men took naps at their positions along the wall. Many dozed off while sitting upright, holding tight to their rifle. I sat beside Flanders while he slept. Instead I kept watch. I could not bear to be out of his sight and had brought over my precious buffalo robe and a blanket to make us more comfortable. The day was a Thursday, not that it made any difference. Warm, with a breeze that might foretell a late-day storm, we all observed the unusual and constant activity outside our gates. Just after dark, the assault began.

Blackfish's warriors ran toward the fort, hollering their war cries and carrying torches and fire arrows. Rifle fire rang out from every available angle into the fort. The sound of so many rifles seemed determined to deafen us, and yet we joined in the cries. Daddy and Captain Billy called out commands. Women, older children, and anyone able loaded rifles and handed them to the best shots. Every man and many women took up positions. I stayed beside Flanders but fired and reloaded my rifle over and over and over again. My hands turned black with the grime of gunpowder, probably my face as well. Thirsty and tired, oh so tired, I kept up the repetition of loading, aiming, and firing.

I worried. Would our ammunition and powder run out? How many would be shot or killed? Would the fort burn? Would this torture, this fear, never end?

The night sky glowed orange with the intense firing. Soon, we didn't need candles or lanterns to see every movement, both inside and outside the fort. Some men and boys had to scramble onto roofs to knock out the fires. Men, women, and children alike screamed in fear, sensing defeat would soon overtake our defenses. We all knew the horrors the Shawnee would bring upon our people. Women huddled to protect their children, some deciding to take measures into their own hands if our walls were overrun. Most planned to take their own lives, and their children's, before allowing them to be captured, tortured, and carried off into slavery.

For an hour or more we battled. Again, and again, they threw every warrior against our walls. On and on they came. My arms ached. I was covered in gunpowder, thirsty, and practically deaf from the noise.

Their tunnel grew ever closer to breaching our walls. Daddy had to pull men off the wall to defend us from their underground intrusion. On and on we fought. Just as it seemed we would be overcome by the fires, and the tunnel would breach our wall, I smelled lightning and heard the crash of rolling thunder. Rain began to fall in torrents.

A thundering storm lit the sky and added to the brightness from the magnitude of rifle fire and fires burning roundabout the fort. The warriors swarming about just below our walls, began to disappear into the surrounding darkness. Then a shout rang out from behind our position.

"Their tunnel collapsed! Their tunnel collapsed!"

Unbeknown to us, one man, William Patton had arrived back from a long hunt after the siege began. He beheld all from a hidden position on Hackberry Ridge. Listening to and observing that night's assault, Will believed the fort had fallen. He fled toward Logan's Station and told how Boonesborough had fallen and all were lost. We learned all this when, a few days later, men from Logan's rode to give aid to any survivors and to bury the dead. They found us alive and well. We were not surprised at Will's believing all was lost.

Here at Boonesborough, we slept lightly that evening, but no more attacks came. The next morning revealed the warriors' camp to be abandoned. Daddy and others scouted the area but came back to tell us the Indians had departed. Later, we found out they had split into several groups and harassed various stations along their return path to the Ohio, killing several settlers.

Fear leaves slowly after such a long stay. Few of us ventured forth into our wooded surroundings for days, even weeks. Mothers continued to keep their children close. Fathers and husbands kept guard as the womenfolk fetched water from the spring to wash away the stench of battle and that of *lingering fear*. Slowly, ever so slowly, fear left but caution and wariness hung around.

Chapter 15
The Trial

In the days following the siege, our lives began to return to normal. We pulled some one-hundred-twenty-five pounds of lead from the fort's walls. Only two men lost their lives at Boonesborough, one white and one black. We buried them in our little cemetery and honored both for their bravery and sacrifice.

Several days later, Virginia militiamen arrived to aid us in our time of strife. Too late for one battle but perhaps needed for another attack.

We cleaned and repaired our cabins and the fort. We stockpiled food, in case the Indians returned. We treated our wounded, rejoiced in our deliverance, and sang praises to God the Father for our salvation.

Flanders and I could have been happy, if not for the charges levied against Daddy by Flanders' uncle and Benjamin Logan of Fort Logan.

Callaway and Logan always strongly believed Daddy'd committed treason by selling out the salt makers and taking an oath to Hamilton and the British. Now, Daddy would be court marshaled. About the fort, people talked of only two things, Daddy's actions before and during the siege, and if the Indians would return.

Will came by to help Daddy with his letter to Mama. Daddy wanted to get the words just right. He explained why he could not immediately travel to North Carolina and reunite our family. I learned one line by heart after hearing Daddy read it aloud to Will. Daddy told Mama his feeling about the British, saying *God damn them, they set the Indians on us.* Now, Daddy never used profanity; never have I known him to issue one such word, and I don't believe he did so in this letter. It was more of a prayer to our Lord asking him to damn the British for their actions. Seemed understandable, given what we'd suffered.

While Flanders, Will, Captain Billy, Uncle Squire, Aunt Jane, myself, and many others understood Daddy's story of the actions he took to assure our safety, others still did not. They held the trial at Fort Logan, and while Flanders attended, I did not, as women were not allowed. I waited at home, waited for word, waited to hear Daddy had been cleared. Because I always knew he would be.

I remember Callaway and Logan brought four charges against him. First, that Daddy handed over the salt makers without their consent. Second, that he consorted with the enemy in their village and in Detroit and bargained with Hamilton to give up the people of Boonesborough to the Indians. Next, they asserted he'd weakened the fort's defenses by taking our men north to scout for enemy actions and to raid the Shawnee village. Finally, they charged him with treason by exposing all our officers to ambush when he asked them to go outside the fort to speak with Blackfish and the other chiefs. Callaway declared certain knowledge that Daniel Boone was a Tory and should be stripped of his commission.

A large contingent of our men left for Fort Logan with Daddy under guard so he could not escape. As if a man as trustworthy as Daddy would even attempt escape rather than face trial. At that moment, I began to pace, to worry, and to pray. Days passed. I helped Jane with the children, gathered our remaining crops, nuts, and wild grapes. I even hunted, as most of the men went to the court martial. Of course, I never went out alone. Most often I took some of the older boys with me. They didn't mind tagging along, as I was a better shot than most and I always shared with those families most in need. At nights, sleep became hard to come by. My thoughts were consumed with worry. I even began to wonder if Mama would return to Kentucky, or if she would insist on staying in North Carolina.

Days later, when Flanders rode in from the trial, he first gathered me in his arms and gave me a big kiss. Uncle

Squire laughed and did the same to Jane, right out there in the commons! Then, we gathered in their cabin to listen to the news. I'd already noticed Daddy was not with them, and despite my knowledge of his innocence, feared the worst had come to fruition. Except, Flanders and Squire seemed to be so happy and full of good news.

Once we settled, they told us what had occurred. Flanders acquainted us with the court martial happenings, and Uncle Squire added details here and there.

"Uncle Dick testified about all he deemed wrong about Daniel's actions. Mima, he seemed even more spiteful and arrogant than usual. I've always known him to be so, but he spoke with such vengeance, many, even those who knew him well, were surprised. Andrew Johnston and William Hancock, the two other escapees who've returned, testified as well. Each one told his story and gave his honest opinion. As you know, Andy held that Daniel was guilty, while Will knew him to be loyal to this fort and its people. Lastly, the court listened intently to Daniel's story. The officers asked many questions. Daniel answered truthfully, explaining each action and each thought. I deemed his words found more believers than before the trial. Then, all the officers retired to make their decision."

"Jemima, you would have loved to have heard your Daddy give his testimony. He spoke for near on half an hour. Kept the audience spellbound with his words. Yet, he made the men all laugh with his story of running the gauntlet!" Squire asserted.

"Oh, Flanders, I can hardly stand not knowing, please tell me, did they decide for Daddy?"

"Well, Mima, I rode back to Boonesborough knowing my father-in-law had just been promoted to major!"

"They promoted him? So, they believed him? Tell me it's so, Flanders."

"Those officers deliberated for only an hour, maybe a bit longer. Then they came back in and acquitted Daniel and promoted him to major! That's why he's not yet returned. They needed to hold some discussions about safety at various stations and especially wanted Daniel's input," Squire answered before Flanders even opened his mouth.

"Oh, Flanders. But how did Mr. Callaway take the news?"

"Oh, Uncle is fighting mad, so is Captain Logan. They expressed their dismay at the verdict in loud terms and curses. They were asked to leave the room, and none too politely, I'll tell you. Uncle sees Daniel's promotion as a personal affront. I even overheard him say *he'd be damned if he'd follow that man.*"

"Your journey back must have been miserable, listening to his tirade," stated Jane.

"Nay, dear wife. We let him ride home alone. Flanders and I stalled around a bit, and then rode back with Captain Billy and Will. We enjoyed each other's company a great deal."

"When Daddy returns, I expect he'll want to leave immediately for the settlements to see Mama and the family. I've been thinking. . ."

"Jemima, we're going with him. You'd be miserable here without him, listening to all the talk, and worrying if he'll return. So, I see as how we should go along," declared Flanders.

"What about your family?" I asked.

"Jemima, I came here without my family. My own parents have been dead and buried for many a long year. I came with only my brother beside me, and one more joined me later. Both are still missing. I don't rely on Uncle Dick for anything and don't want to be around the miserable old fart!"

"Flanders Callaway!" Aunt Jane and I shouted together. Squire just laughed.

"Well, he is. He makes everyone else miserable. I'll take you back to the settlements with Daniel. You're my family now. Then we can make a decision as to our return together."

"No, Flanders, you must promise me we will return to Kentucky when my family does. Of that decision, there shall be no doubt. Where my Daddy goes, I go. I know he'll choose Kentucky. I hope Mama will."

After a long discussion, Squire and Jane determined not to go back to the settlements. Squire aimed to continue work on a cabin he was constructing on nearby land.

⸻ ● ⸻

Within days, Daddy, Flanders, Will Hays, and I rode out for the North Carolina settlements. We traveled light and carried not much more than the necessities of the trail and our rifles. We arrived in early November and found Mama, Israel, and the little ones, living in a cabin on Uncle Billy Bryan's place. Uncle Billy being married to Daddy's sister Mary, they were twice related. Finding the cabin too small for us all, Daddy moved us to a larger cabin on Mama's father's land. There Flanders and I lived with Suzy, Will, and their two little ones, alongside Mama and Daddy and all my brothers and sisters.

Mama and the children listened intently to our telling all that occurred. Mama cried over our suffering during the siege. She cried over Daddy being court martialed. And she cried over Squire's injuries. I do think she shed a few million tears. Yet, we rejoiced in our deliverance, enjoyed Suzy's little ones, and delighted in family once again.

Mama and Daddy often walked out together during the evenings, until the weather turned too cold. They talked and talked. Daddy explained his decisions and his worries. As far as I know, Mama never apologized for believing him dead. Daddy seemed to accept her actions the previous May as right and honest.

Time passed slowly. Daddy and Flanders hunted the Blue Ridge that winter. The rest of us stayed put in North Carolina, safe and happy to be a whole family once again. Seems like Mama, Suzy, and I sewed all winter to supply the family with clothing. I exhibited the most desperate need, having not been able to purchase sufficient cloth in Kentucky. My clothes were threadbare, torn, and plain worn out by the time we reached North Carolina. I worried about Uncle Squire and Aunt Jane and their little ones, but we often received news from folks traveling from Kentucky back to the settlements. We set aside supplies to carry back to them upon our return, for Flanders and I were determined to make Kentucky our home.

We celebrated Christmas and the beginning of 1779 safe in North Carolina. Well, safe from the Shawnee. None felt secure from the British. Many battles took place in South Carolina and Georgia. Savannah fell to the British right at the year's end. In news closer to our Kentucky home, we heard how Kentuckian George Rogers Clark had captured the British fort at Vincennes in late February with many of our Kentucky friends leading the fight.

We got our war news quite regularly from travelers and newspapers. During that winter, we also began to experience the effects of neighbor against neighbor. Several of Mama's brothers and cousins stayed loyal to the King. Patriots treated them and their families with contempt and hatred, on occasion with violence. Talking with Daddy, now a firm Patriot, some Bryan families decided to move to Kentucky. Not all were Patriots. Not all were Tories. We knew, in Kentucky, everyone seemed to accept others' loyalties more readily. West of the Appalachians, we didn't bother as much with Patriot or Tory. We just looked to everyone to defend each other against our common enemy.

Besides, the Virginia legislature, having decided to encourage the settlement of the County of Kentucky, offered cheap land, only $2.25 per hundred acres for up to 400 acres, to any who would clear a set number of acres and build a cabin. Settlers might purchase a thousand additional acres for only $400. Anyone who'd settled in Kentucky before the first day of 1778 received four hundred acres, and if they'd improved their land, they could apply for one thousand more. So, Flanders and I could claim the land we had already improved.

By September of 1779, Daddy'd gathered a large number of relatives and friends to join our return to Kentucky. I believe, to this day, that Mama came back only because most everyone in our family had decided to follow Daddy. Each held their own reasons for making the journey. Why, there were more than one hundred men, women, and children! The largest party to travel to Kentucky up until that time. We left from our old family settlement on September twenty-second. One year after the siege, we headed for home. Oh, how I had missed my Kentucky home. I guess my distance from Boonesborough had erased some of the fear.

Flanders and I had a terrible argument not long before we left for Kentucky. I can rightly remember we at first tried to keep our voices low, but the great intensity of our disagreement caused some shouting.

"Flanders Isham Callaway, I be goin' home to Kentucky with my family, whether you come along is your own decision," I shouted after several attempts to discuss this in a more civilized manner.

"Mima, you can't ride all that way, not now," Flanders shouted back.

"I can't? Who are you to tell me what I can and cannot do? I be goin'."

"Well, you shouldn't. Not in your condition," Flanders said, taking my hands and pulling me close.

As I pulled away, I completely lost my temper, "Well, my condition is all your fault!"

It was this statement that brought both Mama and Daddy to the room we shared. Mama tried to hush me, while Daddy laughed at my last statement. "Mima, understanding more than you about how a man and a woman spend their nights, I truly doubt you had nothing to do with getting yourself with child. Now, as you have shared it with the entire family, just what is this purpose of this argument?"

Flanders replied before I had a chance to even open my mouth. "Daniel, she insists she be goin' to Kentucky before the babe comes. Why, 'tis possible she'll have it before we arrive at Boonesborough. I simply want her to wait until after the babe comes."

"Flanders," I began, now calmer and more determined than ever, "this babe of mine will be born in Kentucky. If it comes while we are traveling, well, so be it. But if I have warning enough, I'll ride hard for Caintuck!"

Seemed to me we were at an impasse, being as how neither one of us planned to give in. 'Twas Mama who put everything right. "Flanders, I understand your concern. Mima's babe should arrive about Christmas, by then we will be in Boonesborough or have moved on to our new home. She's strong, has not had a day of worry with this babe. Besides, there will be plenty of us there in case the babe decides to come early. Just think on it, most all the womenfolk in the family will be with her day after day during our journey."

More talk, this time quiet talk, finally convinced Flanders of my ability to ride to Kentucky while carrying my first babe. Mama helped me pack up the small clothes the babe would need, nappies, gowns, blankets, and such. We wrapped them in a well-oiled deer hide and tied them on just behind my saddle.

What a sight we made—stretched out along the trail. Why, Uncle Billy Bryan's family all rode horses, and they brought along twenty-eight packhorses loaded down with household goods, personal goods, and farming equipment. My that man was wealthy!

Daddy loaded six pack horses, and we brought to Kentucky a load of blacksmith tools, as well as kettles, household goods, and farming tools. We packed all our personal goods and our gifts for Uncle Squire's family.

Daddy packed two small swivel guns, one for use at our new home, as he'd decided not to return to Boonesborough to live after all the talk of his actions and the trial. Some, like Dick Callaway, still held great animosity for him. The other was for Uncle Billy Bryan at Bryan's Station. General Griffith Rutherford, the local North Carolina militia commander, gave us the guns. Too bad those guns proved so heavy. Two draft horses died while trying to carry those guns. After the horses died, Daddy tried dragging them behind a horse, but the load was just too much. So, Uncle Billy and Daddy hid them some six miles after we passed Cumberland Gap. They always meant to return for those guns. Far as I know, those guns still lie hidden to this day.

Now, I can't rightly remember everyone that came to Kentucky with us. I mentioned Uncle Billy and his wife Mary, Daddy's sister. Daddy seemed to have the hardest time convincing Uncle George to go along. With his bad leg, traveling always created problems for George, though he rarely complained. George and Ann's family consisted of five girls, the oldest being fourteen, and three boys.

Then there was Samuel, and his family. Samuel, six years older than Daddy, served as the family's patriarch ever since their father, Squire, passed some twenty years before. Samuel and Sarah Day had previously moved their family to the Camden, South Carolina, area. By 1779, the fighting grew too close and they retreated back to the Yadkin. All Samuel's children came with them except Samuel, Jr., who served in the Patriot army until the war's end. Their oldest, Elizabeth was already married and had two daughters. She and her husband William White came along to Kentucky.

You must realize by now that our family moves together. First England, then Pennsylvania, then Virginia, then North Carolina. A few of us stray off now and then, but very few. So, almost all my Boone uncles and aunts came with us to Kentucky. Even Uncle Jonathan brought his family, there being only a few of those children, maybe four, I can't rightly remember. Jonathan was a miller and often worked for Squire.

Not once during the journey did I feel the least out of sorts. I carried on just as I had at the cabin in North Carolina. All except the day I decided to lead the women across at a rather high river—don't remember which river. That day I rode double with young Jane Dodson. Our whole party had wasted a day waiting for the water level to fall and, being impatient, I announced I would cross first to demonstrate how to cross a swollen river.

I plunged my horse into the water. As the water grew deeper, my horse took to, and we moved right sharply across. Jane and I had almost reached the other bank when something floated by and startled my horse. Dang horse threw us both with his thrashing about! As we hit the water and sank, I heard Mama and Suzy screaming. Being a lover of water, I simply grabbed Jane and helped her to shore where Peter Houston and John Dodson, Jane's father, pulled us up from the water and set us firmly on dry ground. The ground may have been dry, but we weren't. Poor Jane, later in the trip she came down with the measles, and we were delayed for three days until she recovered enough to ride.

When Mama made it across, without incident, she began to scold. Standing there wrapped in a blanket, I answered her sharply, "A ducking is very disagreeable this chilly day, but much less so than capture by the Indians. So please help me find dry clothing and quit your fussing."

Mama stood, hands on hips, and then grabbed me by both shoulders, "Jemima Boone Callaway!" she shouted, "for once in your life will you take care?" Only Flanders, pulling me from her arms and wrapping me in his, forced Mama to let go. Daddy once again came to my rescue by suggesting dry clothing, hot coffee, and rest. He then took Mama off to let her fuss and fume at him, instead of at me.

Chapter 16
Home in Kentucky

Although Daddy rode ahead to Fort Logan for a Virginia Land Commission meeting, the rest of our party arrived in Boonesborough some thirty days after our departure from the Yadkin. Oh, what a sight met our eyes! Once again, Boonesborough's walls stood in absolute disrepair. The fort's ground and its people stank! To think we'd convinced our family to journey to this beautiful, wonderful paradise, only to discover our former home's complete state of disarray from the neglect and laziness of its occupants.

Flanders and I walked toward our cabin and found it occupied by slovenly residents. Mama, fortunately, found their cabin somewhat inhabitable. Uncle Squire and Aunt Jane had once again left for their land nearby, so other family members took over their cabin. While our Bryan family departed almost immediately for Bryan's Station, we settled in. Flanders, Will, Daddy, and his brothers filed petitions for their land and took care of the necessary requirements. Daddy and the menfolk built a cabin some six miles northwest of Boonesborough on some land he'd cleared for corn several years back. Squire's new cabin lay close by.

In the meantime, I gave birth to my first child, with all my aunts in attendance. Mama fretted silently, so as not to worry Flanders, over my condition throughout our journey west, and fretted even more since my dunking in that river. I suffered no ill effects and in early December delivered a beautiful baby girl. I could not have been prouder.

Flanders and I named her Sarah, after Daddy's mother. Flanders attended to my every want and need after the birth. He held little Sarah constantly and fretted something terrible when she cried. You'd have thought the babe was dying the way he insisted I drop everything and grab her up at the least little whimper.

A week or so later, our family prepared to move on to Boone's Station, as it had been named. Flanders insisted the babe and I remain in Boonesborough, but when our family decided to leave the fort and move before spring, I likewise insisted upon going. I won that argument as well.

That year's snow came early to Kentucky, and with it an extreme cold. The Louisa froze solid at Boonesborough, and on Christmas Day in the year of our Lord 1779, we crossed the river and moved to our new homes on that land we now called Boone's Station. All the Boone brothers and sisters joined us, including Squire. The heavy snows that winter made our existence miserable. We built and lived in a cluster of half-faced cabins. I shiver with a chill just remembering those three-walled cabins. We kept a fire burning at the front and used hides and such to keep out the snow and cold. Thinking back, we always called that season *the Hard Winter*. Cattle froze to death in the fields. Wild turkeys froze in the trees and fell to the ground. We could hardly move about the snow was so deep. Too deep to hunt, too deep to trap. Food, once again, became scarce. Many suffered from frostbite and illness. Yet, we survived. I don't remember a single one of our little settlement dying that winter. I will say, at winter's end, many married women found themselves with child.

Throughout the winter, I spent many days with Aunt Jane or Mama as they had full, four-walled cabins. Sometimes, it seemed, the whole of our settlement crowded in those two cabins.

In late February, with the beginning of spring, maple trees released their sap. Our men tapped trees, and we collected and boiled the sap for maple syrup. What a treat. We even ate it poured over fresh snow. Buffalo and deer came from the forest to lap up the syrup; each of those animals too scrawny to kill for meat.

About this time, Daddy left for Williamsburg, Virginia, with over twenty-thousand dollars in Virginia money to register land claims for family and friends. We didn't learn the trip's events until Daddy's return, for on March twentieth near Williamsburg, Daddy and his traveling companion were robbed of all those funds while they slept. They'd taken a room at an inn and kept their saddlebags with the cash and land certificates in their room. Neither man awoke during the night, nor did either one do so until late in the morning. Upon waking and discovering their belongings disturbed, Daddy realized they'd been drugged. He returned downhearted to tell us of the robbery. Will Hays, one of the men who'd trusted Daddy with his money, knew immediately Daniel's story was true. While Hays and Thomas Hart believed Daddy's story, others did not. Again, rumors about Daddy's character surfaced.

During Daddy's absence, we learned about two family members' deaths. First, Shawnee warriors killed sixteen-year-old William Bryan, Jr. Then, only weeks later, Uncle Billy Bryan also lost his life to the Indian constant strife. Like so many who perished, Billy walked out after one of his prize horses and was taken by surprise by the Indians, who'd used his horse to set a trap for him. They killed and scalped him. Within a week, most Bryans, who'd come in September with our party, packed their belongings and returned to North Carolina.

Spring arrived, and our men took to building proper cabins and clearing fields for crops. Next came the palisade to join all the cabins for defense. Those who'd survived the siege knew we were not safe without walls for protection. Flanders provided for us well enough. He often helped Daddy with his surveying work, but mostly he was a hunter and farmer. We rejoiced in little Sarah, our own land, and the beauty and family that surrounded us. Squire or George preached on Sundays, and we gave thanks for our deliverance and our bounty.

The Shawnee defeat at Boonesborough did not stop the Shawnee raids and violence. Using information on the location of various Shawnee towns north of the Ohio gleaned from former captives, the Virginia militia first led raids upon their villages in early 1779. While some tribes began moving farther west, some saw the white settlements all across their hunting grounds and continued their attempts to force us back across the Appalachians. In March of 1780, Flanders and myself, along with others, traveled to Boonesborough for his uncle Richard Callaway's funeral. He was scalped and mutilated while building a ferry across the Louisa River near Boonesborough.

In late June, a large Indian force, backed by British soldiers and artillery, captured both Ruddle's and Martin's stations. The warriors took most of their residents captive and marched them north into Ohio. We learned much later that any who fell to the wayside, mostly women and children, were tomahawked to death. Those residents suffered the fate I had once faced.

Every time our men left our stockade to hunt or farm, we worried for their safety. Indian raids continued all over the county.

Later that summer, Daddy and many of our men joined George Rogers Clark and his army, consisting of eleven hundred soldiers, on a raid north of the Ohio. As our militia approached the Shawnee town called Piqua, the warriors killed many of the remaining captives from Ruddle's and Martin's. A vicious battle ensued and ended with our men burning the village and all their crops.

Returning from the raid, Daddy and Uncle Ned stopped to rest their horses, now loaded with game. In a meadow, Ned began gathering walnuts and cracking them with a large rock while Daddy pursued a bear into the woods. Daddy's shot had just brought down the bear when he heard rifle shots near where Ned sat. He looked back to see Shawnee warriors surrounding Ned's body. One exclaimed loudly, "We have killed Daniel Boone." Everyone always said Daddy and Neddie looked very much alike.

With no choice, unless he wanted to die as had Neddie, Daddy hid in a canebrake. The Shawnee sent in a dog to track him, but Daddy killed the dog and moved deeper and deeper into the cane. Finally, the warriors stopped pursuing Daddy and cut off Ned's head to prove they had killed Daniel Boone and turned off toward the north. Daddy ran all night and arrived back at the station by morning.

I heard his call as he passed our cabin. Placing the tail of Sarah's gown underneath our bedpost to keep her safe, as she now crawled, I ran outside. Daddy stopped and pulled me to him. "Mima, call Flanders, gather up the babe, and go to the station. Warn any others you see," he urged before running off.

Once we had all assembled, Daddy told his story and then organized a few men to retrieve Ned's body for burial. Later I learned that, when they arrived at the spot, a wildcat stood feasting on Ned's flesh. Some men followed the warriors all the way back to the Ohio but found they had already crossed.

I took Uncle Neddie's death hard. So many memories rushed back, him finding me when I lost my way while sangin'. Neddie bringing me Ezekiel, now long buried but a faithful friend for so, so many years. And just for being my father's youngest brother, whom he so closely resembled. I could not help but imagine it being my father who had moved on to heaven.

Given Daddy's high regard by so many Kentucky residents, he was elected to represent Kentucky in the Virginia assembly that same year. He traveled to Richmond. While he was there, the British army approached the city and the legislators adjourned to avoid capture. Daddy and a friend, John Jouett, left for Charlottesville where they were forced once again to flee. Before making their escape, they stalled to try to save some horses. Soon after they left Charlottesville, they were quickly overtaken by British dragoons under Lieutenant Colonel Banastre Tarleton's command. As Daddy and John were dressed in hunting clothes, they were not taken as legislators and managed to talk their way out of trouble, riding along beside the Colonel for several miles. At a fork in the road, Daddy expressed his intention to go the opposite direction from the troops. It would have worked if Jouett had not replied, "Wait a minute, Captain Boone, and I'll go with you."

Poor Daddy and Jouett found themselves arrested and lodged in a coal house. Only held for a few days, Daddy managed to convince the authorities that the title captain was a holdover from his militia days during Dunmore's War. Daddy returned home for the summer. That autumn, he went by way of Pennsylvania to visit relatives when he returned to serve in the legislature. Daddy never dressed for the assembly like his fellow representatives in Virginia. Instead, he left home in new beaded leggings, Indian-made, and a new hunting shirt. When he returned, he told us tales of Thomas Jefferson, Thomas Paine, and other Patriot leaders. His most important news centered on General Cornwallis' defeat at Yorktown.

Daddy returned in August to greet his new son, for Mama gave birth to a baby boy they named Nathan, in March of 1781, just after Daddy departed for Virginia. He was a beautiful baby, and Daddy doted on him and all his grandchildren. Many others in our community also added to Kentucky's population.

Daddy continued to serve in the legislature until 1783. We stayed at Boone's Station for a bit over three years. During that time, Suzy and Will added a son, William in 1780, twin daughters, Susannah and Delinda in 1782, and another son, Boone in 1783. Will continued to beat Suzy on occasion. Daddy, Squire, and Flanders stepped in to intervene when necessary.

I added two boys to our family, John in July of 1781, and James in September of 1783.

━━━━ ● ━━━━

During those years, Indian troubles continued throughout Kentucky. In August of 1782, I once again watched as Daddy rode out to recruit men from Boonesborough to help rescue two boys taken from Hoy's

Station. Bryan's Station's men, planning to join the rescue party, instead found themselves surrounded by over 300 Shawnee, Wyandot, Cherokee, Tawa, and Delaware warriors. As the warriors kept out of sight, hoping to surprise the fort, within it was decided that all the women would go to the spring for water in their usual manner. After falling to their knees in prayer, all the station's women took their pails and buckets and walked out to the springs, talking and gossiping as usual. After carrying the precious water back into the fort, the gates were closed. All knew the fort now contained enough water to survive at least a few days under the hot August sun. While the women carried water, two men rode from the fort and went for help. To continue their ruse, the warriors let them pass.

One cousin later told me how, inside the fort, all continued to carry out their regular routines. Yet the Indians did not attack. In mid-morning, a few cabin doors were opened to the outside of the fort. Their men ran out, firing at the Indians before running back toward the fort. As the Indians attacked, they quickly discovered the sharpshooters inside were prepared, each having three to five rifles ready at hand and women standing by to load each as they were fired. Their rate of fire and effectiveness greatly discouraged the attack.

Then they waited, like we had four years earlier. Their messengers reached Boone's Station, where Major Levi Todd and his thirty men planned to join our Captain Ellis and his sixteen or so mounted men to join the rescue party. Instead, they turned toward Bryan's Station. Under Captain Will Hays' command, the mounted men planned to ride at full speed toward the gate, while those afoot would sneak in toward the back gate through a tall corn field. Those on horseback rode like the wind, stirring the dusty summer dry ground into obscuring clouds of grit. They made it to the gates without a loss. The men in the cornfield were not as lucky, for they encountered many warriors, who forced them to turn back, leaving two dead behind.

It was told that Simon Girty, a brutal white man who'd lived with the Indians for years, demanded the station's surrender, saying their cannons would arrive shortly and they would suffer the same fate as Martin's and Ruddle's. Like our John Holder, Bryan's Aaron Reynolds answered their demand with an inventive string of curse words. Fighting remained light, and by morning the Indians had withdrawn. Bryan's lost four killed and suffered two wounded. One was Will Hays, who took a bullet to the neck but survived. When the relief party's remaining men reached Bryan's Station, they found the fort standing, but all the crops burned and the livestock slaughtered.

Incensed, our militia gathered together some 182 men from Bryan's, Boone's, Fort Harrod, Lexington, and so forth. Without waiting for the forces from Logan's, they proceeded after the Indians. Among those who marched were Daddy, Israel, Flanders, Squire, and so many others of my family. All we womenfolk could do was stay home, worry, and pray.

Days later, Squire told us what happened. The farther they moved north toward the Licking River and the Big Blue Lick, Daddy repeatedly told Major Todd that the Indians numbered much greater than he initially thought. Daddy could tell the warriors walked in each other's steps to disguise their numbers.

As they approached the ravines around the lick, Daddy urged Todd to wait for the reinforcements from Fort Logan. While Todd agreed, Hugh McGary did not. Angry still about his son's massacre and having been called a coward, he insisted they move ahead with their attack. When Daddy and Todd urged caution, McGary took matters into his own hands.

"All who are not damned cowards, follow me, and I'll show you the Indians," Hugh yelled, raising his rifle high overhead.

Daddy answered, "I can go as far as any man," before turning to urge Todd to hold the men back.

Todd instead answered, "Let them go, and we will remain in the rear, and if they are surprised by the Indians, the blame will be on McGary and he will have the brunt to bear."

There are many stories of what happened next. All I know for sure is, as they moved across the river and crested the ravine, Major Todd and Colonel Trigg fell wounded amid the first volley from the enemy. Squire said Daddy yelled for the men to retreat and regroup. Within minutes, twenty-two men lay dead. Soon eighteen more joined them in death. As they tried to retreat, Daddy found a horse and urged Israel to escape west into the forest. Poor Israel, sickened with a fever for several days, was not yet recovered. Instead of riding away, he waited for Daddy to find a horse. Within an instant, he joined the others lost to enemy fire. Cousin Samuel managed to make it across the river and reported Israel's death, and that he supposed Daniel dead as well.

Several minutes later, the retreating militia members witnessed a man and horse crash into the river downstream from their position. Daddy had escaped. He relayed to Todd and others how he had carried Israel's body into the woods, where he'd encountered even more Indians and was forced to abandon my brother. As he told of his escape, his composure collapsed, and he wept bitterly for yet another son lost.

Overall, more than seventy-five men died at the Battle of Blue Licks. Every Kentuckian suffered a loss—a father, a son, a brother, a cousin, a friend. We all fell into mourning, and grief left none standing—none untouched. When Daddy made a trip back to the Lick several days later and returned with Israel's body, we buried another brother. Israel, like James, died away from his family, still young, still vibrant. I missed him terribly.

For the very first time since I heard about this glorious land—this place called Caintuck, this land of milk and honey—I despaired the cost too high.

Chapter 17
My Soul Lies at Rest

Flanders and I slowly recovered from the shock of the Battle of Blue Licks. Mama took Israel's death very hard, yet she and Daddy fell back upon their family and, in time, returned to themselves.

In a show of strength, George Rogers Clark and others led strikes against our enemies. While the Shawnee still carried out attacks and raids across the Ohio, their own strength diminished, and many Indian nations began to move west as more and more settlers pushed west across the Alleghenies and the Appalachians. As the years passed, our own war against England came to a final peace in 1783. We watched as thousands upon thousands of immigrants moved into Kentucky. Many were Revolutionary War veterans, claiming lands promised in return for their service. With the need for additional licensed surveyors, Daddy passed several boards and became a registered surveyor.

Our family grew and changed with each coming year. Suzy and Will added four more children to their first six. Each time Mama and Daddy moved, which became frequent after 1785, Will and Suzy packed up their family and moved as well. Levina married Joseph Scholl in 1784

In the autumn of 1784, Daddy and Mama, all their children and adopted children still at home, Suzy and Will, and Levina and Joseph moved from Boone's Station and settled about five miles away on Marble Creek, north of the Kentucky River. So many things happened to all of us Boones during the coming years I can hardly account for all the family. I do recall that Daddy and Mama ran a trading post at Maysville, up on the Ohio River, for a while.

About 1786, Daddy and militiamen went above the Ohio to try to trade Indian prisoners for white captives. As a group of Shawnee warriors tried to flee from the militia, Daddy recognized Big Jim. That same Big Jim who had tortured James so many years before. Daddy warned the others to be wary of the tall, stout warrior. Still, Jim took one more life and wounded another before being killed. It made no difference in our sorrow.

I remember on that raid, Hugh McGary, who had somehow escaped unharmed at the Battle of Blue Licks, once again showed his temper. He killed the old Shawnee chief Moluntha and attacked his wife before being pulled off the woman. He received a reprimand, and a court-martial stripped him of his commission.

For several years after that raid, Daddy continued his work to free white captives and to exchange Shawnee prisoners. He cared for each the same, feeding them, nursing their wounds, and making sure they survived to return home. One boy, who Daddy managed to exchange, stayed with him and Mama for several years until Daddy finally located his family and reunited them with their son.

Flanders and I pretty much stayed on our original homestead. We added our second daughter, Frances, in February of 1785.

Later that year, Daddy, Mama, and Nathan traveled to Pennsylvania with a load of ginseng. I even contributed some to their load, being as I am an expert at sangin'. Back in his original home, Daddy discovered he had become famous, mostly because of a small book entitled *The Adventures of Col. Daniel Boone, the Kentucky Rifleman* by Francis Lister Hawks. Upon their return, Mama and Daddy came to see their new granddaughter, my Frances. To my great surprise and wonderment, Daddy brought a copy of the book and proceeded to read to us each evening. I learned the beginning almost by heart.

Some men choose to live in crowded cities;—others are pleased with the peaceful quiet of a country farm, while some love to roam through wild forests and make their homes in the wilderness. The man of whom I shall now speak was one of this last class. Perhaps you never heard of DANIEL BOONE, the Kentucky rifleman. If not, then I have a strange and interesting story to tell you.

Each night we listened as Daddy read another chapter. On the fourth night, I listened intently, Frances at my breast and our older three sitting before their granddaddy, hearing for the first time a story we each knew only too well. Of Fanny, Betsy, and myself, the author wrote:

Spring had not passed away, however, before they were in sorrow about these children. When the wild flowers began to bloom in the woods, the girls were in the habit of strolling around the fort and gathering them to adorn their humble homes. This was an innocent and pleasant occupation; it pleased the girls as well as their parents. They were only cautioned not to wander far, for fear of the Indians. This caution, it seems, was forgotten. Near the close of a beautiful day in July, they were wandering, as usual, and the bright flowers tempted them to stroll thoughtlessly onward. Indians were in ambush: they were suddenly surrounded, seized, and hurried away, in spite of their screams for help.

At this point, I rudely interrupted Daddy, "Why that Mr. Hawks, may the good Lord have mercy upon his soul. He has the story all wrong. Everyone knows we were in a canoe on the river. How could Mr. Hawks write such lies?"

Daddy replied, chuckling, "Oh, don't fret yourself, daughter, the lies get worse hereafter!"

Author's Notes

As a daughter of Kentucky, Jemima Boone's story was one I grew up knowing. Over the years, I have read ten or more biographies of Daniel Boone and own even more that I scan for research. My favorites are *Daniel Boone's Own Story and The Adventures of Daniel Boone* by Daniel Boone and Francis Lister Hawks; *My Father, Daniel Boone: The Draper Interviews with Nathan Boone*, edited by Neal O. Hammon; and *Boone, A Biography* by Robert Morgan.

Additionally, I have read *My Blessed, Wretched Life: Rebecca Boone's Story* by Sue Kelly Ballard and *Jemima, Daughter of Daniel Boone* by Margaret Sutton. The latter, I read in the Berea College Library as no other copies were available nearby. I quickly realized why! *Sarah's Courage: A Kentucky Frontier Kidnapping* by Karen Leet gives a fictional account of girls being grabbed by Indians and is followed by a telling of Jemima's ordeal. The book also has a well-researched and well-written entitled "Read More About It" that provides some wonderful, fun facts about early Kentucky and her pioneers.

I have read other early Kentucky historical fiction. My favorite is *Oh, Kentucky!* by Betty Layman Receveur. I have purchased more copies of this book than I wish to admit. Over the years, I have loaned copy after copy to friends and relatives and never saw them again. I purchased my current copy in a used bookstore. It's not going anywhere.

Back to Jemima—I wanted to tell Jemima's story in a way that would emphasize the female perspective of our nation's first major westward expansion—across the Appalachians into the heart of the North American continent. Yet, I needed to tell Jemima's story, not as a biography, but in novel form, so as to bring her to life. Few details of Jemima's early life are known. I needed to "manufacture" her childhood based on the facts presented in historical references. Two additional years of research about early Kentucky settlements, folkways, and the Boone family allowed me to finally begin writing.

I hope you enjoyed Jemima's story as much as I did writing it.

Truth vs fiction:

Most every event in this novel actually happened. The important ones that are truly fiction are Jemima getting lost while hunting for ginseng, the description of her wedding (including time and date), her flirtation with Simon Butler (Kenton), and a few other minor scenes. I kept her personality true to how others who know her described her in various letters and documents.

Learn More:

At www.cmhuddleston.com you can find "What Happened After Caintuck Lies Within My Soul: More of Jemima Boone's Story." There you'll also find maps, images, and book club questions that can be downloaded.

C. M. Huddleston

About the Author

C. M. Huddleston loved history and dreamed of writing a book even as a child. However, she got sidetracked. She became an Army wife, a mother, an elementary school teacher, an archaeologist, and an historic preservation consultant, all before publishing her first book! Since 2006, she has written five historical novels, three pictorials, three histories on the family of President Theodore Roosevelt, one about the enslaved residents of Bulloch Hall, Roswell, Georgia, and two short stories in a collection entitled *Winter Wonder*. All of her writings deal with her love of our nation's past.

C.M. Huddleston has won awards for all of her fiction books, and the collaborative effort *Winter Wonder*, which she edited. *Caintuck Lies Within My Soul* is her fifteenth book. Her sixteenth, a biography of James S. Bulloch, will be released in February of 2020.

Now a full-time author, Connie resides in a log cabin near Crab Orchard, Kentucky, with her husband and their Australian Shepherd Katie. They all enjoy the quiet of rural Kentucky.

https://www.amazon.com/C.-M.-Huddleston/e/B00PMBB1BY/

https://www.goodreads.com/author/show/9860539.Connie_M_Huddleston

https://www.facebook.com/C.M.HuddlestonAuthor/

https://twitter.com/MM_Indie

https://www.bookbub.com/authors/c-m-huddleston

https://www.youtube.com/watch?v=9wjq0Z9fyGk